MW00850141

The Absolution of Mars

T.F. Troy

HISTORIUM PRESS

U.S.A.

THE ABSOLUTION OF MARS

COPYRIGHT © TERRY F. TROY 2025

PUBLISHED BY HISTORIUM PRESS 2025

All persons portrayed in this work of fiction are from historical accounts and/or from historical documents, or from the author's imagination. Author maintained the historical verbiage throughout as shown in historical documents.

Hardcover ISBN 978-1-962465-85-4
Paperback ISBN 978-1-962465-84-7
Ebook ISBN 978-1-962465-83-0

LOC Control Number on File

To my family

TABLE OF CONTENTS

"A stone, a leaf, an unfound door. Where? When?

O Lost, and by the wind grieved, ghost, come back again."

Thomas Wolfe

Look Homeward Angel

FOREWARD
The Proper Truth

It has been said that there are three kinds of truth: Personal, Political and Empirical. Of these, Empirical truth the strongest because it is based on fact and hard evidence. Perhaps the weakest, Political truth is often based on intellectual observation, human association, but it can be manipulated by others through a process known at the time as social conditioning -- as well as our own thoughts and emotions. Personal truth is held in the strong belief of the heart often forsaking the other two.

This is the story of a man of three identities who embraced but one of those three truths, and his pursuer who based his findings on empirical evidence alone. Two men, from completely divergent backgrounds; one of privilege, the other of slavery, thrust together by historical circumstance.

We know today that Jemm Pender was born common chattel, the issuance of Winnifried Pender out of Thomas Pender. Despite being born into the unjust servitude of slavery, he was still the rarest of human being; blessed with an intellect far superior than even the brightest political and scientific scholars of the day. It was that intellect he used to solve one of the greatest mysteries in our nation's history. A tale once told, but thence forgotten.

Until now.

Granbury, Texas, 1873.

In a crowded, honky-tonk on a dusty dry late summer night, a man named Finis Bates meets a liquor and tobacco merchant named

John St. Helen. Both favor strong drink. Bates marvels at how St. Helen recites Shakespeare at length. St. Helen even acts out some of the most complex and difficult passages from the works of the Great Bard.

Four days later, St. Helen falls desperately ill. From his rented room, he summons his new best friend, giving him a deathbed confession:

"I am dying. My name is John Wilkes Booth, and I am the assassin of President Lincoln. Get the picture of myself from under the pillow. I leave it with you for my future identification. Notify my brother Edwin Booth of New York City."

But St. Helen survives his illness, and after a brief, and often halting explanation to his friend, moves to Colorado.

Bates, who was always skeptical of the confession, moves to Memphis, Tennessee losing track of his friend until years later when he was summoned to the Grand Avenue Hotel in Enid, Oklahoma. There a man named David E. George, a house painter who also has an appetite for strong drink and a penchant for quoting Shakespeare, has poisoned himself. Found among his possessions is a paper requesting that Finis Bates be summoned.

Three years prior, George had confessed to Ms. Jessie May Kuhn that he was John Wilkes Booth, saying: "I killed the best man that ever lived." She dismisses it as drug and alcohol induced delirium. But when Finis Bates shows up ten days later, he identifies the body as that of his old friend John St. Helen.

Today, the St. Helen story is widely disbelieved and has faded into obscurity. It did set off a tragic series of events that now serve as a comic coda to our nation's great tragedy. But no one ever asked the question: Why would a man who believed he was dying claim to be the assassin of our most beloved president? Was he seeking absolution for a crime committed decades earlier? Did he want the truth to come out? Or did he want everyone to know that he was somehow involved?

But then again, why would a man who was considered the most handsome and talented actor in America throw his career away on that fateful Good Friday? Was it truly for political reasons? Or was it something more personal?

CHAPTER 1
Battling Blizzard Monster

"Here comes a blizzard," the little boy says. He's only eight years old, a shock of wheat colored hair across his face. He is dressed in a blue suit, with short pants. His ill-fitting white socks are falling into his brown shoes. A little girl, no more than three, is dressed in white with a yellow sweater. She picks up a handful of white apple blossoms, which are carpeting the ground under the tree. She plasters Captain Boyd directly in the face. She runs away giggling in delight, as Boyd raises his hands, contorts his face in mock pain, and falls back on the ground feigning injury.

The little boy in turn picks up a handful of blossoms that are mixed heavily with mud and dirt, he tries to hit Captain Boyd in the face, but is well off his mark. Boyd grabs him about the waist and picks him up as the boy squeals and laughs.

"If you're going to go about fighting monsters, you must perfect your aim," Boyd says, setting the boy back down. "Now go get some more ammunition."

The little girl comes back, pausing directly in front of Boyd.

"He can't aim so well because he needs spec taters," she says.

"You mean spectacles, my blue-eyed beauty," Boyd says correcting her. "Your brother suffers from a very common condition known as myopia. Many great men suffer from such a condition these days."

The sun, which is starting to set, casts an orange glow through the white apple blossoms still on the tree. His traveling companion walks up from the road.

The little girl, becoming bored, picks up some more apple blossoms, hitting Mr. Boyd directly in the face.

"Another blizzard," she squeals, as some of the fallen blossoms find their way into Mr. Boyd's mouth. He makes a comic face as he spits them out, and then picks them out one by one.

A woman comes out of the Garrett House and shouts to her children.

"You two leave Captain Boyd alone," Mrs. Garrett says. "You've both had enough playacting for today...Captain Boyd, do you and Mr. Smith want some supper?"

"Some biscuits would be nice," Boyd answers.

"I'll get you both blankets for tonight, it's supposed to be colder, and that barn doesn't hold too much heat," she says to her guests.

"Thank you so much," Captain Boyd says struggling to stand up on his crutch, "You've been much more than just kind."

He turns to Smith and says under his breath, "We'll leave at first light."

Boyd and Smith head toward the old tobacco barn at the southern corner of the Garrett farm.

Before dawn the next morning, Smith and Boyd, are suddenly awakened by a great clamoring outside. A union lieutenant in charge of the detachment is calling for all in the house to answer and surrender, as the man known as David Smith looks out the slats of the barn.

"Geezus, Union troops, looks like a whole detachment of cavalry," Smith says to Boyd.

"I told you to leave earlier," Boyd says. "Stay here, do not make a move. The Garrett's will have to give us up, and we want no further bloodshed."

"But they're making so much noise, we owe it to them to escape," Smith says.

"It's Boyd, start saying it now, and start believing it now," Boyd says. "It means your life. Boyd. We met up north and you have been traveling with me as a paid companion."

Smith helps Boyd up on his crutch.

"Do not arm yourself," Boyd cautions. "I don't want your innocent blood on my hands, enough has been spilt already. Surrender, and we won't be harmed. And I'll testify as to your innocence."

Through the slats, both men see the Garrett family, children in tow, all brought out to the front porch of the whitewashed farmhouse. A black man servant stands with them, pointing toward the barn, as the eldest Garrett boy, named Richard after his father who is absent on business, chimes in, pointing to the barn for the lieutenant in charge.

"Won't be long now," Boyd says.

"Away there in the barn," the lieutenant calls, as his detail dismounts and starts surrounding the barn in quick order. They light torches and hand them out to each other until they completely encircle the barn. "You are surrounded. We want no bloodshed, especially with innocent children about."

"There is one in here who is innocent," Boyd calls out to the Union detachment. "He will come out first, and I will follow, unarmed!"

"I'm glad we can settle this like gentlemen," another lieutenant calls back. "Surrender or we shall burn the barn and have a bonfire and a shootin' match."

Smith heads out first, his arms in the air.

"Lez burn him with perditions flames," a Union sergeant with a scraggily beard and unwashed hair says, tossing his torch toward the base of the barn.

And with that, all the soldiers start tossing their torches toward the base of the barn as well.

"Hold on. Hold on. I am coming out. I surrender!" Boyd says from inside, as the barn quickly catches fire.

Boyd stands, has trouble with his crutch and tosses it down. From the barn slats, the soldiers looking inside see him drop the crutch, and make for the slightly open door of the barn, struggling with his left leg in a splint.

Peering through a slat, the sergeant sees the man known as Boyd making his way for the door. He raises his weapon and fires, hitting Boyd directly in the back, a mere seven inches down from the skull. Once he sees that it wasn't an immediate "kill" shot, the sergeant moves quickly in.

"Dammit. Dammit," the lieutenant screams. "Who shot that? Who shot that?"

"I was the avenger," the sergeant says.

"Why did you disobey my direct order," the lieutenant adds.

"Providence directed my hand," the sergeant snaps back. "I did it for the 'Greater Glory of God.'"

As other soldiers look on, the barn starts to burn more ferociously, the sergeant and two other soldiers run inside.

"Pull him out. Pull him out," the lieutenant orders, his horse circling, and becoming fractious at the building flames.

Before the men could even grab Boyd, the sergeant is on him, searching his pockets, pulling out a billfold with more than $1,000 dollars in it, a red journal, and three newspaper clippings.

The other two soldiers grab Boyd by the armpits, his legs dangling and dragging behind him, unconcerned about favoring the leg in the splint.

Boyd sees red, then white. As they lift him up, he comes to and feels his neck bend awkwardly to one side. Nothing is working.

Boyd sees red then white. As the soldiers pull him up the steps to Garrett's porch, he comes back once again. He tries to spit up the blood and phlegm gurgling in his throat, but is unsuccessful. He starts to choke.

Boyd sees red then white. He coughs up blood and wakes. His breath gurgles, as he continues to spit blood and phlegm from his mouth. The lieutenant stands over him.

"The wound looks fatal," he says to Boyd. "Do you wish to make a last statement."

Boyd looks at him, realizing his situation, and tries to nod his head but is not successful.

"Smith, Smith is, paid…paid companion," Boyd says, as blood flowed from the corners of his mouth. His eyes roll back in his head. "Not a part of this."

Boyd sees red, then white.

One of the two soldiers who had carried him, speaks up.

"Corbett grabbed some personal belongings," he says.

"True," says the sergeant. "Lookey here, what we got. More than

$1,000 in U.S bills, plus some clippings here."

"Garrett, I need some brandy, a sponge," the lieutenant says. "I want a final confession."

Richard Garrett dutifully steps inside the house, his frightened family and man servant still on the porch as the first pink and grey slivers of dawn can be seen on the horizon.

Boyd sees red, then white.

"Anything else?" the lieutenant asks the sergeant as Garrett steps inside, but the sergeant ignores him.

"I said anything else sergeant!" lieutenant shouts louder, bringing Boyd back to consciousness.

"Journal. My journal," Boyd says, passing out again. He comes to as Garrett applied the brandy to his lips. "Journal explains," he says, as his eyes rolled back in his head. "Bell, Bell."

"Ask Not for Whom the Bell tolls," the lieutenant says, quoting John Donne's immortal poem and hoping to give a man he saw as an actor a great last line.

"He musta dropped that journal in the barn," the sergeant says.

Boyd tries to shake his head and coughs. Blood begins flowing freely from the corners of both lips.

Boyd sees red, then white.

His brother comes down the steps of his home in Maryland and smiles at him. His mother comes out from the kitchen, a concerned look on her face. "Why?" she asks, as Boyd is jolted back to consciousness.

Boyd sees red, then white. A sharp pain comes from the base of his neck, as he opens his eyes and sees the lieutenant.

"Tell my mother I died for my country," Boyd says. "Raise my hands. Please raise my hands, that I may see them one last time" he pleads.

The soldier that helped carry him to the porch raises his hands up to Boyd's gaze, and Boyd shakes his head slightly.

"Other, other side," he gasps.

The soldier turns Boyd's palms toward him, and the man known to the Garrett family as Captain Boyd whispers his last words on earth. Words that would be later used to confirm his identity.

CHAPTER 2

12 Days Earlier

At just over six feet tall, Jemm Pender is only slightly above average, but his thin, athletic build makes him seem at least a couple of inches taller. He has a "baby" face that makes him look younger than his years.

But his physical appearance is not what sets him apart from other men.

A single distant scream pierces through the misty night. Down U street and up 10ᵗʰ the lamplighters have done their job as they had done the night before for the Grand Illumination, kicking off a weekend of celebration. Flickering gas lamps shrouded in a halo of pulsating golden light—lining the streets — the city alight with the potential for an all-night celebration.

But something has gone terribly wrong,

Jemm doesn't know how he knows, he just knows. And he feels a pit in his stomach, his arumbo, as his ancestors called it, a sixth sense that tells when trouble is coming. Marnie had predicted something like this. But Jemm thought himself above her predictions, which seemed childlike, denying even his own arumbo.

A man of science and observation, Jemm has no time for tribal shibboleths and superstitions. But Marnie does have a knack for things like this. And she does have the Ovambo talent for reading people. It not only commands Jemm's respect, sometimes it scares him.

Jemm sits in the window of the fourth floor of his dwelling in what the whites call "darkie town" where Marnie has made a home. Early on in the Great Conflict, even before the Emancipation Proclamation, President Lincoln freed more than 3,000 slaves, most now working as servants. Many live in this neighborhood, which is attracting more freedmen and women heading north to freedom every day.

From his perch above the city, Jemm sees the trouble moving its way across town, fanning out in a concentric circle; moving from house to house, from street to street, to neighborhood and neighborhoods beyond. The town reacting to desperate news in the middle of the night.

It was just as his Aunt Cordelia said: You could see trouble moving, through nature, or through men, not by the trouble itself, but its effect—just as you couldn't see the wind, but you could see how it would bend and sway trees—or how birds would fly or small animals run away from danger.

A foggy night with cold and rain in the offing, Jemm can smell it in the air. The stove by the window, takes the chill off. Marnie is still asleep in the ondijungo, but Jemm knows she will soon travel back to the living.

Jemm spots a single lantern in the spire of St. John's on Lafayette when he hears the first bell. Then a light from behind throws flickering shadows on the wall in front.

It's Marnie.

"Here it comes, just like I told," she says, grabbing his shoulders.

The night before she had one of her dreams. Aunt Cordelia had taken her hand and walked her in a strange shape.

"Dis the way it got to be Marnie. Dis here da way it is," Cordelia says to her from the ethereal.

When she waked the next morning, Marnie realizes she's been walked in the shape of a coffin. Someone important to her is dead or going to die.

Thundering footfalls just blocks away as horses, men and wagons are sent crazily in motion, as if infected by the diseased news coming ever closer. A block over, a shriek and another yell, then all at once a gunshot so shockingly close that it makes them both gasp and fall into each other's arms.

A driverless horse and wagon career down the street. It tips over as it turns up 10th Street spilling sacks of beans and rice breaking onto the street below.

The news comes from unknown and unrecognizable voice below.

"SHOT. HE'S BEEN SHOT!" a faceless male voice outside screams.

"WHAT?" another man screams.

"SHOT."

Banging on the door. Sam the cook is there, tears streaming down, panic on his face. He stammers twice laboring to get out the news.

"Shot! Father's been shot!" He looks around, comes in and sits at the grey table, the lamp throwing flickering shadows against his large brown face.

"Shot. Shot." Sam whispers. He looks down and covers his strong face in his huge hands, shaking his head slowly from side to side.

"It was da same men," Sam says. "Dose same men from Gautier's. I know."

Marnie pulls a chair next to Sam and puts her arms around him, as he sobs uncontrollably. She looks at Jemm as panic takes over.

"Who shot him? Where was he shot? Who did this?" Jemm asks.

Sam's attitude turns from abject despair to disbelieving reality. He looks out on the room in an almost catatonic state.

"Father went to see play-acting with his missus. A man shot him. It was those same men from Gautier's. They came back d'other night. They shot the father, I know it was dem."

"Is he dead? LOOK AT ME SAM! Is he dead?"

"No one…who knows…What happens now? What now?"

The clatter of a wagon and men on horses draw up outside, Marnie moves to the window, a lamp in her hand, and looks four stories down.

"Dey's here all right," she says.

Outside the door, they hear footsteps coming up the stairs and the muffled voices of men talking. Then an abrupt loud banging on the door. When Jemm opens it, a bird colonel with a thick mustache and a sergeant with red hair at his temples stand there. The sergeant takes off his cover before entering. He's balding on top.

The colonel offers no such acquiescence. His cover remains firmly on, but a thick crop of dark hair with streaks of white grows out from underneath. His nose is long and thin and his piercing blue eyes give a hint at his intensity. But his uniform is strangely disheveled. Jemm sees that the buttons of his coat are mismatched all the way up. The sergeant had taken better care of his appearance.

Must've dressed in a hurry, Jemm thinks about the colonel. The sergeant is clearly on duty, but his right arm is missing, the empty arm of his coat pinned up against the shoulder.

"Sgt. Pender?" the colonel asks.

"Yes suh," Jemm says coming to attention. He feels awkward because he is still in bed clothes.

"You are hereby directed to accompany me and my detail. Get dressed."

"Yes suh," Jemm answers.

"Not in uniform," the colonel says flatly.

"But he had nothin'…he's here with me the whole night…he never…" says Marnie rising from the table.

"Sir," the bald sergeant says under his breath. "I'm not sure this is the best of ideas, especially tonight. People will think…"

"Those are my orders sergeant," the colonel says even more matter-of-factly. He turns to Marnie and his demeanor changes immediately.

"We know that mam," the colonel answers, politely, almost reverently. "We need your husband to come with us. His country needs him now. His Father needs him."

"Will Father be okay? Will he live?" Marnie asks.

"We don't know yet, but he still breathes. And where there's breath there's always hope."

Jemm goes behind the curtain separating the living area and the ondijungo and begins to dress.

"Can I ask where and why we're going, sir?" says Jemm from behind the wooden screen.

"The Secretary wants to see you at Petersen's Boarding House," says the colonel. "Something about a peanut vendor."

CHAPTER 3
The Trip To Petersen's

Colonel Well's wagon sits outside along the wooden planked walkway in front, its two horses becoming increasingly fractious as the once slumbering neighborhood awakes and is instantly agitated. A light misty rain begins to come through the late-night fog. In addition to the bald sergeant who has followed them down the stairs, there are two escort riders, a sergeant and a corporal, who are trying to calm the wagon's two hitched horses.

The colonel motions for Jemm to sit between him and the sergeant, the latter looking out on the confused city in both fear and amazement.

"Geezus, sir. This whole thing could get totally out of hand in about half a heartbeat," he says to the colonel.

Gas lights flicker up and down U Street, as the wagon makes its way toward 10th Street. The same wagon that had tipped over at the intersection has been set afire, and freedmen and contracted servants on the street are working to put it out. Its lone horse now de-harnessed, is walking calmly across the lawn at the corner, nibbling at freshly sprouted specks of green grass here and there.

Petersen House was only about two miles away, but the ride seems to take an hour or more. At Cribbett's Market, Jemm sees Joey Burroughs flying by, running for his life along the grey dirt that is quickly turning to black mud in front of the store. When he sees Jemm, his eyes fly open, wild with fear. His left eye looks like he's been in a fight, and he holds his left side, like he is either out of breath or nursing a wound there as well.

He ditches in the alley along Cribbitt's and hops a wooden fence to the rear of the store, his head going down and bottom up, asshole over tea kettle, as he flops on the other side.

"A friend of yours? Colonel Wells asks.

"An acquaintance," Jemm answers. "Maybe we should go back…

"No, the Secretary needs to see you first," the colonel says.

"But sir, that could…"

The colonel shoots Jemm a look that says "don't argue." And Jemm complies.

They never want to listen, even if it's for their own benefit, Jemm thinks. But his arumbo comes up from his stomach and sticks in the back of his throat. His methodical brain going through the details. Joey worked at Ford's selling peanuts. Play-acting. Why was he running? What do you know, Joey?

The bald sergeant shoots him a look.

He knows something, too and he's not telling me either, Jemm thinks.

At K Street, Jemm's fears are realized. A group of scraggily looking white men with torches and rifles travels along like a pack of wild dogs, looking for a victim. One of them spots Jemm sitting between the sergeant and colonel, looking like he has just been apprehended.

"Look dare, dare it is right thar!" a man screams pointing at Jemm as the sergeant shakes the reins and the wagon picks up speed. "Right thar, jus' like I said. A darkie, they got him right thar."

The group starts off after the wagon but are no match as the sergeant puts on speed and distance.

Colonel Wells finally gets it.

"Coming out of uniform might not have been the best idea," he says to Jemm.

Jemm sees Sam the cook running up H Street, his strong face beading sweat, or maybe it's the sticking fog. How the hell did he get there so fast? He looks out of breath. He stops at 10th as the wagon rumbles by, looking at Jemm between the two soldiers.

He's heading for the spire and school, Jemm thinks. I hope he doesn't get a case of the dropsy.

As strong as Sam was, when he was overworked, he got the dropsies, but was usually okay once he cooled down.

His body and muscles are just too big for that heart, Jemm thinks.

The scene at the Petersen house is chaotic. A crowd has gathered outside and is growing angry as rumors swirl with the quickening wind. There are shouts of "Burn the Theater" and plenty of torches in the crowd to do it, throwing an orange glow against the misting but dark night and dampening and darkening dirt streets below.

As soon as they pull up, a white man with so much hate in his soul it causes Jemm to look away screams: "THAT'S HIM! THAT'S HIM! Told you it was a nigger!"

The crowd becomes incensed, screaming for revenge, Jemm its target. Several nooses are hoisted above the agitated crowd. Screams from men and women fill the air, the latter calling for immediate sexual mutilation. The sound rises to a crescendo, when all at once the cacophony of anger is cut off by a bullet from the bald sergeant's gun.

The colonel rises in the wagon, both arms in the air.

"FOLKS, NOW BE QUIET FOLKS!" the colonel yells as the

crowd quiets. "This is not the man, but he is helping us catch the man. Please let us through! Let us through!"

Why didn't he tell them who did this? Jemm thinks. Why did he not assuage their anger? What do you know? This isn't about peanuts or Joey.

Then it came on him and he all at once knows. Joey didn't do anything, but he knows something. And the Secretary sitting inside the Petersen's house knew that Jemm knows where to find him.

There are four guards at the bottom of the stairs of the Petersen's house as well as four by the front door, but they wouldn't be enough to hold back this crowd. On the roof, several sharpshooters poke up their heads from time to time, looking down on the crowd.

A captain with seedy-looking blonde sideburns comes out the door of the Petersen's house, walks down the steps to the street and approaches the wagon.

"Round back, sir," he says to the colonel, but is looking nervously around. "We're lucky we didn't get him lynched. The Secretary is waiting inside."

The colonel steps down, offering Jemm a hand as they make their way around to the servant's entrance of the Petersen's house, away from the now quieted crowd.

"As you folks like to say," the colonel says to Jemm as they near the door, "the Man will see you now. Good luck."

The colonel spins around, and says, "well that's done," but looks down at his coat, then over at the bald sergeant.

"How the hell could you let me go out like this, Henry?" he says to the sergeant after looking at his mismatched buttons. An argument between the two ensues, as Jemm enters Petersen House.

They have arguments between master and servant, too, Jemm thinks.

CHAPTER 4
A Rail Splitter

Inside the house, Jemm hears the peal of the emergency bell at the newly finished spire of a soon-to-be built church and school just six blocks away. What are the sisters doing? Jemm thinks. They've done nothing.

But they have plenty to fear. Before the morning dawns, the African residents of U Street and other neighborhoods gather at the spire on L Street, the site that will soon be the first African church in the capital. While 70 percent of the City wants justice and answers, they are also quick to blame what they see as an inferior race—the easiest of targets and a convenient repository for their ire. The other 30 percent, the freedmen, are gathering at various places to flee, or seek umbrage against the anger that is sure to come their way.

Downstairs, Colonel Wells has finished his admonishment of Sergeant Henry for letting him go out disheveled.

"Henry, you'll be shadowing Sergeant Pender during his investigation. You'll report to me anything he uncovers, before it becomes official. And he should never know that you are so ordered in this capacity. Is that clear?"

"Of course, sir," the sergeant says.

"You will have various field contacts, who will identify themselves by saying, 'this is Rome' you will then identify yourself by saying, 'we are Caesars' is that clear sergeant?"

"Yes sir," Sergeant Henry answers. "This is Rome, we are Caesars."

"After the appropriate sign and counter sign, you will then answer the agent's questions, and follow his directions and orders as if they were my own," Wells says. "Is that clear sergeant?"

"Crystal clear, sir," Henry says.

But the sergeant is also concerned about why a freedman needs to be shadowed. Was he a part of what was already being described as "a larger conspiracy?"

Upstairs, the Petersen house is quiet, sullen, as dignitaries file in and out of the rear bedroom. Jemm catches a brief glimpse of the room, smaller than his own and sees where the stricken president is laid out catty-corner on a bed that's too small for his six-foot-four-inch frame.

The room is overly crowded, and people speak in hushed tones, except for Mary Lincoln, who occasionally cries out, and speaks to her husband as if he might somehow respond and wake up.

Jemm is led to the front parlor, where a small fire makes the room too hot for his overcoat. Two oil lamps at either end of the room throw dancing shadows against the wall.

In the rear parlor, Secretary of War Stanton has his lieutenants gathered around him, and is giving orders in hushed tones, speaking softly so the people coming and going in the rear bedroom can't hear him. Jemm recognizes Corporal Jim Tanner sitting next to Stanton at a small round desk, taking notes and writing orders and dispatches, disseminating them to runners who seem to appear out of nowhere, then head out into the misty night.

Tanner was a regular at the War Department, often filling in when there was need for someone experienced in shorthand. When he lost both his legs at the First Bull Run, he decided to stay on for the cause, becoming an expert at the art of shorthand. He had been staying at a boarding house a few doors down, but was impressed into midnight service to take notes from the many eyewitnesses at Ford's.

Jemm catches Stanton's eye, and the bearded man nods quickly and appreciatively, but turns back to his work. While many in government fear him and consider him duplicitous and Machiavellian, Secretary of War Stanton looks and acts more like a grandfather to Jemm, with weak frail round spectacles, and a long beard with two broad white streaks down the front that had been growing ever wider since he started prosecuting the deadly insurrection.

Whatever the War Secretary wants, Jemm will have to wait.

"Good morning James," Stanton says finally. "Would you like to go in and pay your respects?"

"Yes, suh," Jemm answers formally.

"I was kind of hoping that you would," the Secretary says, he clearly has an ulterior motive.

Stanton nods quickly once again, a lieutenant close by leads Jemm into the room, as soon as a general leaves to make enough room. Jemm feels a sense of pride at being allowed into a room, which is closed to most. He is at the absolute highest levels of government and is trusted. But still doesn't understand why he is there.

The President lay, his head bandaged on his left side, the dried blood now turning brown and cracking. There is blood on the linens that has spilled over onto the floor that is also beginning to dry. The president's right eye is swollen but oddly shut, just like Jemm had seen with Sam's eye the night of his beating for simply reporting a crime. And the President's mouth is cocked oddly to his right, like he'd been punched in the side of the head.

There are two physicians in the room, arguing quietly on how to extend the President's life. The President draws long hard breaths, his chest heaving upward each time, but they grow fewer and fewer. Jemm sees his large strong arms, much larger than would seem possible for his tall lanky frame.

A rail splitter, Jemm thinks, and quite a wrestler.

A third physician, and obviously senior to the other two, shows up and concurs with one of the younger physicians that the wound is "absolutely mortal, and it is impossible for the President to recover."

But Jemm decides to make his own cursory examination.

The ball was large enough in size to do extensive damage, but had not exited the cranial cavity, meaning that it was probably of a lower velocity. The bullet had entered through the occipital bone, about an inch to the left of the median line and just above the left lateral sinus, which it had opened judging from the blood that has dried when coming out of the President's nose, down his mouth and onto his beard.

But the bleeding here has not been excessive, no major arteries have been destroyed. Judging from the President's bulging right eye, the projectile has lodged somewhere underneath the right orbital, or perhaps coming to rest under the right corpus striatum.

The projectile has pierced the dura matter of the brain, and there would be some damage from bone fragments, but the wound is not "absolutely mortal."

Had the projectile hit a major artery, the President would already be dead. A skilled surgeon could ascertain the projectile's velocity and make an educated guess as to where it came to rest.

Then, using techniques that were perfected by the ancient Egyptians and still taught by Mauser's work on brain surgery, remove the bullet from the other side, thus alleviating pressure on the brain caused by internal hemorrhaging within the cranial cavity. There would be no need to be continually poking fingers or probes into the President's wound to alleviate the growing pressure within the cranial cavity. Of course, there was always the risk of hemorrhagic stroke…

The president could live but might wind up a vegetable. Still, where there's breath, there's always hope, Jemm thinks.

Jemm wants to speak up but knows his cursory examination would incur the wrath of the physicians in attendance. Perhaps if the library at Alexandria had not burned, these doctors would have a better working knowledge of how to operate on the brain—but that knowledge was forever lost to the ages, and certainly to these physicians.

Then Jemm recalls the last time he had played the role of physician. It earned him his manumission, but almost got him lynched. While impressed as slave labor at a plantation called Orange Grove along the Ashby River in South Carolina, the master, Edward Perroneau's, second son Maurice had become ill with what was diagnosed by the local physician "as an infection of the lower bowel causing a proliferation of gas."

But Jemm didn't buy it. Being on the patient's right-hand side, it was acute appendicitis. Jemm begged Monsieur Perroneau to let him treat the man, who was Jemm's half-brother. Had he not been blood, Jemm wouldn't have even tried. His father acquiesced, and by feeling the lower right side of Maurice, Jemm realized that the situation was much more dire than even he had thought. Realizing that the appendix would soon burst, Jemm moved forward. But the nearest anesthetic was at least two days away, and the infection would not last that long before bursting the appendix—then the cause would be lost.

Jemm's mother put the young man into an Ovambo trance, a dream-like state, the tribe's women placed on the sick whether human or animals, The art was not lost on Jemm's family, and Jemm performed the delicate operation.

But Maurice fell into a catatonic state, induced by a shock to the system. As he lay on what many thought would be his death bed, word had spread throughout the county that "Jemm's black magic" had killed, or was going to kill, a white man.

It wasn't long before a crowd wielding torches and a rope

showed up at Orange Grove, demanding that Jemm be turned over. Just before Perroneau acquiesced, Maurice regained consciousness. And was, in a matter of a few hours, walking as good as new.

Jemm feels a warm hand on his shoulder.

"What do you see son," Secretary Stanton whispers, but it is within ear shot of the older attending physician who looks up clearly offended.

It took longer for the crowd wielding torches to leave Orange Grove that day, Jemm recalls. And the torches outside of the Petersen's boarding house bring the memory back into much clearer focus. Anything I would say to that doctor, would only be taken as an insult from an inferior, Jemm thinks. Besides, if the President were to live, incapacitated, the government could be subjected to a protracted power struggle.

There is no means for succession in the event of an incapacitated president. It might even cause Sherman's Army to pivot back toward the capital, where it could easily assume total control—even though Sherman was not a man of political ambition, having such a prize easily within his grasp might prove to be too much of a temptation...

No, the President must die, for his good and the good of the country, Jemm thinks. And especially for my good.

"The wound is absolutely mortal," Jemm tells Stanton, lying.

Senator Sumner, a radical abolitionist, looks down on the dying man, and whispers what Jemm thinks is a prayer. He nods his head several times, the back of his thick flocked head resembling a duck's tail. The President's son stands next to him, and when the prayer is through turns into the Senator's shoulder, gasps and weeps briefly.

Mary Lincoln sits at her husband's head, whispering into his ear. Vice President Johnson, who Stanton had sent for earlier, shows up and Mary Todd sees him in the outer hallway.

She looks at Jemm, and all at once begins to wail loudly. She stands abruptly and faints, or rather fakes a faint, for dramatic effect, falling to the ground then wailing loudly. Jemm thinks that somehow his presence has frightened her. That somehow the presence of a freedman in the death room is to blame for her agony.

In the outer room, Jemm hears Stanton dismiss the Vice President as if he were subordinate. It is more than obvious that Mr. Johnson is intoxicated, and he obeys the God of War humbly.

He always enjoys being in charge and giving orders, Jemm thinks. Somehow, the Secretary enjoys all of this. When there is chaos, he is in charge.

Stanton comes back through the door of the death room.

"Get that damn woman out of here!" he shouts, pointing to the writhing Mary Todd. "And see to it that she doesn't come in again."

The Secretary of War abruptly leaves the room to let others carry out his wishes. With the President drawing his last breaths, Stanton has no patience for Mary Todd's antics. Jemm finds that disconcerting. In fact, it brings up his arumbo. Stanton is acting in a way that seems somehow inappropriate.

Senator Sumner leads Mrs. Lincoln away, his comforting arms wrapped around her. Jemm stands still, and silent, hoping no one would notice his presence.

Soon Stanton comes back into the death room.

"She's been doing that all night," he whispers in Jemm's ear. "When you're through, come back into the rear parlor, we have a few things to discuss."

Jemm steps out of the room across the front parlor and onto the porch overlooking the street. The crowd has quieted but is still anxious. More and more freedmen mingle into the crowd, making Jemm feel safer.

Jemm returns and sits at the small round desk in the center of the parlor, waiting for the Secretary's return. Soon, he feels Stanton's hand on his shoulder, the same reassuring hand he felt before. The same kind hand that told Jemm he'd have another job to do.

"I'm afraid you won't be getting much sleep tonight" the Secretary says to Jemm. "None of us will. This appears to be a part of a much larger conspiracy—one that you are all too familiar with. This could be the work of the Knights of the Golden Circle…or maybe the Copperheads."

It isn't the first time Jemm has worked all night. It isn't the first time he has tangled with the Copperheads and Knights. It certainly isn't the first time he's been pulled away from his warm bed and wife.

The Secretary has a reputation for working all night and well into the next day. But he also admires Jemm's dedication to the cause, and most recently how hard he worked uncovering Lafayette Baker's indiscretion as head of the National Detective Police.

Jemm knows that his next assignment will be equally important. But he also knows that the Secretary wants access to Marnie, and what she might know from Aunt Cordelia, a spiritual advisor to Mary Lincoln and a servant in her kitchen at the Executive Mansion.

That's one of the reasons the Secretary had taken Jemm under his wing in the first place, He was a left over from Allan Pinkerton's security, which had been purged by Stanton to bring in his own men. But Jemm's experience, education and intellect were just too valuable.

Jemm also represented an acquiescence to radical abolitionists, a political group that Stanton needed and had used before. And since Jemm had shown devotion to his new boss, Stanton treated him more like a stepson than a subservient.

The Secretary leans in closer.

"According to eyewitness accounts, this heinous act was committed by Booth, the actor…

"Then he'll be traveling under James William Boyd."

"We're still not sure they're one and the same," the Secretary of War says. "That's part of what you'll be doing…"

"It's pretty hard to imagine that a man of his reputation would be involved," Jemm says. "But I think we've established a pattern of behavior…But what would the motive be? Why would he give up such an illustrious career?"

"Half of the audience at Ford's, including its employees, swear he was the man who leapt from the Presidential Box. Shouted something, too: 'Sic Semper Tyrono. Be it avenged. The Bell Avenges…' we're not really sure, but we're nailing it down right now…"

"But that's only half of it, Secretary Seward and his son were attacked this very night. Secretary Seward is at present on his death bed…"

CHAPTER 5

Eight Hours Earlier

A large fist knocks on a wooden door. It's opened by a young black servant still dressed in evening tails despite the late hour. The visitor's large imposing shadow is as wide as the door.

"I'm from Dr. Verdi's office. It's medicine for the Secretary."

"But sah, I'm not supposed to let anyone in, specially at this hour," the black, formally dressed butler says.

"Look you fool, if Mr. Seward doesn't get this medicine, it could mean his life," the hulking figure says from out of the shadows.

"Well, let me go check with Mr. Fredrick," the servant says.

As he turns, the servant is shoved violently to the ground as the stranger leaps out of the shadows and bounds up the stairs. He's met halfway down, by Fredrick Seward, the Secretary's son.

"Now see here, just where do you think you're going," Fredrick says, trying to stop him.

"Medicine. Medicine for Mr. Seward," the man says, pushing the smaller Fredrick easily aside.

"But I'm Mr. Seward," Fredrick says.

Lewis Paine stops his assault, his blocky chiseled face looking genuinely confused as he thinks for a moment that he is in the wrong house.

"I'm his son," Fredrick says.

"I was told to give this to no one but Secretary Seward," Paine says, reaching for the revolver hidden against his back in the belt of his trousers.

"I'll see if he can see you," Fredrick says, trying to diffuse the situation.

Fredrick climbs the last three stairs and traverses the short hallway to his father's room. Secretary Seward is sleeping quietly in the dimly lit room, a male nurse at his side. The Secretary is recovering from an earlier carriage accident. Fredrick shuts the door and returns to Paine, who is still about three steps from the top.

"He's sleeping," Fredrick says. "You'll just have to leave the medicine with me, and I'll see to it that he gets it."

Paine makes like he's reaching inside is waistcoat with his left hand, while his right hand finds the revolver tucked in his belt. He pulls it out and pistol-whips Seward's son, knocking him out immediately. Paine bounds the last three stairs in one step, takes a knife out from his waistcoat and pounces like a lion on the sleeping man slashing his face and neck. The male nurse jumps on Paine's back, but is no match for Paine, who throws him off and onto the floor.

Screams and shouts are heard by Seward's second son August, who rushes to his father's room only to see the carnage and blood from both his father and the male nurse. Paine, who looks more like a wild animal than human starts screaming, 'I'M INSANE...I'M INSANE.' But he hears a third set of steps on the stairs outside the door, it's a messenger from the State Department.

Paine turns and rushes out the door, easily pushing past the messenger, who is totally befuddled. Out on the street Paine continues his rant "I'M INSANE! I'M INSANE!" as he runs off into the night. He can be heard screaming until he's a good half mile away.

CHAPTER 6
A Door Left Open

Gideon Welles, the Secretary of the Navy, comes to the entry of the rear parlor, and motions with his tilting head for Stanton to join him outside. Clearly, there has been a development.

That gives Jemm the chance to talk to his friend Tanner from the War Department, who sits at the table taking Stanton's orders.

"Hey, Stumps…how long you been here?" Jemm asks the crippled corporal.

"Well if it ain't the know-it-all nigger who walks like a thief in the night," Tanner says, returning the insult. They often traded barbs like that, each trying to outdo the other.

It is the way of the subservient to trade insults, Jemm reasons.

"Been here since right aroun' midnight, somethin' like that," Corporal Tanner says, shaking his head. "I was on the better side of sleeping off a pint when they woke me. Got here bout two and a half, three hours ago. The old man has the whole War Department up." His voice lowers to a whisper, "they found Sergeant Peters in a hostess house!"

"How long has the old man been here?" Jemm whispers.

"Got here before me, I really don' know how long," the corporal continues in a whisper. "Do you have some of that willow bark extract you make? My head is killin' me."

Jemm fumbles around in his pockets. He just happens to have an eye dropper of the extract in his coat.

"He said it was Booth?" Jemm asks, handing over the dropper to Stumps.

"That's what everyone is sayin'…Booth," Tanner says, squirting down the medication. "Someone who makes that much money. Someone that famous. Can you believe it?"

"No," Jemm answers half-heartedly. But he also knew that a confederate operative named James Boyd, may have been involved in an earlier conspiracy to kidnap the president. That Boyd was in fact, a confederate spy, a commissioned officer in confederate intelligence service. And that Booth and Boyd may be one and the same.

"Well that's what everyone comin' in here says," Tanner says. "That asshole General Auger has been in and out of here all night. Said Ferguson knows for a fact it was Booth. Then Carter and Stanton held court here, with Ferguson and even Hawks, the guy from the play, who said they know it was Booth. I've been taking affadavies all night. Fifteen hundred people in that damn theater and not a one of them has the same story—except about it being Booth.

"So I take it Charlie's been sending out the dispatches?"

"That's what I can't figure out," Tanner says, still whispering. "Not one dispatch sayin' it was Booth. Rumor is, someone has cut all the dispatch lines."

"What about Grant? Was he hurt?"

"He wasn't even there," Tanner says anxiously, "backed out at the last minute."

"But the papers…"

"We're wrong…Grant's up in New Jersey or Pennsylvania

somewhere," Tanner whispers anxiously. He looks through some earlier dispatches until he found his notes. "Burlington, New Jersey, left on the train at six."

"So, you're telling me that no dispatches…"

"We sent tons of 'em, by rider, the whole city is on lock down," Tanner says. "We sent dispatches to every damn fort and command, my hand is numb. But all they included was a description of the assailant…and the fact that he was headed in their direction."

"Which direction?" Jemm asks.

"Mostly north, but every direction, you know how the ole man is," Tanner says. "Wants them all on their toes. The ole man kept sayin' sumptin 'bout a Captain Boyd, and how he'd be headin' North."

"Tell me what you have sent," Jemm asks.

"One went up to Darnestown, for scouting up north," Tanner says. "We have three squads out all along the Potomac, covering the roads toward Barnesville, Tennellytown all the way up to Frederick. We even sent one to Gen'l Slough in Alexandria."

"And the Navy Yard Bridge?" Jemm asks.

Corporal Tanner looks over at Jemm, afraid to answer the question.

"Please tell me a dispatch was sent to the Navy Yard," Jemm begs. Jemm's arumbo came suddenly back up into his throat.

There is something wrong, and it is all leading back to Stanton. The two sat in a confused silence, a brutal realization coming over them. Jemm is the first to speak.

"So Grant wasn't even there? Where were his guards? Who was guarding the President."

"Some guy named Parker," Tanner says.

"That's it?" Geezus, not Parker, Jemm thinks. How could they let a drunk like Parker guard the president?

"He was here. They questioned him and let him go, but I couldn't hear what they were sayin' to him. It looked everythin' was all honkey dory. I'd a kept him 'round, sure."

"So who was in the box with the President?" Jemm asks.

"A major named Rathbone and his girl," says Tanner fumbling again through his notes, "A Miss Harris...but Lincoln asked for Eckert."

"That nut who breaks fireplace pokers over his arm?"

"The same," Tanner answers. "But Stanton refused, said Eckert was going out of town on business. Turns out Eckert was right here in town all the time, asleep at his quarters."

Stanton bursts back into the rear parlor, a sense of urgency on his face. He looks at both Tanner and Jemm as if he knows what they are talking about.

"James, I need to work with Tanner alone here," the Secretary says, motioning with his head for Jemm to leave the room. "Tanner, I want dispatches to all, everyone on our list. The assassin is John Wilkes Booth. Make sure Charlie gets this at the War Department, he'll have the list."

"Are the wires open?" Tanner asks.

"They are now, something went wrong at the main," the Secretary says over his glasses.

"Something went wrong at the main."

Jemm had heard that one before. It was a lame excuse that kept turning up like a bad penny. It was also an easy excuse coming from the man who controlled all the telegraph lines into the War Department, the same man who controlled all the cipher codes and orders heading to Grant's field headquarters. Was anything said to Grant to send him up North, or at the very least, allowing him to go?

And if it is Booth, he's probably already across the Navy Yard Bridge, Jemm thinks as he steps out of the room and into the front parlor, now out of earshot. He's headed south and we've already missed him.

Soon, the oil lamps in the front parlor aren't burning as brightly as when Jemm first arrived. Clearly, they have been burning all night. Here, too, people speak in hushed tones, but not out of respect for the dying president. It was as if they all had some dirty little secret, Jemm thinks, some tidbit of information they were all withholding.

The night churns on, occasionally a voice will rise above the din, catching everyone's attention. Soon, the oil lamps in the two parlors are barley flickering, having used up their reserves. As dawn starts to break steel grey, a slow steady rain begins to fall.

Just then, a round faced Lieutenant bursts into the rear parlor.

"Sir, you'd better come quick, Reverend Gurley is in with him."

Stanton gets up and looks over at Jemm. He motions for Jemm to come toward him in the rear parlor.

"The bottom line is, I'll need to see you in my office when this is all over, and that could be very soon," he whispers. "Lafayette is back and is already heading out to the Surratt house on High Street."

Lafayette's return worries Jemm, he also could detect a quiver in the Secretary's voice. It was the first time Jemm had ever seen any indication of weakness from Stanton, who now sounded more like the grandfather figure he'd come to know in private than as his superior and employer. But what did he know and when? Why was he so nervous? Why was he so slow to tell everyone involved that Boyd and Booth could be the same man?

Lafayette's return, Jemm thinks, brings out dangerous liaisons and professional jealousies.

But Jemm is also relieved. Maybe it wasn't Joey Peanuts. Maybe he wasn't mixed up in all this. But why was he running? Why was he afraid? Why were people on the street accusing "a darkie?"

Jemm stands and hears the reverend begin his prayer: "Let us pray." But he can't hear the rest of muddled words. The room is too crowded for him to see in. He hears the reverend, say "Amen," to which everyone answers. Not another word is said, until Stanton finally says, "Now he belongs to the angels."

Those words stick with Jemm for some reason, as if the Secretary is personally conveying the president's spirit over the river Styx into hereafter.

Then Stanton does something quite unexplainable. He grabs his hat from a nearby table, and with an outstretched arm, places it ceremoniously on top of his head, as if he is crowning himself King of the United States. He quickly removes the hat, and walks back into the parlor, Gideon Welles at his side.

Jemm wants to hang his head in respect, but his arumbo tells him otherwise. The Secretary takes off his spectacles and wipes them off on the front of his shirt. When he looks up, it is Jemm's first chance to have a look at those kind, stern eyes. But he is unprepared for what he sees. Where he sought comfort, he only sees fear, and guilt. Stanton glances at Jemm and looks away quickly.

What did you do? Why can't you look at me? Jemm thinks. You have all the power of the government right now. Would you be willing to answer a few questions?

"James, I need to see you in my office as soon as possible,"

Stanton says. "Start heading there now. See Colonel Wells at the back door. He has an escort for you."

"Thank you, sir," Jemm says formally.

But why do I need an escort? Jemm thinks. Why did he even bring me here? Was it just for my examination?

At the rear entrance, Colonel Wells, who had been downstairs in the basement keeping the Petersens quiet, orders the bald sergeant to escort Jemm to the War Department, just on the other side of the Executive Mansion.

"You'll be working with Sergeant Henry on this one," the Colonel says to Jemm. "The Secretary wants you both in his office immediately, but you can expect a wait, he's pretty damn busy as you might imagine. Both of you grab some shut eye in his parlor outside his office while you're waiting. It might be the only sleep you get for a couple of days."

As Sergeant Henry and Jemm start for the War Department on foot, they hear a long, low distant wail, a grieving wind on a steady rain against a steel grey morning. There are still a few golden gas lamps flickering, even though it is clearly dawn.

As they walk closer toward the Executive Mansion, the wind becomes alive. But as they drew closer, they see the sounds of grief come from a large crowd of freedmen, who have gathered with their families outside the mansion, bemoaning their own fate, now that their father had passed. The truth, at least for them, has been lost, cast upon the wind.

"Poor bastards," Sergeant Henry, says to Jemm as a tear rolls down his cheek. "If I were them I'd be crying too."

"But you are crying," Jemm says.

"See there," Sergeant Henry answers. "And I don't have nearly the reason they do."

Bastards, good word, Jemm thinks. Now we're all bastards, born into a world of new-found freedom without direction, without a father.

"We are all bastards," Sergeant Henry says, as if reading his mind.

Sometimes it was like that with Jemm's gift, people could read his mind as clear as day—without him saying a word. Jemm tries to clear his mind as much as he could. As they pass to the side of the Executive Mansion, Jemm puts his hand on Sergeant Henry's shoulder.

"I need to leave you here, sergeant," Jemm says. "I'll catch up with you in the Secretary's office."

"But I have orders, you're to…"

"I'll only be a couple of minutes, go ahead and I'll…"

"But what if the Secretary…"

"He'll be late, he always is. You'll still be waiting when I get there," Jemm says.

"But…wait."

Jemm turns and looks back at Sergeant Henry, who is still in a state of confusion.

"Just go. I'll be there. If the Secretary asks, just tell him I went to see my aunt. He'll know."

"But I've never…what sort of man is he?" Henry asks.

"You'll find out today."

CHAPTER 7
The Executive Mansion

Jemm walks quickly down the steps to the service entrance of the Executive Mansion, bounding down the brick steps to the red door. Mr. Slade, the head of house servants and majordormo, sees him coming and opens the door, tears of grief streaming down his strong African face, his lower lip trembling. Balding but grey at the temples, he's stout, but has dignified carriage. And he runs the staff at the Executive Mansion like a well-trained military unit, Across town church bells begin to peal.

"He's gone, isn't he? Gone?"

"Yes he is," Jemm answers grimly.

"She's waitin' for you. Knew you would come. It's important, too. She's in the kitchen. I cleared it out for you. You'll talk there."

Mr. Slade and Jemm walk down the long hall past the ice cabinets lining either side toward the bright light of the main kitchen beyond. The hall was always damp from melting ice, but for some reason today is dry, their footfalls echoing strangely as they walk along the clay tiles.

Ahead, Jemm sees Aunt Cordelia seated at the butcher's table. Her back is to them. She has a shawl over her stooped shoulders, the top half of her body moving forward and back, like she did whenever she got nervous.

Jemm hears the rain plinking against the curved window and glass blocks of the kitchen as hanging pans on the oval rack overhead throw grey shadows across the tables inside. The large stoves against the far wall normally provide plenty of warmth, but only one of the ovens is lit.

Cordelia doesn't turn around when they enter the room. Jemm walks around in front of her. She never even looks up but stares off into space as if in a trance. In front, the butcher's table is freshly brushed and sewn with salt. In front of her, is a small blue vase with a single, but very large white rose.

Jemm points at the rose and looks over at Mr. Slade.

"Hot house," he explains.

"How are you Cordelia?" Jemm asks.

Without looking up, or even acknowledging his presence, "Troublin'" she answers.

"I have to go over to Secretary Stanton's office…"

"I know'd you'd come here dis mawnin," she says again, without looking at him. "Just like I knew dis would happen."

"You've got to tell me about Joey. It's the only way I can help him. What did Joey do?"

"Father knew it, too. Dreamed it da night afore," she came to, as if coming out of her trance. "Told me 'bout his dream of a ship not reachin' the shore…What you askin' bout Joey for?"

"They're lookin for him. He's involved. I need to know what you know about Joey."

"Joey ain't do nothin' child. He jus' in the wrong place is all. Dis ain't 'bout Joey. It's bout dat man. Da man with da bad hands."

"What man?"

"The man who came to see da Father," Cordelia says. "He da one, all right. I see it clear now."

"You know he did it, sure?" Jemm asks.

"How Marnie is?" Cordelia asks.

"Never mind…fine, upset but who isn't? I only have a few minutes," Jemm says urgently. "Tell me about the man who came to see Father."

"Bad hands that one," Cordelia says, looking off into the distance again. "Saw it right off. Should have shooed him on outta here minute I saw it, but Father wants to see him."

"He was here? When?"

"Jus over dar. They talked right by that sink dar. Came here bout his friend."

"When was this?"

"Father only saw him on account Massa Robert."

"When!? Cordelia!" Jemm says forcefully, trying to get her attention again. "When did this happen?"

"At a train station, months ago…"

"No! No!, when did the man come here? Cordelia!?"

"At night, late night," she answers falling into a scmi-conscious state once again. "You know the Father, he loves his cornbread and honey, comes down late at night while his missus is asleep."

"No. What day? What day did the man come?"

"Bout a month after da Lord's birfday…maybe a little more."

"So not in the last few days? Weeks?" Jemm asks.

"No…but the other one, he come, Stanley his name," Cordelia says. "He got sompin to do with it too… He's da one…I just know. I feel it. I should have known, after Father told me 'bout his dream. I should have stopped it."

She's emotional, blaming herself for something she couldn't have possibly known, let alone stop, Jemm thinks.

"Where's Joey?"

"Hidin'…hidin' where he always hide,. With that tramp he keeps I spect," Cordelia turns to him smiling, coming out of her trance. "You find him dar all right."

"I'll be back Cordelia. Try to remember everything you can from that night, but don't tell a soul except me."

"Here," Cordelia says handing Jemm the rose. "Take dis to Marnie for Easter."

"I can't…what's this all about?"

"Your dinner guest, he'll know." Cordelia answers.

"But I don't have a dinner guest."

Jemm looks over at Mr. Slade, who hears the entire conversation. He just shakes his head as if to say, 'I don't know what the hell she talking about.' Mr. Slade picks up the rose.

"I'll send this on," he says to Jemm.

Jemm isn't worried about Mr. Slade. He is a man of very few words. And rarely offered any of his own.

"Is there anything else you can tell me about that visit?" Jemm, asks her.

Cordelia nods yes, but Jemm knows he is running out of time, especially if he wants to make it to the Secretary's office in time.

CHAPTER 8
An Unexpected Promotion

Back at the War Department Sergeant Henry sits outside Stanton's office worrying that Jemm is not there yet. He hears the Secretary come back into his office through a rear door and becomes even more anxious. Jemm shows up and bounds past the two sentries and in the outside parlor just as the Stanton begins barking orders to Sergeant Roscoe Peters. The two men sit briefly in silence.

"I was afraid you wouldn't get here in time," Henry says finally.

"So was I," Jemm answers, his breath heavy from the quick pace he put on from the Executive Mansion.

"You're sweating like a stuck pig. Was that really important?

"Turns out it might have been," Jemm says. "But the information was sketchy, inconclusive—based on conjecture and circumstance, more than actual fact. I'm afraid that's the way my Aunt Cordelia is —wise, but there's no figuring her—at least not logically."

The parlor was always dark, especially in the morning when the light didn't shine through the western window. A single gas lamp throws flickering light. It too, has burned all night.

Inside, they hear Stanton speaking in muffled tones to his aide. Occasionally, a harsh voice rises, and a part of the conversation audible. But mostly they speak in hushed tones.

"So?"

"So what? Jemm asks.

"What sort of man is he?" Henry asks anxiously.

"He doesn't suffer fools," Jemm says. "A bit of advice, better to be quiet and appear foolish, than to speak up and remove all doubt, as our President used to say. Keep your eyes open and take in all details, that will tell you what manner of man he is."

Inside, they hear the Secretary still talking with his aide, the voice still muffled. Then, Sergeant Roscoe Peters opens the door abruptly. Before he could speak, the Secretary intervenes.

"Henry, James, get in here," the Secretary shouts. "Get that wire off this morning, Roscoe," Stanton says to his aide.

Jemm and Henry stand in front of the Secretary's large L-shaped desk. It is clear of all paperwork with a large decorative copper lamp with light blue-green patina. Against the far wall is a small circular table next to a large window with a red-draped curtain, with piles of paper and maps. Clearly, this is where the Secretary preferred to work, leaving his desk clean for more formal meetings. Behind that small desk, was a large map of the United States, delineating the areas controlled by the Union.

Also on the desk, Sergeant Henry sees a black obsidian ashtray, large enough for the largest of cigars, but remarkably clean as if it had never been used. Stanton sits at the desk, without looking up, working on yet another dispatch. Behind him, war maps and a portrait of the late president are hung on the federal green wall.

To the left, there's ship's portrait of a side-wheel sail steamer hung above a horsehair lounge covered in a ratty old patchwork quilt in tan and alternating red, green and blue patches. It seems to complement the green pattern on the wall. But it looks like it should be used as a dog's bed rather than on the lounge of the Secretary of War.

I wouldn't use that thing to cover my horse, the balding sergeant thinks. I wonder how many nights he's slept covered in that thing? A feather pillow at the head of the lounge, is grey, unwashed, and equally gross.

Stanton looks up at the two who are standing at attention.

"Stand easy, gentlemen. Roscoe, get this off to Grant, he should be on the train back. If not, make sure it follows him all the way back here if necessary. We're expecting him back in town this morning."

Sergeant Peters comes back in, picks up the dispatch and carries it through an anti-chamber behind Stanton's desk and into the large Telegraph Office beyond.

The Telegraph Office cipher room was the former library of the War Department, which is right next to Stanton's second floor office. Inside are two sets of telegraph operators sitting face to face at stained and varnished wood stations. At each is an operator, who takes down the ciphered message, which are then passed onto an intelligence officer, who translates them and passes them onto Sergeant Peters. This is the nexus of all communication during the war, and it came in from virtually anywhere in the country where a rail line existed, transferred literally at the speed of lightning.

From the constant clicking of the wires in the next room, it became apparent to Jemm that if the lines had been cut, they had been cut selectively

"Why are you sweating James?" the Secretary asks, looking back down and starting yet another dispatch.

"Sir I…"

"You stopped at the Mansion, didn't you?"

"Sir I wanted to see…"

"What did she say?"

"She talked about some man with bad hands, then something about the president's dream…"

"We already know all of this, just a waste of time."

The Secretary grows noticeably agitated.

"It was my intent for you both to come directly here. I guess I didn't make that clear. Sergeant Henry, you were to accompany him…"

"Sir I thought that since it was such a small distance…"

"Never interrupt me again," Stanton says, looking down at a folder that he has opened. "This makes a little hard for what I am about to do this day sergeant."

"Where can we find the peanut vendor?" Stanton asks. "I've already given the order to apprehend Spengle, Spengley, Roscoe what the hell is that man's name?" he shouts to his aide in the other room.

"Spangler, sir," Sergeant Roscoe Peters says. "He should be in custody within a day or two according to Lafayette."

"Joey Burroughs is probably hiding with a lady friend," Jemm says. "I saw him running by Cribbett's Market earlier this morning."

"What's your feeling?"

"He's scared, knows something, but I don't think directly involved…I'd almost stake my reputation on it."

"Give the address to Roscoe before you go. He won't be hurt. We'll need to interview him as soon as possible.

"This is a very important mission that will require someone with the grade of a commissioned officer to be in charge. But regardless of rank, you will conduct this investigation as equals. No one will be in charge of the other, is that clear?"

The two men nod. The Secretary reaches for a folder and opens it, reviewing its contents.

Jemm's heart wants to burst out of his chest. Finally, the promotion he deserves. A commissioned officer in the United States Army! His name will go down in history with, or maybe even supersede, Lieutenant Reed, and Colonel Singleton, or Lieutenant Becker of the 55th Massachusetts.

But this promotion will be even more important. He isn't a part of a "colored" regiment. He isn't in charge of "colored" troops. He will simply be an officer in the U.S. Army—working in intelligence at the highest levels of government!

Stanton had always told him that this would be his ultimate destiny and reward...especially after the investigation that revealed the corruption of Colonel Lafayette Baker—head of the National Detective Police. Stanton had furloughed Baker, based on the results of that investigation, but now Lafayette Baker was back. The promotion would be Jemm's reward.

He didn't care that he would have to act as an equal, despite out ranking Henry. The fact that he would be an officer was more than enough.

"Okay then, here it is," the Secretary says at last.

The two men are assigned to investigate the travel and habits of a Captain J.W. Boyd, a Confederate spy, who has taken part in raids from Canada, and who is believed to have operated with a ring of spies out of Toronto and Montreal.

All interviews are to be conducted out of uniform, and while all information gleaned was official, the Secretary didn't want the people being interviewed to feel like they were under oath. This would be especially important in Jemm's case, as he would often be interviewing maids, servants, and colored help who might not want to talk to an official of the government.

Stanton looks up and realizes how dirty his round spectacles are, the misting rain had clung to the lenses and made them cloudy as they dried. He takes them off and cleans them meticulously on the front of his shirt, putting them back on and refocusing his eyes.

"We have reason to believe that this is a major conspiracy involving the very highest levels of the Confederacy and certainly the Knights of the Golden Circle and the Copperheads," the Secretary says. "And we need to prove it in short order. You are to trace the movements of Captain Boyd and ascertain his movements for the last two years."

"Do you think there's a relationship between Boyd and Booth?" Sergeant Henry asks.

"That's what your investigation will ascertain. We know that Boyd planned and almost executed a kidnap attempt against the president earlier this year. He was also involved in a piracy of a vessel on the Great Lakes. The burning of hotels in New York last year and may be involved in trying to derail a train with prisoners at the Suspension Bridge by Niagara Falls. We have a complete dossier on Boyd—which James already has in his possession," Stanton answers. "As you may know, I've also ordered Colonel Baker back here."

"Will he be in charge?" Jemm asks.

Stanton shot him a look that said I thought I told you not to interrupt.

"Sorry sir," Jemm says looking down.

"Sergeant Henry, you will interview all officials, government, railroads and the like. James, you'll do your usual job of interviewing the coloreds, Chinese, servants and the help.

"Sergeant Henry, James is very good at his job, and the information he will glean from the help can be every bit as important, if not even more so, than the officials you interview. James I want you to start with the help of..." then shouting once again to Peters in the next room, "Roscoe what the hell was the name of that place?"

"Gautier's, sir," the sergeant answers from the other room.

"Right, Gautier's," the Secretary of War says. "That's where we uncovered the kidnap plot. But it was also where we believe the kidnappers were warned of our trap and called the whole thing off.

"Go there by Monday morning latest. You will share equal responsibility and equal ranking on this detail. As I said before, no one in charge of the other.

"Although there will be no differentiation in rank, this detail also requires a ranking officer. To that end, Sergeant Henry, the War Department of the United States and I as its Secretary have seen fit that you be commissioned as a second Lieutenant in the United States Army. So, in recognition of your service in Tennessee, please raise your right hand and repeat after me..."

The words shoot through Jemm like a knife. After all the months of service to the Secretary. After working late nights helping the Secretary investigate members of the cabinet as well as officers like Colonel Baker himself. After all that he had sacrificed—in the end, he is just a freedman, nothing more than chattel. And he hates the new Lieutenant Henry because of it. But he looks again at Henry's missing arm.

Oh great, another gimp—why do I always get these basket cases? Jemm thinks but dismisses it almost immediately.

At that moment, Jemm knows this is his last assignment—the last detail. He'll carry it out to the letter but he won't offer any additional insight nor information. He's had enough of white promises.

CHAPTER 9
A Drunk Guard and a Stableman

As the newly commissioned Lt. Henry and Sgt. Jemm Pender leave the War Department, the misty night has become a day of solid steady rain, almost as if heaven had opened to grieve for its assassinated son. It was well past noon and both men could feel pangs of hunger. The two stopped and stared at each other before looking back at the War Department."

"Something's wrong here," Jemm says finally.

"I agree, but I couldn't really turn down a commission directly from…"

"That's not what I'm talking about lieutenant," Jemm says.

"I know that you are a very experienced investigator, and I will of course, follow…"

"Listen to me," Jemm says firmly. "I said something's very wrong here."

"How do you mean?"

"Grant's supposed to go to the theater, and then backs out. Half the people who went to Ford's went there to see Grant. So Lincoln goes to the State Department and asks for Major Eckert, but Stanton refuses and Lincoln ends up going with Rathbone, some Major he only marginally knows.

"How do you know all this?"

"I talked to a friend of mine at Petersen's who was sending out the dispatches. But there's more to it. Every avenue of escape is cut off, except the Navy Yard Bridge. If you were a Southern sympathizer like Booth or an agent like Boyd and had just shot the president, which way would you head?"

"Toward the Navy Yard Bridge," Henry says, realizing the implication of his statement.

"Exactly. So why would Stanton leave it virtually unguarded? It gets worse, I have reason to believe that Stanton visited the president recently."

"That's not exactly unusual…"

"But the visit came late at night, when the President was sneaking honey and cornbread…why would Stanton need to visit the President at night—especially when he spent so much time in Stanton's office awaiting ciphered dispatches. My Aunt mentioned something about a train platform and Robert, but I can't put the two together.

"Listen Lieutenant, before we head out in search of Captain Boyd who might have headed up north, we need to find out when Grant left and why he left," says Jemm. "You head out to the train station…"

"You're not thinking…no!"

"I'll go find out who was guarding the Navy Yard Bridge last night."

"If the old man is involved, we could be in a lot of danger," Henry says.

"Let's meet at my place tomorrow," Jemm answers.

Jemm turns back to the War Department to do a little digging. Whenever he needed a little information about the goings on at the

War Department, Jemm knew the first place to start was always Geoffrey, head of housekeeping and hospitality.

Geoffrey was a freedman, but every bit the professional man servant. He was dignified in his carriage, strong of gait, tall and proud with fine almost European features that belied his African heritage but spoke volumes to miscegenation. He was articulate, soft-spoken when necessary, but stern with underlings when he had to be. And he studied the classics and could quote them verbatim. While his avocation was to the theatrical arts, he also knew that he would never realize his dreams.

He had become so good in his duties as an overseer of houses across the South, that his talents were sought out by all the major hotels in the Capital, including the National, once news of his manumission had leaked out.

While he had his choice of positions in hospitality throughout the Capital, Geoffrey chose the War Department. He'd grown sick of catering to "rich white folks, who couldn't think" for themselves. Geoffrey was 20 years Jemm's senior, which always caused tension between the two. Geoffrey treated Jemm as an inferior, constantly quizzing him and testing his reasoning—something Jemm hated. But the information the interaction yielded made the brief humiliation more than worth it.

Like any good information resource, Geoffrey was all ears and treated information they way it should be treated, always in the strictest of confidence.

Geoffrey's "office" was no more than an over-sized storage closet. Yet Geoffrey maintained it better than the offices of many of the War Department's senior members. It was meticulously clean and well ordered, the same traits that made his information so valuable. He heard Jemm outside before he knocked.

"Come in," Geoffrey says, "Kind of thought you'd be here sometime this morning. Kind of surprised it took you this long."

"This thing really has the whole place in an uproar."

"This place was in an uproar long before that man pulled the trigger," Geoffrey answers. "I heard Roscoe was found in a hostess house. I long expected that man of spending a little too much time in the water closet, loping the proverbial mule if you get my bent..."

"I need to find out..." Jemm interrupted trying to avoid the topic.

"Why Major Eckert wasn't protecting the president," Geoffrey says, interrupting him. Jemm hated when he did this but wasn't in the mood to argue.

"Precisely," Jemm says.

"Master Secretary had a more important job for him to do," Geoffrey said sarcastically.

"What job could possibly be more important than protecting the president?" Jemm shoots back.

"Precisely," Geoffrey says, mocking him. "Think of urgency. What would make a job more urgent and important than protecting the president?"

"If you were certain an attack was going to come from another direction, at another time," Jemm says.

"Or if you thought the attack was going to come on someone else," Geoffrey says, almost as if schooling him.

"Was that why Grant left for New Jersey?"

"Maybe, but I think it was to get him out of the city than to put him out of harm's way," Geoffrey says.

"So Stanton knew there would be some sort of trouble?"

"Precisely," Geoffrey says again, this time standing and facing away from Jemm.

Jemm grows impatient. He knows, he just wants me to work for it, he thinks. Surely, he overheard Stanton giving the orders to Eckert.

"Sometimes the most important information is that which is worked for, it sticks with you better," says Geoffrey, as if sensing Jemm's frustration.

"Please, just tell me, I don't have much time," Jemm pleads.

"Mr. Stanton assigned Major Eckert to duty protecting Secretary Seward…"

"But Seward was attacked," Jemm says.

"It seems the Major retired a little too early. He was only assigned to protect Seward until ten o'clock. After that, it was thought the attack would not come…Only it appears that the would-be assassin waited for Major Eckert's departure."

"And there were plenty of people in Seward's House to protect him," Jemm says.

"So 10 o'clock comes and there's no attack, so Major Eckert retires for the evening. The assassin must have seen him leave his post, and went ahead with his mission," Geoffrey says.

"But why would Stanton think that Seward was in danger?"

"Better still, why would he think that Seward would need protection and not the president?" Geoffrey says.

Geoffrey turns back toward his charge, to see Jemm looking at him with an inquisitive look, asking Geoffrey to answer his own question.

"I have no idea, truly," Geoffrey says. "That's something you'll have to find out on your own."

"Did you hear about any visit to the Executive Mansion?"

"There've been plenty of visits," Geoffrey says, mocking him. "You mean the latest one?"

"I mean any that might stick out, any that might arouse some sort of suspicion?" Jemm asks.

"Mr. Slade tells me most of the visits have been about pardons and paroles," Geoffrey says. "There were two meetings that stick out."

"Any that created a stir around here?"

"There was a midnight meeting, more like an evening meeting about a commutation," says Geoffrey. "But it was between the Old Man, Seward and Dix. They wanted to stop a commutation of a brigand.

"That one put Secretary Stanton and Seward on serious edge," Geoffrey adds.

He could sense that Jemm is getting close. "They cleared out of it in a hurry once they heard about it. Went straight in to see Father about it too."

"Who paid the president a visit in the kitchen late at night?" Jemm asks, recalling Cordelia's comment about the man with bad hands..

"There was four of them, Mr. Slade tells me," Geoffrey says. "There was an attorney from Baltimore, a man named Ritchie and another named Wheatley, but the only one that got into see the Father was Senator Browning, President knows him cause he's from his home state."

"Any idea what it was about?"

"Like I said, a pardon or some sort of clemency for someone held in a prison up north," Geoffrey says.

"Any one with bad hands—ever hear someone talk about bad hands?"

"What?"

"Sorry, just something I heard from Cordelia," Jemm says.

"She's a wise woman, why not ask her?" Geoffrey says.

"I'm sure it's nothing," Jemm says, "doesn't seem to fit with any fact pattern...Stanton also left the Navy Yard Bridge virtually unguarded," Jemm adds, tossing out the fact to see if Geoffrey would bite.

"Virtually, is one of the trickiest words in the English lexicon," Geoffrey says. "It leaves open endless possibilities while throwing off the intellect in another direction."

"There was one guard," Jemm says.

"Then I'd start with that guard," Geoffrey answers.

# # #

With the help of Roscoe, Jemm soon finds out that a sergeant named Silas Cobb was in charge of the bridge detail at the Navy Yard Bridge that night and had been relieved at one in the morning. He had standing orders to not let anyone cross the bridge without having a pass.

When Jemm pays a visit to Cobb at the 10th Regiment Veteran Reserve Corps, the unit in charge of guarding the bridge, it is early afternoon. The rain has abated, but the day still cloudy and everything seems damp. Cobb is quartered in a large white tent outside of headquarters with three other men, who were now on duty. Cobb should be the only one in the tent, he is told by the duty officer.

Jemm approaches the door.

"Away in the tent, can I enter?"

"Come," comes the voice from inside.

Jemm enters the tent, the floor covered in hay damp from the rain. He sees a man with blue union trousers without his shirt. He has just soaked his head in a bowl of water and his brown hair was wet and disheveled. He has a horrific scar up by his left shoulder that looked like it had carved out a groove from front to back.

"Whaddya you want? I didn't order anything boy," the man says, rubbing his eyes.

"I'm looking for a Sergeant Silas Cobb," Jemm says, offering his credentials from the War Department.

The man glances briefly at the credentials without really inspecting them. He motions for Jemm to sit in a chair as he puts on a t-shirt that has greyed from so much use. He pulls up another chair and sits across from Jemm, staring down between his legs unable to look Jemm square in the face. He looks like a guilty man.

"I heard they was alettin' coloreds in, didn't spect they'd be workin' for the War Department," the man says.

"I'm looking for Silas…"

"I'm him," says the man still looking downward, as if accepting his fate. "I figure I'm in a peck of trouble."

"How'd you get the wound?" Jemm asks.

"Petersburg, at a pontoon bridge, curtsy of Dr. Minnie. "Yuns here to arrest me?"

"How many people crossed the bridge on Friday after nine? Jemm asks.

"Just three, a fourth tried to, but I stopped him. No wait, it was only three," Cobb says.

"You sure?"

"Three," Cobb responds, "after I found out roun bout the president at roun two this mawnin, I had a few drinks, maybe too many. I figure I might hang…should I be getting my things together?"

"So the first?"

"Was a man named Boyd, but he had a pass," says Cobb.

"Who signed it?"

"Johnson," Cobb says. "Yeah, it was a Vice President Johnson."

"Johnson. You sure?"

"I'll take my oath on it," Cobb answers, looking up directly at Jemm. "Hurt his foot getting offa his horse. Said he sprained it earlier, but I heard something pop."

"So he's hurt?" Jemm asks.

The sergeant shook his head affirmatively.

"Who was next?"

"A man named Smith, said he was headin to White Plains, visiting a lady on Capitol Hill and couldn't get away until then."

"And you let him pass?" Jemm asks.

"Said the lady wasn't his missus, and he was in trouble. I took pity on him. I was in a good mood, bein' that the secesh had surrendered an all."

"Were you drinking on post?" Jemm asks.

"We're you drinking on post?" Jemm repeats.

"Might have been," Cobb says, looking back down again, "but not drunk, at least not while on the bridge. Everyone was celebratin'."

"What did this Smith look like?"

"Clean shaved, hair parted on his left. Wore a string tie and a wide lapel coat. Kind of an oval face, ya know the kind, had floppy ears that he tried to cover up with his hair on the sides, too…"

Sounds like David Herold, Jemm thinks. The same man who was suspected of having supplied the kidnap conspirators just a month back.

There is an awkward silence, before Cobb stands and walks away with his back toward Jem.

"He had a horse with him, a pinto," Cobb says. "I only mention it on accounta the stableman come by right after sayin' that he rented him the horse, and it was overdue. He wanted to follow this Smith to get the horse back or get more money out of him."

"So you let him pass, too?"

"I told him he could cross, but wouldn't be able to get back until the next mawnin'. By that time ah had ta put my foot down. Am I unda arrest?"

"Not by me," Jemm says. "What was his name?"

"Smith."

"No the stableman," Jemm asks.

"Fletcher," Cobb says. "John Fletcher, He works…"

"I know him," says Jemm as he stands and walks toward the tent's door, "much obliged for your time sergeant. Please keep this confidential."

# # #

At Nailor's Stable, Jemm runs into John Fletcher, who is gathering his things. The stable is well kept, but still smells of dung. It has broad wooden ceiling beams painted brown that contrast with the golden hay spread copiously across the wooden floor. Fletcher is near what looks to be the rental office. It looks like he is preparing for a hasty exit and a long trip. He has straw colored hair that matches the floor covering and two front teeth that want to pop out beyond his two round lips.

"Ain't got time for no coloreds," Fletcher says. "I have to get back to Genr'l Auger's office pronto."

"Did you try to cross the Navy Yard Bridge last night?" Jemm asks.

Fletcher doesn't answer, instead opening a black locker box and pulling out what looks like a change of clothes, a razor and soap mug. He puts them into a bummer's bundle that would be tied to the end of a long stick.

"You goin' somewhere?" Jemm asks.

"Like I said boy, I got to get back to Genr'l Auger," Fletcher says, looking up from his packing up. "Ain't supposed to talk to nobody neither."

"You were at Navy Yard last night, weren't you?"

"Goin' after a pinto that was overdue," Fletcher says.

"You sure it was your horse?"

"I was kinda far away when I saw him, but the bridle and saddle were definitely ours. I could tell them a mile away."

"Do you remember who you rented him to?" Jemm asks.

"Ain't supposed to say," Fletcher responds.

"I work at the War Department, and…"

"Genr'l Auger hisself told me not to say, that okay with you boy?"

"Yeah…yeah that's fine, you told me all I need to know," Jemm says. So it was Herold, Jemm thought. And Auger is going after him for the glory, using this half-wit to identify the saddle and bridle. There will probably be a reward, too.

CHAPTER 10
The Peanut Man

Joey Burroughs, also known as "Johnny Peanuts," sits in a barren room on a wobbly wooden chair, his arms in shackles behind him. His top half is bare, and there is a bruise forming on his left rib cage. His left eye is closing, as if he has been in a prize fight.

Why me? Joey thinks. All I did was hold a man's horse for a quarter.

The room is painted tan and the windows at the very top of the wall throw in enough just enough light to provide the most basic illumination. The black wooden floor is scuffed in many parts, revealing the white oak below.

Joey hears the door behind him open and close, and the footfalls of two men who enter behind him.

"So this is our peanut vendor," one man with a gravely voice says.

"Yes, sir. Picked him up yesta-day hidin' out and fornicatin' with a women of the night," says the other in a squeaky voice that sounds like a boy's voice that hasn't changed with adolescence.

A colonel with piercing blue-grey, almost silver eyes, high cheekbones and the beginnings of a full beard walks in front of Joey. He has large strong hands and a thin waist and hips that look almost too small for his broad shoulders.

"So you're the peanut man at Ford's," the gravely voice colonel says, standing uncomfortably close and looking Joey up and down.

"Yes, sir," the man with the squeaky voice says from behind.

Joey gets a pit in his stomach and becomes instantly afraid.

"Sergeant, we had orders from the Secretary that this man was not to be harmed," the colonel says, looking at Joey's injuries.

"That's how they picked him up, sir."

"No fight in him?" the colonel asks.

"He came along peace-able," the sergeant answers, walking around to the front. Joey can see that he is slender with light brown hair parted in the middle and pasted firmly down. He isn't' wearing a cover and his uniform is field worn but not wrinkled. His dull grey eyes peer out from under a deep-set brow that gives him a constant scowling look.

"Maybe you got these from your whore," the colonel says. "She beat you boy?"

Joey shakes his head.

"Not too talkative are you?" the colonel says.

The sergeant is slowly wrapping a leather strap around his right hand.

"I'll tell it just like I did before..." Joey says. "I didn't...

The colonel holds up his left hand to quiet the prisoner. He walks around to Joey's right, when all at once there is a blinding white flash, that sends Joey's head violently left. The room blurs and comes back into focus as his head pounds with pain. He tastes coppery blood as it floods his mouth and comes out his nose.

"You needed your right eye to match your left," the sergeant says. "We got us a real nice tree outside where we're gonna string up your black ass, peanut boy."

So this is how it ends, Joey thinks. Just like momma said it would. Hang around whitey long enough, and he'll find a reason to hang you proper.

"That's enough sergeant," the colonel says.

The next assault came to his right ribs, taking his breath completely away.

"I said that's enough sergeant!" the colonel repeats. "Any more and you'll be sitting in that chair, got it Corbett?"

"Ned...it was Ned," Joey coughs. "He had to go set the stage and told me to hold the horse."

"Booth's horse?" the colonel asks.

"Yes, sah," Joey says. "I didn't see him get off it, but it was Mister Booth's. I saw him on it before."

"So you never saw him get off it?" the colonel asks.

"No sah, but I saw him get back on—right after I heard the shot."

"And you didn't try to stop him?"

"He come runnin' out and hit me with the butt end of his knife and knocked me down. When I got back up, he kicked me here in the chest."

"And it was Ned who told you to hold the horse?" the colonel asks.

"Spangler," the sergeant squeaks from behind. "He was released after questioning yesterday."

"Yes sah, it was Ned, gave me a quarter," Joey says.

"Good, very good," the colonel says calmly. He walks over behind Joey and pulls another wooden chair up to his right side, putting its back to Joey and straddling the seat with its back in front of him.

"Now you're gonna tell me everything, aren't you. We're gonna go over it again and you're gonna tell me everything," the colonel says, his gravely voice taking on an almost avuncular tone.

"Sergeant Corbett, have them men pick up Mr. Spangler, I believe he'll be at that boardin' house, or maybe at the bar across the street," the colonel says. He turned back to Joey. "Now boy, you're gonna tell me all about Mr. Booth, what he said, what he looked like, everything."

CHAPTER 11
The Petals of a Rose

When he ties his horse outside of Jemm's later that night, Lt. Henry is immediately confronted by a man in an elegant black suit. He's clean and closely shaven and wears a bowler style hat.

"This is Rome," the man says.

"We are Caesars," Henry replies obediently, holding his horse with one arm.

"Where are you going next?" the man asks.

"Gautier's on Monday," Lt. Henry says.

"Where they hatched the kidnapping plot," the man says. "We'll see you right after."

The man raises his hand to the bowler, tipping it slightly.

"Now then, have a good evening Lieutenant."

#

The pounding at the door wakes Jemm out of a dead sleep, black and without dreams. From his bed in the ondijungo he sees the shadow of Marnie through the curtain, moving toward the door. He sits up in the bed and rubs his hands across his face, trying to come back to the land of the living.

"He's here, all right, Missa Henry," Marnie says. "Come on in.

He jus came in and pass right out. I couldn't let him sleep all night. By da way, congratulations! I heard the Secretary gave you a commissen. Oh lookie dare it is in gold on that shoulder. You look quite the handsome in that uniform, too."

Jemm comes out from behind the curtain, still in his bed clothes. It's getting on to late Saturday evening. Jemm was hoping to get a few hours of shut eye after the long night and day. His eyes focus on Henry, slightly out of breath. He detects the urgent nature of the visit.

"I thought you'd still be sleeping," he says to Lt. Henry.

Why the hell did he have to wear that uniform? Jemm thinks. Why the hell did Marnie have to congratulate him? What's he tryin' to do, rub it in my face? Make me feel small? Well good ole bearded Billy Boy with the specs had already done that.

But once again, his gift turns on him.

"I couldn't help it," Henry says, looking down at his uniform. Jemm sees his eyes turn from urgent to genuinely apologetic. "I know we're supposed to be out of uniform, but I just had to see what it felt like walking around town. I just wanted to see people's faces one time."

"Forget it Ollie," Jemm says. It was the first time he'd addressed Lt. Henry by his first name. Before it was always his last name or rank. And Jemm isn't sure it's appropriate, or appreciated, until he sees Henry's wide smile.

"So what brings you here?" Jemm says.

Henry's attitude quickly changes back to its sense of urgency.

"They beat him up."

"Who beat him up? Who got beaten?" Jemm asks, rubbing his brow, still trying to push the cobwebs away.

"That Joey you know, I heard about it at the War Department. That 'Greater Glory of God man' Corbett."

"He is a strange one," Jemm says. "I figured it would happen. It usually does."

A white man can't interview a freedman without drawin' a little blood, Jemm thinks. It just ain't in his nature.

"Missa Henry, Jemm why don' you come over here and sit at the table and have sumpin' to drink," Marnie says. She had brought two tall glasses of lemonade and set them on the table right between the stunning white rose in the blue vase.

Henry is almost immediately transfixed on the white rose. He points at it and looks over inquisitively at Jemm.

"Hot house grown, her aunt sent it over for Easter," Jemm explains. But Henry still had some questions.

"She gets them for free, works for, well, used to work for, the President…as an advisor."

Astounded, Henry asks: "Helps with entertaining the cabinet?"

"More like the kitchen cabinet, really a spiritual advisor," Jemm says, "one of several. Mary Todd befriends a lot of the Negroes."

"Like her best friend?"

"Her dressmaker, Mrs. Keckley. But she doesn't work at the mansion, owns a dress shop on 12th Street. Cordelia works in the kitchen for Mr. Slade. She is said to be blessed by precognition."

Henry nods, finally understanding, but still a little perplexed. "I don't believe in that non-sense," he says.

"Neither do I," Jemm answers.

"He's out an out lyin' to you missa Henry," Marnie says, in an almost childlike tone. "He's as superstition as they come. Every time he travel to New York, he sees an old gypsy woman to get his fortune told…

"Not for my fortune," Jemm interjects, she just happens to make the best sausage sandwich you'll ever have…"

"But they give him the wind sumpin' terrible," Marnie adds. "Don't let him stop at that sandwich stand, or you'll be payin' for it the rest of the trip."

"So her only real prognostication is that the sandwich will give me gas," Jemm adds.

Henry smiles broadly again. He takes a long slow drink of the lemonade in front of him. It was half gone before he sets it back down.

"Well Jim," Lt. Henry says almost without thinking. "Can I call you Jim?"

"No you can't."

Lt. Henry's heart sinks, he has so few people left in the world, and most of them are back in Ohio.

Jemm senses it immediately. "That's because my name's not Jim, it's Jemm."

"But the Secretary calls you James and the diminutive…"

"Is Jim, but my name is Jemm."

"A family name?"

"In a manner of speaking, it comes from Jem Cato of South Carolina, leader of the Great Rebellion…"

"Of 1740," Henry interrupts. "I went to a lecture in Hudson, Ohio to hear Reverend Brown talk about it…"

"Before they strung him up, after Harper's Ferry."

"But only after he took over an armory," Henry says, correcting him in a congenial manner.

The two men sat smiling at one another.

"Jemm is fine."

"So you just let ole Stanton call you by the wrong name…"

"Every time without even trying to correct him. It's even on all my military papers," Jemm says. "Let's keep it our little joke."

"Why you sly old dog," Ollie Henry says. "I knew there was more to you than meets the eye."

There is another one of those odd silences that always seem to come when people need to digest a little information.

"I didn't just come about Joey," Ollie Henry says. "I have some serious concerns, not just about this investigation, but about why Colonel Baker is back in town, why we're being sent out of town—and just how easily Booth or Boyd made his escape.

"Everyone is saying he crossed the Navy Yard Bridge without being questioned or even stopped. What did you find out?"

Jemm tells Ollie Henry about the interviews with Sergeant Cobb and John Fletcher, and how a man named Boyd crossed the bridge first, with someone named Smith following closely behind. Jemm also tells him that he believes it was David Herold, who had been involved with a previous plot to kidnap the president with Captain Boyd.

"But that leaves the obvious question: Why didn't our great

Secretary of War have these men under observation? Why didn't he put everyone on alert, or make sure...

"He might not have thought they were capable," Jemm says. "Being a part of the failed kidnap, they did seem like a bunch of amateurs...

"Still he had to know, once he got the word, that it would be these same men who..."

"Or maybe grandpa Stanton was just out of place," Jemm says. "I heard he was at the Seward House and went back there before he even heard about the President. Having a friend attacked like that while recovering from a carriage accident is enough to put..."

"I agree, but Grant was also supposed to accompany the President, then declines out of nowhere and gets on a train to New Jersey—to see his kids?"

"It's not unusual for a soldier to want to see his family— especially after so long a time away," Jemm says. But he felt strangely as he said it. Why was he defending the Secretary? True, Stanton had been kind to him, but was there any reason beyond that to protect him now? After being passed over?

"Grant's son Jesse was with him at City Point a few weeks back and both his wife and Jesse were with him here in Washington and boarded the train with him for Burlington, according to the station master," Henry says.

"You spoke with him?" Jemm asks.

Henry nods and pulls out a folded paper from his uniform's right front pocket, his one hand fumbling as he tries to unfold the paper and hand it to Jemm.

"I know he also saw both Jesse and Fred at Christmas," Ollie Henry says. "What does that tell you?" Henry adds, his chin motioning at the paper.

Jemm looks down at the paper, a train schedule of the Camden and Amboy Railway out of Washington. Jemm always hated quizzes but was always very good at them. Was Lt. Henry going to be another Geoffrey? Jemm didn't think so, but this did set a precedent.

"He left at six," Ollie Henry adds.

After studying a few minutes, it became very clear. With the connection at Philadelphia, Grant could have easily left the next morning, and still been in Burlington for the family visit only a few hours later than if he'd not taken the train the night before.

Were those few hours enough to turn down an invitation from your Commander-In-Chief to attend the theater? Jemm thinks.

"Do ya see it?" Henry asks.

Jemm nods.

"There's even more troubling news," Jemm says. "I was going to spare, you but…"

Jemm tells Ollie Henry about his day at the War Department, confirming what he had heard from Tanner at the Petersen's house. Both Stanton and Eckert said they had very important business to attend to that night, Jemm says. But in the end, Stanton had only gone to look in on Steward, who was in bed. And Eckert spent the night alone by his own account, but Geoffrey confirmed that Eckert was only assigned there for protection until 10 pm.

"It's almost as if the Secretary knew what was going to happen," Ollie Henry says, hollowly. "If that's the case…"

Our lives could be in grave danger, Jemm thinks, this time purposely trying to put the idea in Henry's head.

"We're either on a fool's errand, or it's a good thing we're getting out of town," Lt. Henry says at last.

"Do you have fambly in town, missa Henry?" Marnie asks.

"No..."

"Well then why don' you come here for Easta suppa? You can be our dinna guest."

"Why thank you, that would be lovely, yes," Ollie Henry says.

With the abrupt change in plans, Jemm looks over at the white rose, and back at Marnie, who looks back at him innocently.

Dinner guest? Jemm thinks. What do you and Cordelia have cooked up beside dinner?

# # #

Back at Stanton's office at the War Department, Colonel Lafayette Baker is pacing back and forth in front of the Secretary, who is looking at him from behind his L-shaped desk. Baker's tall stature looming over the Secretary.

"You're sure he didn't break his leg on the stage?" Stanton asks.

"Sure of it," Lafayette Baker says, his voice a little less gravely than when he handled his interrogation. He looks out the window of the War Department office and onto the city spreading below, purposely turning his back on the Secretary. The sun is just starting to part the steel grey clouds that had shrouded the city since the assassination. The sun would be out the next day.

"He wouldn't have been able to hit Joey Peanuts with his knife, let alone kick him in the ribs. Impossible. Besides, he'd never have been able to make it to the bridge," says Lafayette.

"I understand he's very good on a horse," the Secretary says.

"You ever try to ride with a broke leg? Near impossible to go 100 yards at quick pace let alone several miles. No, he was fine despite his clumsy exit from the theater," Baker says. "Sergeant Cobb said he swears he heard something pop when he got off his horse, and I believe him."

"So you're sure he's hurt?" Stanton asks.

"Can't say for sure, but if he is, he'll head for Mudd's."

"You know for sure?"

"That's where we tracked him to last time, didn't we?" Baker says, turning back to his host.

"You sure he isn't hiding somewhere, maybe at the National..."

"Naw, he left town all right. I have to talk to that Paine or Powell whatever the hell he's goin' by this week. We should pick him up in a day or two...not too bright that boy. And when I talk to him, that will be the last time for him," says Baker, his voice getting low and intense.

It scares the Secretary to see him like this, unafraid of his position and superiority. Lafayette Baker steps behind Stanton at his desk, between him and the cipher room. Stanton looks up at Baker, his visage now blurred and out of focus over the top of his glasses.

"You keep that boy of yours off my ass this time," Baker says, almost as if giving an order. But he knows that he has the Secretary over a barrel, especially if he wants his help. "I heard he was already out to the 10th VRC talking with Cobb. That boy is a natural born hound dog.

"Come to think of it, I just may need him," Baker adds. "Do I have authorization?"

"Sure, but he'll be off on Tuesday chasing Captain Boyd from Gautier's up to Canada," Stanton says. "I sent the newly commissioned Lieutenant Henry with him to keep him in line. That should keep them both busy, and it might even give us more information on what's going on up in Canada."

"They are way too smart," Baker says. "Besides, these two may both wind up dead. Especially, if they run into Burley."

"He's incarcerated," Stanton says.

"Where?!" Lafayette asks disbelieving, as he steps from behind the desk.

Stanton looks down and picks through some papers, before he reads from the proper document, just to be sure he has the city right.

"Civilian Jail in Port Clinton, Ohio," Stanton says, looking up and talking off his spectacles. "Ashley the master from the passenger ferry swore out a complaint, and Canada threw him back to us."

"What?" Baker says again in disbelief, trying not to laugh out loud. "Sent him back for a petty robbery?"

"I know, I know," the Secretary says chuckling along with him. He starts cleaning his glasses, which were perpetually dirty, even when immaculate.

"Do they even know who they have?!"

"I doubt it," Stanton says.

"He'll be escaping soon," Baker says.

"And when he does, I'll instruct Jemm and the good Lt. Henry to follow him back to Montreal, keeping their distance..."

"And what if they find out too..."

"Relax Lafayette, I'll simply instruct them to track a fugitive."

Baker smiles. He likes the sublime nature of the plan.

"So who will you want?" Stanton askes, finally.

"I want my cousin Luther and his team to be a part of the party, with maybe Lt. Dougherty in charge of the actual military detail," says Lafayette.

"And I want Sergeant Corbett to be a part of the detail as well," says Stanton.

"But he espouses bizarre ideologies…his poor bedeviled mind is poisoned and lacks critical thinking skills," says the Colonel. "He scares me because he's unbalanced, a religious fanatic."

"But do you doubt his devotion?"

"No…no I don't. Who can?" Baker asks rhetorically. "But I want to be able to call Jemm back here—his work with the coloreds and the Secret Line could be very helpful if we run into a jam."

"You know they'll be headed for Cox, and then…

"Yeah, but they'll need a good guide through the swamps down there, and Jemm has contacts that know them roads and paths better than anybody."

"Call him back only if you have to then."

CHAPTER 12
A Holiday Suppa

I t is early Easter Sunday afternoon, the sun rising majestically in the sky.

Across the room, Lt. Henry smells the cottage ham that Sam the cook has brought up. With the cover off, the smell of cloves permeates the room. Sam had left and was now on his way down to the school, and probably at least halfway there, carrying Easter dinner in wooden baskets for the sisters and all who would be eating at the church.

"It sure smells good in here," Lt. Ollie Henry says. "Bet you could smell it three blocks away."

"That's Sam, you can smell his food for miles," Marnie says. "We even have sweet taters and other trimmins today."

As they sit at the table, Marnie makes sure to say Catholic grace in English instead of a prayer to Kalunga the Creator, out of respect for their guest. When they finish, Marnie cuts up slices of ham and gives them to her husband and Henry, but then she notices that Henry is having a hard time cutting the meat with just his left hand. Jemm notices as well and is about to offer some help cutting the meat, when Marnie shoots him a stern look that tells him not to interfere.

"Looks like you almost got it dar," Marnie says, as Ollie Henry gets close to creating a bit sized piece. "Don't worry too much bout ya manners, we pretty informal round here. When it looks like it might fit, just go about stuffin' it in."

They all share a brief laugh.

The three sit in silence, the food just too good to withstand any kind of conversation save a complement about its taste. Seconds are had by all, with Henry and Jemm finishing off the cottage ham with a third helping that is paired with dinner biscuits that melt in their mouth.

Marnie brings out a steaming pie made with apple preserves and a hot pot of special cider tea that she has brewed for the occasion.

"Here you eat dis pie, and make sure you drink that apple tea," she says to Henry. "It will make you relax and help get all that meat through ya system."

Jemm knows at once what she is up to.

"You know, I had a grandma named Marnie or Mamie back in Ohio," Henry says.

"I think everyone has a grandma named Marnie or Mamie or some such thing, makes me feel old," she answers with a laugh.

"It is kind of strange though, don't you think," Henry says, his full belly and the tea are making him just the slightest bit drowsy, but he is able to fight it off.

"Time and people flow through life like a river," Marnie says, as she stands and goes to the bureau by the stove where she had been keeping the white rose. She brings it back to the table and sets it not too far in front of Henry. The sun, which is now just beginning to set, reflects off the windows on the building on the other side of the street, casting the white rose with a strange orange fiery glow. "All of time and people flow through this world as if in the same current."

"How the hell did you get to the War Department?" Lt. Henry asks.

"Our people are Ovambo, from West Africa," Jemm says. "We were sold to the Accabee Plantation, which is now Orange Grove. It eventually was bought by a man named Perroneau. I earned, or maybe should say was granted, my manumission by Perroneau after I saved his son, who was really my half-brother. After Monsieur Perroneau died, my mother and I moved up here."

"If you stayed in South Carolina, you'd only be sold back…"

"It was just a matter of time," Jemm says. "So I went to work as a janitor at the War Department and Allan Pinkerton…"

"Not the?"

"The same," Jemm answers, motioning with his chin toward the white rose. "He's a chartist…and you know…"

"That's one beautiful center piece, for a wonderful meal," Lt. Henry says.

"You like it," Marnie says, "Look closer at how that sun plays wit da edge of each petal, do you see that missa Henry?"

Her voice drops low, almost monotone, "how many petals can you count on that rose? They must be a hundred."

Marnie reaches over and starts to slowly twirl the rose as Henry became transfixed.

"Now jus' look at the rose and relax, missa Henry, you with friends in this house. Put everythin' out ya mind and relax."

"How many rows of petals did you count?" Marnie asks quietly.

"There have to be, 20 or 22," but Lt. Henry is having a hard time concentrating. It seems like his vision was beginning to narrow, his head becoming lighter.

"It's easier if you start at one hundred and count backwards, can you do that?" Marnie asks. "You and I, we count together."

The count got to 87, when all at once Marnie tells him to relax and sleep. He is among friends. She snaps her fingers and Henry finds himself strangely relaxed, as if this was all a dream.

"You're relaxed just like yous at home," Marnie says. "Now tell us now what the Colonel Wells said to you on Friday."

Strangely, and without hesitancy, Henry says, "I'm to report to the Colonel Wells and the War Department anything that Jemm turns up and I'm to do so without his knowledge."

"But now you're gonna tell Jemm exactly what you will tell them, but you'll tell Jemm before, because we're friends, right."

"Of course, it wouldn't be right goin' behind my partners back like that."

"Partners...I like that. Have you told them anything so far?"

"No, but they want to hear from me on Monday, right after we go to Gautiers."

"But you'll tell Jemm what you're going be saying, right?"

"Of course, like I said, it wouldn't be right."

"And when they start with them questions, you will get all fuzzy and relaxed, jus like you is now," Marnie says. "You will only tell 'em what Jemm tells you to say, on accounta we friends...Now when I count three and snap my fingers, you gonna wake up, but you ain't gonna remember what we was sayin...ONE. TWO.THREE.

Marnie's finger snap jolts Lt. Henry back from the etherial and he realizes where he is at.

"Whoah, I must have been day dreamin,' or dozed off. I'm

sorry," Lt. Ollie Henry says.

"Oh don't worry 'bout it, we's all friends here," Marnie answers. "So now tell us 'bout your arm and your fambly, they back in Ohio ain't they?

Comfortable among friends, he tells them all about his grandmother Marnie who owned an apple orchard, and his brother Fitzroy, who had lost his life in the Battle Above the Clouds.

CHAPTER 13
A Troubled House

H enry House in Parma, Ohio had stood for more than 50 years, and the apple orchard behind it and its cider house had supplied much of the Cleveland area before its owners, the Henrys had fallen on hard times. The remnants of the family still lived in the shell of the once grand house, but its orchard and cider house were in a state of disrepair and had been so since the day that Grandma Marnie died.

Marnie's daughter, Norma had married a man named O'Higgins of some means, who had absolutely no interest in running an orchard or cider press. When the Great Conflict started, he balked at enlisting, and finally paid the commutation fee of $300 to avoid the draft in 1863. But the man who he had paid the money to turned out to be a jumper, which meant O'Higgins would have to join a unit—a fate which he didn't relish. He left one day in early spring, and never returned, leaving the Henrys to deal with his dishonor.

It wasn't long before Norma's sons Fitzroy and Ollie enlisted, keeping their mother's last name Henry, eventually joining Joe Hooker in the fight in Tennessee. They may have saved the family's honor, but they also deserted both Marnie and Norma to run the house and the business. Norma took to making preserves, jams and pies, which became very popular—especially with local restaurants. But she also had a hard time controlling the help, which often stole inventory.

That's when Marnie started holding the séances, where she would speak with the dead. At first it was a dodge, to make money and keep the place afloat. But the seances took a more sinister turn, as some of Marnie's predictions started coming true. There were whispers in town, suspicions, accusations. The local clergy naturally condemned the activities.

Then, one beautiful November day, as she was out back of the orchard on a horse drawn cart, with the men preparing the orchard for winter, they all saw something fall into Mamie's lap, dropped from a black bird overhead.

In turn, they dropped their work and surrounded the carriage, amazed by what they saw.

It was November 24, 1863, and 603 miles to the south Fighting Joe Hooker and 12,000 Union men had naively crossed a small creek, where they were ambushed by Confederates, expertly dug in and camouflaged in the short woods on the other side of the creek against a wall of granite known as Lookout Mountain.

It was the start of what would become known as the Battle Above the Clouds. It would also create the ominous military saying, "taking a long walk through a short woods." Despite the ambush, the Federals carried the day. But Fitzroy was carried off the field. For Oliver Henry, it was where he lost his arm..

There was no need for a letter. Back in Ohio, Marnie was riding in a buckboard when she saw a crow flying overhead. It dropped something from a great height. Looking down in her lap, Marnie Henry picked up a white rose, a flower obviously out of season. She looked over to the men working in the orchard who were stupefied by what they saw. She picked up the flower and said, with tears rolling down her cheeks, "Fitty is dead."

Marnie Henry was never the same. The séances abruptly stopped. The apple orchard fell further into disrepair. It was chopped down for firewood, all except two trees; one for each of her children; one for living Ollie, the other for Fitzroy buried somewhere in Tennessee. The Henry's cousins moved in to save the house and orchard, but Marnie was still off, distant, only talking with her five-year old niece Janie, who she had befriended following the tragedy. And then, almost exactly one year later, Marnie Henry simply disappeared.

She came to Norma's daughter Janie in dream one night, waking her and walking her around a room.

"This is the way it has to be," Marnie Henry said to her granddaughter. "Tell everyone this is the way it has to be."

The next day, Janie went downstairs to tell everybody about the strange dream, as Marnie had told her to do, walking them around in that strange shape. At first they dismissed it. Then they pondered it. Finally, they realized that Janie had walked them around the room in the shape of a coffin.

Later that night, a lone rider came with the news. Marnie Henry had been hit by a train. She was dead, but there wasn't a bruise on her body. It was almost as if the train had knocked her soul right out of her body, leaving her remains intact, pristine. The next day, they brought her back and laid her out in the parlor.

Since then, there had been trouble in the house. Disturbances. Furniture and pots moving on their own, Fires alighted in the fireplace, while no one was home. Marnie Henry's spirit was not at rest.

# # #

"I just heard about it in a letter the other day," Ollie Henry says, coming out of yet another dream. "I don't believe any of it. That's why I'm looking forward to getting back to Ohio. I need to see just what in the hell is going on."

CHAPTER 14
After Dinner Visitors

It is dusk, when Lt. Henry leaves. Jemm walks him down the four flights of stairs, just to make sure he gets down safe. People just out of a trance can sometimes stumble over their own feet. And Ollie Henry was in one of the deepest trances that Jemm had ever seen.

They walk over to Henry's big red horse with a patch of white on his nose tied up to a railing outside. Jemm is surprised at how nimbly the Lieutenant mounts the large beast, at least 16 hands high, with just one arm.

Jemm's gaze follows Lt. Henry as he makes his way up U Street. The lamplighters are out, the lamps already starting to throw golden light on the dirt street below.

He'll get home fine, Jemm thinks.

A gravely-voice from behind startles him, and Jemm knows all at once who it is, afraid to turn around but does, only to see Lafayette Baker standing at the corner of his building.

"How are you Jemm?" says Lafayette Baker, a small slender cigar hanging out from the corner his mouth glowed bright orange as he inhales. "Why did you betray me?"

"I took an oath to the Constitution…not to you."

"A document that doesn't even recognize coloreds as people, at least not yet, completely," Baker says, interrupting him. He takes another draw on his cigar, pulls it out of his mouth and examines its growing grey ash before flicking it onto the street.

"Isn't your allegiance to the Union?" Jemm asks.

"You know my loyalties," Lafayette Baker says. "Your people will never be accepted in our glorious new union. You know that."

Jemm doesn't answer, looking away. There is an element of truth to Baker's comment.

"Didn't it happen just like I said it would?" Baker asks. "Two states entirely devastated by Sherman. The white secesh trash, once high and mighty, now all turned into refugees. More than a million acres that could be turned into an Ovambo Republic—run by coloreds for coloreds. Maybe even an Ovambo Kingdom here in the New World…but you let that all go, didn't you?"

"I took an oath…and frankly Lafayette, colonization and repatriation are hard sells, especially after the Freedom Proclamation. After what happened before, how many negroes do you think would be willing to get back on a boat—you certainly couldn't make them pay any kind of fare…"

"I suppose not…"

"Most of my people have been here helping to build this experiment in freedom and humanity for almost 300 years. We're supposed to give that up and just move on? Like I said, I took an oath..

"You took an oath, that's rich…to whom, that old man!? The same old man you won't let call you by your proper name. Does he even know the origin of that name?" Baker asks.

"Like I told you before, it has to do with cultural expediency, of…"

"How about intellectual dishonesty?" Baker says. "The same way you yassa-boss any whitey you cross."

Baker steps around to the front of Jemm, his large, high-cheekbones and blue-silver eyes eventually coming within inches of Jemm's face.

"Well, I'm back now," says Baker. "And you're gonna be working with me again. Get used to it."

"I have direct orders, from the Secretary, to track a Captain Boyd…"

"You're chasing a phantom, and you know it," Baker says. "We already ascertained that there are several men named J.W. Boyd, and several of them are Confederate officers…

"We need to ascertain whether the men involved with the kidnapping are the same…at least there seems to be some new found urgency at least on the part of the Secretary. We need to confirm that the J.W. Boyd spy is actually J.W. Booth…"

"You know they are," Baker interjects. "Besides, I just got approval from ole specs himself. You go on, chase your ghosts. When I need you, I'll call.

"Got something for you—you'll like this," Lafayette Baker says trying to change the direction of the conversation. He hands Jemm a part of what he's been working on.

Jemm holds the three printed images of John Surratt, David Herold and John Wilkes Booth.

"Remarkable, Lafayette truly remarkable."

"We're combining photography and lithography, printing the images so they can be easily distributed to law enforcement across the area. I have three sets you can take with you up north. Give a set to that partner of yours. We're going to put these on a poster as well with a large reward. They won't be making a move without everyone knowing who they are."

Understandably proud Baker awaits additional forthcoming praise from Jemm. But none comes.

"Well…"

"I'm not sure Lafayette…"

"It should at least give us some positive identification between Booth and Boyd, or even confirm that they two are one and the same."

But Jemm hesitates.

You uppity nigger, Baker thinks, can't give me any kind of credit. Always thinkin you're better, smarter…

"It's just that, well one of the worst things you can have is an eye witness," Jemm says. "You know mistaken identities, false reports and accusations. I can see spreading these to law enforcement, but this could also give sympathizers the ability to better aid and abet."

Baker is still fuming.

"You know I'm against using the public for any kind of law enforcement," says Jemm still trying to defuse the situation.

You just don't want to share any of the glory, do you? thinks Lafayette. Always got to be better.

"These are very powerful," Jemm adds. "They are tools that really should be evaluated, before they go into the field.

"Besides, the same technique could be used against us in the field as well," Jemm continues. "That could expose under cover operators…"

Baker liked the compliment, but it still bit cold, especially with his failure in the field. He had tried to be a field agent but was dangerously inept at subterfuge. He once adopted the name Sam

Munson, tried to fake a Southern accent, and was almost immediately arrested as a spy. After being interrogated by Confederate General Beauregard at Manassas before the first battle there and then taken on to Richmond, he was able to convince his captors of his innocence and head back to Washington. That, and the fact that Jemm was such a proficient field agent, stuck in Lafayette's professional craw as well.

"Yeah but you don't have to worry, you're way too ugly for anyone to ever want to take a portrait of your black ass."

Jemm lets out a gaffaw. And Lafayette breaks into a smile.

"At least have your partner up there take a look, what's his name?

"Cao, Inspector Cao," Jemm answers. "I haven't even told him I'm heading there yet. Come to think of it, these might be helpful if used properly. It is brilliant Colonel Baker. But I think we only need two sets—the fewer that could fall into Thompson's hands, the better."

"Someday, I envision a time when we'll be able to send these lithographs much in the same way we send telegraphs today, all over the nation in the blink of an eye," Baker boasts.

"It'll probably be a few years before we send anything like these through wires," Jemm answers, "but think of it, being able to communicate that way at the speed of electricity—almost instantaneously. It does boggle the mind..."

"Ya know what Jemm, you're just old," Lafayette Baker says. "Don't like the new ways of modern law enforcement. But you're a fine old hound dog. Go up north and chase your ghosts. If I need you, I'll call...

"Oh wait, there is one more thing," Baker says as he turns back, "it true they caught Roscoe Peters in a hostess house?"

"I don't know…" says Jemm, hoping to drop the whole issue.

"Well if anyone would know, I thought it'd be you…"

"Heard he got caught with his trousers round his ankles…"

"Tried to run and fell, I heard that one too."

"Bare ass up and face down."

The colonel begins to chuckle. "Say hello to Marnie for me," he says.

Lafayette Baker heads back down the side of the building. Jemm hears him mount a horse, and head back down the alley behind.

Tomorrow he'd head to Gautier's, no matter what Baker said. And if he found anything wrong, he'd report it just as he'd done before. Even if it meant ending up on the wrong side of Baker's murderous ire.

As Lafayette Baker rides off, Jemm's arumbo comes on strong once again sending flutters up and down his spine. It is not in the form of a warning as it had been with Lafayette, but one of friendly familiarity.

Under a tree across the street, he sees the figure of a friend holding a glowing pipe. He smells the acrid smoke of fine Virginia tobacco. He knows all at once who it is.

It immediately confirmed Jemm's recent hypothesis: that pre-cognition isn't really pre-cognition at all, but something more out of the preternatural--the ability of the subconscious mind to process minute information in brief flashes the conscious mind could not grasp nor process.

"How are you Jemm," the accented voice comes, as Allan Pinkerton steps out of the shadows.

"Fine, sir, didn't expect you back…I thought you were in New Orleans…"

"I don't want Mars to know I'm in town He'll be getting a telegraph from me from New Orleans in a few days. I fear he may play a role in this."

Pinkerton takes a long draw on his pipe.

"Do you have Lt. Henry mesmerized?" Colonel Pinkerton asks.

"No, but Marnie does," Jemm answers.

"Sure…you know how I disapprove…"

"It's something my people have done for centuries, like your healthy mistrust of the British. Besides, it's just for protection, you know how Marnie is…we've also implanted a suggestion that will prevent him from divulging any information."

"It still scares me," says Pinkerton.

"Perhaps because you don't understand it."

"Or how to control it," adds Pinkerton. "There's a chance of suggestion under trance, that could lead to the creation of a false history that becomes fact for the subject. Besides, there's a very base aspect of it that runs contrary to my Christian education."

"But it is a safeguard…"

"Which, as always, is a wise precaution," says Pinkerton. "How is Marnie?

"She's with child."

Pinkerton's smile grows warm and wide.

"Congratulations, Jemm. Do you have a midwife?"

"I'm afraid Cordelia will insist."

"A good woman," Pinkerton answers. "Do you need anything, maybe a surgeon's kit?"

"That would be helpful, just in case anything unexpected were to happen."

"And it always does," Pinkerton adds.

"I suppose you know why I'm here."

"You know why I'm being sent on this errand?" Jemm asks.

"I only know that you are being sent," Pinkerton says. "I suspect the Secretary has an ulterior motive for confirming that J.W. Boyd and Booth are the same individual.

"I suppose we have Geoffrey to thank for that," Jemm answers as Pinkerton nods sightly.

"How are you getting along with Lafayette?"

"I guess you saw that."

"I know you two aren't the best of friends, but his heart is in the right place."

"But maybe not his fists."

"You are on the same side in this one—in that much, you can trust him. I have already spoken to him. He doesn't like you, but he does respect you—at least your intellect."

"So, who's in charge—

"I thought I left you in charge," Pinkerton says.

"Oh that it were true."

"But it is," Pinkerton interjects. "Why do you think the old man called for you instead of Lafayette? He needs you on this one, and he knows it. You know more about the Copperheads and Knights of the Golden Circle than anyone...As for Lafayette, he's afraid of your intellect, that's what causes him to assert his physical dominance and his ego. Remember how bad he was in the field... But he'll do as you tell him. Remember, men are not governed by borders, but are ruled by their own fear or ideals."

"I mean officially…"

"Lafayette, and ultimately the Old Man. I've authorized the use of the Post Office—so you'll have that to travel in--You know Lafayette's not going to give you any reward money."

"As I had surmised, maybe he can get me that surgeon's kit?"

"Wouldn't be a bad trade off—and he'd feel like he was actually giving you something," Pinkerton says. "I heard you were passed over this weekend. How is that sitting?"

"I don't think my people will ever be taken seriously," Jemm answers.

"Don't be disheartened," says Pinkerton. "I'm sure that the Old Man put the good Mister Henry there for a reason that had very little to do with his race…"

"Or intellect…

'Or intellect. He needed someone to keep tabs on you during your investigation," says Pinkerton. "Do you think Booth's mesmerized?"

"Hadn't really thought of it," Jemm says. "I'm not sure. But he may have been socially conditioned."

"Duck. Duck. Goose?"

"Except this isn't a kid's game," says Jemm.

"What about Lafayette?"

"He's not under a spell."

"Blinded by your own outrage over being passed over for what you thought were racial reasons…not like you Jemm."

"If he is mesmerized, we'll find it out," Jemm says. "Probably was a good thing to plant some suggestions with Lt. Henry."

"Just don't overuse it," Pinkerton says. "You may need him, or come to like him as a partner and a friend…As for the racial thing, can't say I blame you. But don't give up on this country son, your people have too much sweat equity in this country, over 236 years. You can't just walk away from that, it would be an insult to your ancestors, your family."

"Who have built much of this country without remuneration or even acknowledgement of their services. Sometimes, it's all I can do just to keep my mouth shut."

"I know son, but don't despair," Pinkerton says, while taking a larger draw on his glowing pipe. "Think of the skills your people have learned…

"By being subjugated! Next you'll want us to pay for the boat ride over, or perhaps our matriculation earned at the end of a whip… Have you been to the refugee camps? Have you seen the scars from the lash? Do you have any idea…?

Jemm could tell the words burned a little too deep.

"It's not what I mean colonel…"

"Sure it's what you mean, and rightly so," Pinkerton says.

"Think of all that has been lost. The knowledge, the science, all lost through a process of conquer and assimilation," says Jemm. "I was lucky. Thanks to our marketable skills, we were allowed to educate—even after the Great Rebellion and Purge. How many like me have been lost?

"Did I ever tell you the story of Negro Tom, the Virginia Calculator?" Jemm asks. "He came from the slave coast of Africa, just like my people. Because he was captured, and couldn't speak the language, he was thought to be illiterate—but he demonstrated to his masters, Presley and Elizabeth Cox, an unusual talent for solving complex math and geometric problems. He was soon used in the management of every phase of their plantation. My family's first master family, the Pender family, who were friends of the Cox family, learned the value of intelligence of the Africans. Tom is the only reason we were allowed to pass down traditions, knowledge..."

"Even forbidden practices like mesmerization," says Pinkerton, probing.

"Yes, even forbidden knowledge," Jemm says. "Think of the knowledge that has been lost by the African people brought to this country for agricultural work—now think of the knowledge lost by the native people here—how many natural cures grow wild on these shores? How many practices can improve the human condition? I've made it my avocation to save that knowledge—and once truly made free, once by manumission and next by military furlough—I will continue that quest."

"And I do hope it comes soon," says Pinkerton. "But now for the real reason I came here. Beware of Secretary Stanton—and this investigation. He not only sees you as an intellectual rival, but a potentially dangerous adversary."

"Then why hasn't he furloughed me already? I can put in my request now that hostilities have ceased. And he can..."

"No, he wants you on this investigation for some reason. He may be looking for a reason that might justify getting rid of you, and I don't mean in a kind way."

"I'm not afraid of that old man…"

"But what about Marnie, and your new family. They will need you more than your country."

"You don't really think…"

"I told you I have never trusted him. He's motivated by power but is also greedy. And thoroughly Machiavellian. He'll stop at nothing."

"Why am I even working for him?"

"He's afraid you'll go over to the other side, or some faction that might work against him. It's the old Roman adage Jemm—keep your friends close, but your enemies closer. Politically, having a colored on the National Detectives also gives him a political leverage with the radical abolitionists…"

"Which would make it harder to bump me off…"

"Unless he can find a way to make you seem dangerous, then you, Marnie, and I fear Cordelia are all gone…and it would satisfy any sort of deep-seated guilt on killing you—if it would become a necessity…But the Old Man is up to something. Haven't been able to put my finger on it yet. Is he trying to blame someone else for what Booth did? Is he trying to help Booth escape, if so, why? Or is he a part of a larger plot to use Booth as a fall guy, a diversion, and use you to facilitate the assassin of the assassin.

"As we said, have you suspected that Booth himself may be a product if not of a spell, than of social conditioning? Why would someone with his illustrious career want to kill anyone for a political reason? It just doesn't fit—there has to be more to it. And why would Stanton send me on an errand to find out what Boyd is up to, when he damn well know that Boyd and Booth are one and the same? That doesn't make sense either.

"But it sounds like you're already starting to narrow down your empirical questions," says Pinkerton. "Answer those and all your other answers will fall into place. I know that's a lot to digest right now. Almost certainly Booth is a victim of some sort of conditioning or at least circumstance," says Pinkerton. "And if you find that out, is Stanton hoping you might have some sort of 'accident' in the field."

"How so?"

"Be careful Jemm," Pinkerton warns. "You'll possibly come up against a man in Canada called Jacob Thompson…"

"Our former Secretary of the Interior, he's already in our discussions."

"Resigned at the start of the Rebellion, the Inspector General of the Confederate Army. He was named by Jefferson Davis to head up the Confederate Secret Service out of Montreal."

"I already know all of this…"

"Through Inspector Cao, no doubt. Remember, Thompson is not a man who believes in politics. He is driven by money and greed alone. He controls a good portion of the Confederate Treasury—which he considers his own. He is ruthless and will stop at nothing to make sure most of that Treasury lines his pockets now that the Rebellion is over."

"We're supposed to track the enigmatic Captain Boyd, and possibly someone named St. Helen, who I suspect to be Surratt. Baker gave me some lithographs, which will help in identifying the suspect."

"The two are pseudonyms…"

"I always suspected so."

"I don't know exactly what to make of Mr. Stanton sending you up north," Pinkerton says. "I don't know of any special relationship between Stanton and Thompson, but they certainly know each other. I'm not sure of Stanton's motivation—he's politically, rather than financially motivated—but you know I have never trusted him.

"He's also made certain that I am not on the investigation," Pinkerton adds solemnly.

"I don't understand that…"

"Perhaps it's easier to get rid of the investigators if they turn up something that is not of his liking," Pinkerton says. "Like I said, watch your top knot. I don't want you to end up like Agent Webster, or Scobell."

"But does anyone really know what happened to John?" Jemm asks of Scobell, a freedman also considered a legend in the intelligence community. "He may have just disappeared into a crowd."

"I'm glad you're an optimist," Pinkerton adds, obviously still suffering the guilt of two previously lost agents. "You remind me a lot of John."

"Cept I don't sing or dance," says Jemm.

"But your just as good at Yassa-bossin!"

"Why don't you come up and see Marnie?" Jemm asks.

"No, but give her my regards," Pinkerton says. "I have to get back down south."

"But you're not under any obligation…"

"Only to our former Commander in Chief," Pinkerton says. "I'm keeping an eye on Sherman."

"He's never had any…"

"But he's in command of the most powerful and largest Army on earth...an Army, I should remind you, that has demonstrated its ability to supply itself by foraging. It's an instrument of terror and death that..."

"I don't agree. I've met Sherman and he's never..."

"Met him? I work for him! Just like I worked for McClennan. No, he doesn't currently have any ambition beside quelling the rebellion. But a man with that much power can always be tempted."

"Do you think Stanton has been tempted?"

"That's something you will have to figure out, Jemm. Good luck."

CHAPTER 15
REE-WARD! REE-WARD!

By the time Sgt. Jemm Pender and Lt. Oliver Henry, leave for the interviews at Gautier's Monday morning, the town is already on edge, security is everywhere. The two meet at the corner of K and 6th, Lt. Henry having a little trouble with his tan steed with a U.S. stamped on its left rear cheek, yet another new mount. Jemm rides atop an Army mule.

"He looks a little balky," Jemm says, as he rides up to Lt. Henry, who is out of uniform as ordered. With his left hand, he is pulling his mount to the left and then back to the right, the horse fighting him at every turn.

"Just not used to my reins," Henry says, becoming annoyed at Jemm's constant observations. "Just when I have a horse get used to one hand, they end up giving it to someone else. I think that damn stableman at Camp gets a kick out of seeing me struggle."

"Want me to pass the word?" Jemm asks genuinely hoping to help.

"And end up riding a mule?" Ollie Henry says, still annoyed. But his attitude quickly changes after he says it, as if he knows the words would cut too deep.

"Better for a freedman to be seen riding a mule, than an Army mount," Jemm says.

"Did you bring the items I asked you to bring?" Jemm asks.

"Paper, pencil, pocketknife, why not a pen?"

"Too sloppy," Jemm says. "The ink could also spill."

Henry gets his mount headed in the right direction south down 6th Street, and the two ride south toward Gautier's, which sits on the corner of 12th and Pennsylvania. It is a short ride, and means backtracking slightly up Pennsylvania, but Jemm is in no hurry, wanting to brief Henry on the previous investigation.

The day had dawned overcast cloudy and grey, but is warm. Along 6th Street shop owners and bodegas open doors as merchants sweep dust off wooden steps and into the street below. The newsstand on the corner of H Street is doing a brisk business, four boys dressed in street rags holding up papers high with the fresh news, as people mob the stand buying the Monday morning paper.

"Ree-ward, ree-ward!" the boys cry out. "Read about the bigges' ree-ward ever!"

"Govament to give 100 grand for information on killers!"

The Post and other papers are reporting rumors, which would two days later turn out to be true, that the War Department is issuing a $100,000 reward for information on Lincoln's assassin and any conspirators.

Henry holds his rein tight as he rides by the stand, his horse becoming a little excited by the commotion, Jemm's mule calmly walking by.

"Well, that tears it, let the nonsense begin," Jemm says barely loud enough for Henry's ears.

"Don't you think that the more men…"

"They'll only work at cross purposes and slow the investigation," Jemm says flatly. "There's only one man who will catch Booth, and if I'm not mistaken, we'll see him up ahead.

The two cross H Street, Surratt's Boarding House on the corner, Henry notices Jemm looking around, as if hunting for someone, but the house looks vacant and quiet.

"You know someone there?" Henry asks.

"I served as a freedman handyman and servant there," Jemm says. "Initially, they didn't know I was with the National Detective Police. We needed information on the people who lived there or passed through. After a time, I think they began to suspect something or someone, especially Booth."

At G Street, they see a large contingent of DC police, as well as Major H.W. Smith and Lafayette Baker, who leads some men Jemm recognizes from the National Detective Police. As they ride by, Henry feels the silver, blue eyes of Baker, staring at them.

Jemm tips his hat, but Baker gives no response, just a threatening stare as if they are invading his territory.

"That's one scary man," says Ollie Henry, under his breath.

"Yon Cassius hath a lean and hungry look," Jemm says. "Such men are dangerous."

There is an awkward silence, only the muddled footfalls of the animals, and sounds of the city waking up could be heard.

"Think they're gonna raid that boarding house back there?" Henry asks.

"Know they are," Jemm says. "They'll get most of 'em back there, if they're the ones who planned this."

Lt. Ollie Henry is genuinely surprised.

"So Baker will get all of them back there? How does he know? How do you know?"

"Because they're the same ones who tried to kidnap the president a few months back," Jemm answers. "Sam, the cook and a server at Gautier's uncovered the plot, which we believe was supported by spies frequenting that boarding house. That's why I was there last month.

"We're kind of covering that same ground today. Mary Surratt, who runs the house, is the mother of John Surratt, a young man who we believe works from Canada for the Confederacy. We heard about it around the beginning of February."

Jemm pulls his mule closer to Henry's horse and begins to speak in hushed tones as the two ride. The proximity of the two animals, and the quiet voices calm Lt. Henry's mount, as Jemm tells him about the first interview at Gautier's.

# # #

The suspected kidnap conspirators were regulars at Gautier's, one of the city's finest dining establishments, often renting out the back room for a private party. They were generally well dressed save two, the one suspected to be David Herold, and another who was unidentified, but was large and brooding and went by the name Powell—this could have been Thomas Paine, the man who attacked Seward the night of the assassination.

The bill was always paid in full, and with a generous tip, by James W. Boyd, a man with greying hair and bushy eyebrows and a beard. But one of the female servers at Gautier's recognized the beard as a fake, and the hair color brushed on.

"It clumped in spots," she said, "almost as if done in a hurry."

So Boyd was in some sort of disguise, Jemm had surmised, seeing this as at least circumstantial evidence that Boyd was familiar with the theatrical arts and makeup. It furthered his suspicions that Boyd and Booth were one and the same.

According to Sam the Cook, and other servers and freedmen

who worked the back room, the group had met at the restaurant often, the management becoming familiar and comfortable with them. Long before there was any talk of a kidnapping, the group had often spoke of shipments from up north, as well as travels to Montreal and Canada when the names Jacob and Clement were frequently heard as a part of ongoing conversations.

So the kidnapping suspects were a part of a larger ongoing trade, perhaps gun running, Jemm had initially suspected, but then rejected as a theory. The shipments would have to be too large to run through the Capital without raising suspicion. And the trail from Canada just too long. It really couldn't be gold either, although it may have been money or foreign currency. None of the servers knew. And the management at Gautier's was reluctant to talk about payment in any form.

# # #

"That's what you will try to find out when you question the managers," Jemm says to Lt. Ollie Henry as they ride. "Remember that they will be hostile, and reluctant to answer any specific questions because they will be protecting people they see as good customers. Perhaps they may even be sympathetic to the Confederate cause. See if they ever paid in gold, and if so, what form.

"Take copious notes," Jemm advises. "Use breaks in the conversation and let them become urgent about the conversation restarting. It's a move that is threatening without being directly threatening—which puts the subject ill at ease.

"Read their mannerisms, sometimes it's not what you hear, but how they say it," Jemm adds. "Look for flash facial expressions that can pinpoint whether the subject is telling the truth or not…"

"Remember, small seemingly insignificant information, can sometimes be the most valuable, especially when it can be compiled and used to support a fact pattern. That's another item crucial to a successful interrogation."

"Are there any others?"

At that point, Jemm realizes that Lt. Henry could not possibly learn all the essential interrogation techniques. He decides to skip any advice on forming hypotheses or using empirical questions to ascertain truth.

"If things stall, just ask innocuous questions, like what the weather was like that night or how late they came into work and why, whether they have family and how close their home is but remember everything they say. Or write it down. Remember they are more nervous than you could possibly be. We're not really expecting too much out of management, so anything you uncover will be a plus. My investigation of the servers and freedmen should uncover much more."

Word had been sent ahead to have Gautier's evening shift ready in the private dining room beyond the main bar and oyster room. Booth had now been identified as the assassin and was traveling South with a man called Boyle or Boyd or even Smith, the papers didn't know.

"But why do you suspect the actual killer is Boyd and not Booth?" Lt. Ollie Henry asks, as they drew closer to their destination.

"You're actually missing the bigger question," Jemm says. "If this is a major conspiracy targeting all upper levels of our government, why wasn't Stanton targeted?"

"But why would Boyd want to kidnap Lincoln?"

"To use as a leverage to free or exchange Confederate officers held in captivity," Jemm answered.

"But if Boyd is Booth, why is he using a pseudonym to cross in and out of Canada?" Jemm asks.

"Obviously to keep his name clear if suspected of doing some sort of illegal activity," Lt. Ollie Henry says. "But there were several raids, and they really didn't amount to all that much."

"Or he didn't want to sully his family's good name. Which begs the question, why the haphazard and so obvious attack upon the president and his staff?" Jemm asks rhetorically.

"Desperate times call for desperate measures." Jemm answers. "The Confederacy has been desperate since they lost Vicksburg to Grant and Gettysburg to Meade. This isn't the first time the Confederates have tried such desperate measures.

"We first heard about a kidnap attempt from Sam back in January, he said they were contemplating it for some time, maybe as early as November. The attempt was to take place at Ford's Theater sometime in January. The kidnappers would enter the Presidential booth, incapacitate any resistance, and then chloroform the president, dropping him down to the stage and making off with him to Richmond...

"Sounds like the stuff of great theater, something someone like Booth would surely concoct—but not very practical," says Lt. Ollie Henry.

"Precisely, the other conspirators thought so as well," Jemm says. "That's at least one of the reasons they didn't pursue it. Until February, when all at once it took greater importance.

"Then another plot was concocted, to take the President while on the road in a carriage when he was coming back from a play. He was supposed to watch a performance of Still Waters Run Deep at Campbell Hospital, on the road to the Old Soldiers Home. On the way back, they would take him on Boundary Street and cross Benning's Bridge instead of at the Navy Yard."

"So what happened?" Henry asks,

"Stanton advised the President not to go, and the trip to Campbell was cancelled. We filled the carriage with agents. We also had the road heavily guarded and under surveillance."

"Why weren't these people picked up then?"

"They got spooked, didn't do anything. They simply watched the carriage drive by. You can't very well arrest someone for watching the Presidential carriage ride by."

Booth, says Jemm, had enlisted the help of some regulars at Mary Surratt's boarding house and other sympathizers in the area, who had subsequently met at Gautier's to plan the kidnapping of the president. They had all been identified. These included John Surratt (Mary's son), Samuel Arnold, George Atzerdot, Michael O'Laughlin, David Herold, Louis Weichmann and Lewis Powell or Paine depending on what he was going by that day.

"Why didn't they pick them up on suspicion?"

"I'm not sure. Maybe it's because we only had the word of one white man, Weichmann," Jemm says, "who got spooked, and decided to turn coat. He may have even tipped off the kidnap conspirators in the first place."

"The same Weichmann who is now out in the field with General Augur?"

"The same."

After this failed attempt, which was bankrolled by Jacob Thompson out of Montreal, some in the group gave up the hunt, hoping that their involvement had not yet been discovered, says Jemm. But Weichmann had been very thorough in the information he had given to white officers. Still Arnold and O'Laughlin had returned to Baltimore and Surratt had disappeared back to Montreal, something that Jemm wanted to confirm at Gautier's today.

"But what about Sam? Couldn't he have uncovered the plot

and had them all picked up on a conspiracy charge?"

"Reliable for my purposes. Reliable for solving an investigation. But unprovable in court. And certainly not for prosecuting a federal investigation. A freedman's word just doesn't hold up."

"So why are we going back today? Sounds like were simply rehashing old territory."

"Maybe so," Jemm says. "Maybe it's just my inquisitive nature. But I just gotta see why they were so desperate to free confederate officers."

"To refill their ranks, and bring in leadership, obviously," Henry says triumphantly.

"Ever see what an officer looks like after they have been paroled from prison? They're lucky if they can lift an arm to feed themselves," Jemm says, almost derisively. "Wouldn't be much in a battle until after about three months of bed rest and feeding. On top of that, parolees are forced to take an oath of allegiance—and believe it or not—Confederate officers are almost insane about their word of honor.

"No there's got to be more to it. It didn't come to me until the night of the assassination. They met at Gautier's two weeks earlier toward the end of February, and this is when I expect their plans became more intense. What had set Boyd or Booth off and why? No man would risk a career as brilliant as his, without some sort of motivation that went beyond politics. He may have been mesmerized. He may have been socially conditioned—and if so to what end?

"Something happened before January, and then something happened just before March that made the plots that much more urgent—and I can't help but think that the good Secretary Stanton is somehow involved."

# # #

Just a few blocks from the Executive Mansion on Pennsylvania Avenue, Gautier's was known as a very generous employer, paying the highest wages for its cooks and servers. It was also where Sam the cook worked every day, except Sunday, when he would cook for the sisters at the church. He managed one weekend off every month, which was exceptionally generous.

Sam the cook, the originator of the kidnap attempt investigation, had helped Jemm and Lafayette Baker uncover a honeycomb of Southern sympathizers and spies in Northern Virginia and Maryland all the way up to and including Baltimore. Many of these same suspects were already under arrest or being doggedly pursued by General Auger's Police or Baker's men by the time Jemm and Henry got to Gauthier's early Monday afternoon. But this time, they weren't there to uncover a plot, but to ascertain a motive, and what happened to Captain Boyd immediately afterward.

# # #

The private dining room used by the conspirators is just off the oyster bar, which is in the room behind the main bar. The bar, which is open only after five, is dark with only a few gas lamps throwing golden light. A small amount of light also comes through two small windows covered by English lace curtains at the front.

Two bartenders, both dressed in white shirts, dark trousers and working smocks that came well down the front, are re-stocking the bar, filling up deep wash buckets with ice to help cool down kegs of beer. Considered management, they will be interviewed later by Lt. Ollie Henry.

Jemm catches a glimpse of himself and Lt. Ollie Henry as they walk past the long bar on the left wall, catching his reflection as he passes each of the three mirrors directly behind the bar, the middle one raised slightly higher than the other two, but each a good four feet high.

Like the main bar, the oyster bar is being stocked with crushed icc for thc coming night. The evening help, which has been invited in early for interviews, sits in the back private dining room at the very front table, just as Jemm has requested,

Long and rectangular, the back dining room is painted white with black gas lamps on the wall that match the black wood crisscrossed beams on the ceiling. Otherwise, the walls are bare white until halfway down, where wood paneling painted black stands waist high on all four walls. The room has no windows, so the gas lamps are alight, throwing golden flickering light and shadows against the far wall.

The room holds seven heavy wooden tables lined up front to back, each with four high back wooden chairs. There are four booths along the rear of the room as well.

As Jemm walks past, he recognizes the faces from the previous investigation. Sam is there, smiling broadly, following both Lt. Henry and Jemm as they set up shop in one of the rear booths, just out of ear shot of the others seated at the front of the room.

Jemm starts out with Sam, who isn't as helpful as Jemm hopes he would be. He tells Jemm about running to the Sisters that frightful night, and seeing Joey Peanuts coming down the street in a big hurry, but that's about it.

"So you sure it was the same men involved with the kidnapping plot," Jemm asks him, slipping into drawl that seemed more comfortable to those of his own race..

"Sho as anything."

"When this was?"

"Bout, oh maybe a couple of weeks, two weeks before Father got shot, but on a Thursday."

"We're dey all here?" Jemm asks.
"Couldn't rightly see. I was in back and only came out for a

second…I had to get the oysters out."

"So they ordered the same thing they did last time?"

"That's how I could tell it was them. Ten dozen, with six more cold on da half shell."

"But did you see their faces?" Jemm asks.

"Only the one time when we was settin' up the chafers. But I caught a good glimpse. It was dem, all right."

"Think again, were all of them here that night?

"I think so. I only remember on accounta the young one John says he's headin' back up north to meet with Jacob. Then Captain Boyd say he supposed to call himself St. Helen, like before."

"You didn't catch a last name of who he was supposed to meet, did you?"

Sam sat for a moment, a little befuddled, then blurted out, "Thomas, it was Thomas, or somethin' like that," he said.

"Thompson?"

"That's it, Thompson!" Sam says obviously pleased.

"Did you ever hear them mention something about a parsons, or a priest, or a bell, an avenging bell?" Jemm asks.

"Naw, didn't hear anything like that," Sam says dejectedly. "I don't think they ever said nothing about no priest."

"In all the time Captain Boyd came here did his demeanor change?"

"What's a meaner?" Sam asks innocently.

"I mean to his behavior…did it change? Did he start to act differently?"

"You know, he did. He was usually all business with everyone and happy. But long about March, maybe end of February, he starts drinkin a lot. Stayin' after when everyone has left. Sittin' right there at the bar drinking and mumblin' 'bout an old goat—sometimes he finishes off a whole bottle, sometimes he takes it with him. And you could see the hate in his eyes mumblin' 'bout his density…"

"You mean destiny…"

"Yeah, that's it!"

Jemm calls Sally Clements next.

Sally Clements is a freedwoman, and while exceedingly beautiful, she always dresses down, wearing a shawl and plain brown clothing that hide her ample breasts and cat-like figure. She had been raped once by a group of white men, and this is her first line of defense.

"Make yourself unattractive Sally, and they's less likely to come at you," her mother told her once.

But she didn't listen and paid the price. Sally is the chief server at Gautier's, a position that paid her well enough to afford nice clothes, a luxury that she chose to deny given the circumstances.

#

Like Sam, Sally is convinced the men overheard in Gautier's are the same men who had attempted the earlier kidnap plot, but this time, they changed the mission to assassinate Lincoln and all high-level members of his cabinet to throw the Union into chaos.

"But yaw sure it was Boyd?" Jemm asks.

"Oh it was Boyd all right," Sally says. "I could tell the way he looked at me. You know the eyes, all right. And everyone in the room, callin' him Captain.

"Something happened, first in Canada, and then New York. Something about a parson, a parsonage. They sayin' something like that, like I couldn't understan' and didn't know what they was sayin."

"Did they say anything about a bell? Jemm asks.

"Avenging bell," Sally said. "Heard it outright…you don't suppose it was some sort of signal do you? You know, like when to pull everything off?"

Jemm remembered that night, hearing the peeling of the bells from the tower of the sisters. But it had come after the assassination, and Paine's attack. Maybe it was a signal that told other conspirators that the deeds had been done, the mission accomplished.

"Can't say," Jemm says, "but you've been very helpful. Do you remember when Boyd started drinking a lot?"

"Right around the end of February,' Sally says.

# # #

After four other interviews, it became clear that Lt. Ollie Henry and Jemm would have to travel up north, to retrace the footsteps of the man who traveled under the name of James W. Boyd.

Lt. Henry's efforts with the management at Gautier's were far less successful. They only knew that a middle-aged man named Boyd had always paid the bill—usually in Union—and always left a substantial tip. They did admit that he would occasionally over drink and would sometimes keep his horse out front, management sending him home in a carriage. They also said he started drinking heavily around the end of February.

# # #

Henry rides with Jemm in silence back to his home on U Street. After they split, Lt. Henry turns and the man with the same bowler rides up alongside. This time, he is dressed in a worksuit that is more appropriate for the neighborhood but makes his bowler strangely out of place.

"This is Rome," the rider says.

"And we are Caesars," Henry says immediately, but his head becomes fuzzy and he is unclear as to where he was at, or what is being said.

"Where are you going now?" the man with the bowler asks.

"I'm heading home," Henry says blankly.

"No, I mean where are you and Jemm heading next?" the man says, annoyed.

"North," Henry says, becoming even more cloudy in his thinking.

"Where? When? By horse? By train?"

"Train, I think. He didn't say," Henry answers.

"Have you been drinking? The man with the bowler asks.

"No. Not since Sunday dinner," Henry says.

"Why the hell did they put you on this anyway," the man says. "You are one simple son-of-a-bitch."

The man pulled away up 10th street, and Henry watches him ride away, his mind begins to clear.

"That's right," he says to himself out loud as if he were just remembering. "The train station tomorrow. I must be tired."

CHAPTER 16
Let the Nonsense Begin

Word of the reward sent thousands of men into the swamps south of town into Maryland and Virginia to hunt the assassins. It was the biggest manhunt ever assembled. Some were military, others police, still others private investigators and bounty hunters.

Worse yet, the lithographs that Lafayette Baker had produced had already been printed onto posters with the Reward information —there was no secret about who the government was looking for and how much could be earned for turning them in or offering information.

The military would eventually put more than 1,400 troops into the field: 700 men of the 8th Illinois Cavalry; 600 men of the 22nd Colored Troops and 100 men of the 16th New York. The Washington DC police, investigating a murder thought to be under their jurisdiction, put hundreds of inspectors and officers into the field, leading to a department that was understaffed in the city, which contributed to a sense of lawlessness in the town.

While the Great Civil War was thought to be ended it wasn't exactly over. The Union Army under Sherman was still pursuing Johnston in North Carolina. With more than 100,00 men under arms, and an estimated 20,000 bummers who supplied his Army under pillage rights. Sherman could easily move on the Capital. And no one, not any force on earth, could ever hope to stop him. Not even Grant.

The chief of the DC Police, Superintendent Richards, had

interviewed Weichmann who had an idea that the assassination attempt was linked to the earlier kidnap investigation. This, of course, was almost common knowledge among the National Detective Police. But now, Weichmann, along with Fletcher the stableman who had pursued "Mr. Smith" to the Navy Yard Bridge, were under the protection of General Augur, who led the troops and military police protecting the nation's capital.

General Augur, in turn, told Lafayette Baker that his services as head of the National Detective Police would not only be a distraction, but were not at all welcome—which didn't make one bit of difference to Lafayette Baker. He would just as soon see Augur die in the field by an "accident" while the manhunt was on.

For his part, Stanton did very little to coordinate troops, the investigation, nor the politics surrounding the manhunt. He retreated into his office, sticking his head ostrich-like in imaginary sand, as if hiding against some untold truth that would eventually come from the investigation.

So politics and greed would come to play an even bigger role in the manhunt for the President's assassins than patriotism and duty. Over the next few days, the troops in the field would only work against one another, as Jemm had predicted. The politics and inter-relationships between those of the rank of Major and higher would only obfuscate the issue.

The only investigator that really mattered was Col. Lafayette Baker, and he would see to it that he would apprehend the assassins and get more than his fair share of the reward money.

Make no mistake Col. Lafayette Baker was more than capable to the task. But it was not his skill as a detective, noticing small details and assembling fact patterns that helped him. It wasn't an innate ability in marshalling troops in the field toward a single cause, nor creating strategic alliances among mid-ranked officers, although he did use some in the final analysis.

Nor was it his dogged work and tireless interviews that led him to his quarry. He didn't beat the information out of anyone, although he tried. He simply knew the names and whereabouts of just about all the conspirators all along. Every one of them had been involved with an early plot to kidnap Lincoln.

While it was Weichmann who was reported to have overheard the plot at Gautier's, and fed the information on to the authorities, it was Sam the cook who had told Jemm, who had first interviewed the staff at Gautier's. And it was Jemm, who had later reported it to Col. Lafayette Baker, who had in turn, passed the information onto Stanton.

Of course, Baker had to make sure of the information coming from Sam, so he had him tied to a chair, and beat him. No sense in taking any chances. Sam was subservient and obedient. But when you're beating a man as big as Sam, you just didn't want to take any chances. So you tie him down.

Of course, once Jemm found out about the beating, there was another investigation. Turns out Colonel Baker, while having a little fun with the restrained Sam, had also relieved him of his week's pay. Which at the time, was Lafayette Baker's only crime. No crime to beat up a suspect. No crime to beat up a witness, either. And certainly no crime to beat up a freedman, no matter how unfair the fight.

All this was reported to Stanton, who took Jemm's word as gold. But Colonel Baker denied the allegation, leaving Secretary Stanton with a "he said, she said" decision. So Jemm enlisted the help of Geoffrey, who had found out that Baker had been spying on Stanton, intercepting telegraphs from the War Department. Stanton couldn't have this. Colonel Lafayette Baker was officially, and somewhat unceremoniously reprimanded, with the sword of Damocles of a potential court martial hanging over his head. He was sent to the field office in New York City. In addition to Jemm's mentor-mentee relationship with Pinkerton and Baker's failure as a field agent, this was yet another source of the bad blood between Jemm and Col. Lafayette Baker, the man Jemm now had to work for under Stanton's direction.

As Baker was awaiting an official hearing about his misconduct, he came back to Washington to aid in designing a trap to capture the Lincoln's would-be kidnappers. That was in mid-March. And it was the first of several notable deeds by Lafayette Baker that helped to re-establish his credibility in the National Detective Police.

Something had happened in February, and it set off the man the people at Gautier's knew as James W. Boyd. A man whose violence and hatred for the Union seemed to have boiled over into the irrational. There was also the issue of Weichmann, who was also a regular, maybe even one of the conspirators and the man who Jemm believed may have tipped off the would-be kidnappers. The same man who was now on the trail of Booth heading South. Would he mis-direct the manhunt for Booth in the field? Only time would tell.

# # #

CHAPTER 17
Pinkerton's Post Office

Tuesday, April 18, 1865

It is still dark the next day, when Jemm meets Lt. Ollie Henry outside the entrance of the B&O Rail Station on New Jersey Avenue. The first slivers of dawn are behind the newly completed Capitol dome, the gas lamps flickering gold against the city's new horse drawn street cars, which are already busy bringing people into the station. Just over ten years old, the brick, stucco and brownstone building is the shining star of the B&O Railroad, modeled after a large villa in Tuscany.

The building's four-sided clock tower rises 100 feet over the city towering over every other building in the neighborhood except the almost-completed Capitol dome to the north and east. Inside there are ladies and gentlemen's saloons, among other amenities for white travelers. While large when first built, the station is now overcrowded with passengers almost every day.

Colored passengers have a separate entrance near the freight depot, but still enjoy some of the comforts of their lighter skinned counterparts. Despite the new Emancipation Proclamation, and the support and sacrifice of colored troops in the field of battle, they still can't ride in the same car as whites—especially when traveling through Baltimore, which is laced with Confederate sympathizers.

Lt. Henry, by reservation through the War Department, is traveling in the first-class coach. His ticket waits for him at the ticket office, being turned over once he shows his travel orders. As he steps off the horse drawn urban line, he sees Jemm smiling out front. He has a huge stack of files in his arms.

"We should get our tickets," Lt. Henry says to Jemm, looking down at the files.

"I don't need one, they've made special arrangements at the War Department," Jemm answers.

"You know, that's just not right," Henry says, "through all of this…"

"What did I tell you about social expediency," Jemm says. "Don't worry, Ollie, I'm more than satisfied with my accommodations."

"So, if I need you during the trip…what are all those?" Henry says, his curiosity getting the best of him.

"Just a little refresher course for the trip," Jemm says. He looks up and sees an urban car pull up about 200 feet away on Indiana Avenue. He motions with his chin for Lt. Ollie Henry to look over at the person stepping out. There was no mistaking the silhouette of the figure, nor the face illuminated by golden whisps of gaslight.

"Superintendent Richards, what the hell is he doing here?" Lt. Henry asks.

Surely, the chief of the Washington police should be in the field with his men, directing their efforts in the capture of Booth and his traveling companion. He would want to at least have a stake in the reward money.

"Obviously on his way to New York," Jemm says.

"Shouldn't he be down south on the hunt?" Lt. Henry asks. "You would think the police chief would want to be close to home."

"No, this is the right move, the smart move," Jemm says. "He's heard a lot of information from Weichmann and General Auger. He's probably gotten wind of our trip up north. He's as greedy as anyone on this manhunt."

"Which brings me back to my original question, why wouldn't he be in charge of his men?"

"Which would be more valuable to you, Ollie? A mere $100,000 split a hundred or more ways, or possibly a big chunk of the wealth of the Confederacy? There's a lot of money missing from this equation, and I have a feeling that someone in Canada just may know where it's at."

"Then this might not be the fool's errand we thought it would be," says Henry. "So will I be able to get a message to you in the colored car?" Henry asks.

"Send it back to the postal car, that's where I'll be."

"That's totally unacceptable, I'm going to see about this…"

"No, you're not Ollie, like I said, I'm very satisfied with my accommodations. I'll meet you on the platform at the stop in Baltimore."

Lt. Henry watches his friend head back to the freight entrance at the rear of station. He isn't even allowed to use the colored entrance.

"How does he do it?" Ollie Henry wonders. "A man with his intellect, who takes no objection over how he's being treated, just because of the color of his skin. He's got a lot more tolerance than I would certainly have."

Just before the Baltimore Station, Lt. Henry awakes from his train-induced rattling slumber. The morning is in full bloom, sunny, with clouds that might turn into showers later in the day. Lt. Henry receives a message from the conductor.

"Come back to the postal car, when we hit the station. We have some studying to do before we hit New York."

At the station, Henry walks back through the second class and standard coach cars, but exits the train just before the colored car, where his presence might stir up indignation. He had mistakenly walked through a colored car in the past, which provoked a scuffle, and was awarded a black eye for not keeping to his own car.

The Postal Car is just like any other, painted barn red that is showing signs of age. Across the side, you can see small holes, less than an inch deep, that had been painted over in the same color as the car. From a distance, you can't see them. But up close, you can tell by the slight discoloration of the new paint that they are there.

Along the side, there are two large freight doors, there to accommodate larger packages. Up top, there are two small smoke chimneys, one belching a thin stream of white smoke. At the front, three steps lead to a small platform and a front facing door, which is the entrance to the post master's office.

When Henry bangs on the door, he is greeted by a large-framed man, with a full brown mustache, big hands and a postal cap that looks out of place against the man's razor jaw. Henry recognizes him immediately as Agent Beckwith from the War Department.

"I'm here..uh..to see," Henry stammers.

"He's waiting for you," Beckwith says, expeditiously.

It is the first time that Lt. Oliver Henry suspects that his friend, partner and fellow agent Jemm, has an actual rank in the intelligence community that is higher than his own. That Jemm's word and standing within the War Department and the National Detective Police are superior to his, despite their actual military ranks.

For the most part, the post master's office is very typical. With dispatches on the walls, and bills of lading stacked neatly on a desk. Lt. Henry walks through the office and opens the door to the freight compartment but is not ready for what he was about to see.

The freight compartment is a fine office, with two long beds, a large oak desk, wrought iron oil lamps festooned to the walls, and a red wool rug down the center. The walls, which are also oak from the ceiling to waist high, are lightly stained a honey yellow to reflect light. Windows on the side provide ample light as well. From the floor up, the car is ironclad, underneath the oak.

Jemm looks up and smiles broadly.

"Hi Ollie, welcome to Pinkerton's Post Office," he says.

"Where the hell did this come from?" Lt. Henry asks, his suspicions confirmed. "And how do you rate an agent like Beckwith?"

"Protection."

"Then why…how come I don't have…"

"You do. There are four agents on this train," Jemm says. "Two for you and two for me."

"Then how come? Why do you have?"

"I told you I was satisfied with my accommodations," says Jemm. "Besides, we needed people to see you get on this train."

"Like Richards?"

"And a few others," Jemm answers. "Let me give you a quick tour."

# # #

Initially built to protect Samuel Fenton, president of the Philadelphia Wilmington and Baltimore Railroad in the event of an emergency, Allan Pinkerton, had designed the faux postal car before he became Lincoln's Spymaster and Head of Union Intelligence Service and National Detective Police, Jemm explained. Pinkerton chose a postal car because they were already well fortified against potential robbers. But this postal car was a marvel of modern technology. In addition to the ironclad sides, there was a large iron plate that ran along the floor underneath the wood flooring and red carpet, creating a bullet proof sanctuary should the car ever be attacked.

"It's said to be able withstand a keg of black powder from underneath," Jemm said, "although I wouldn't want to be in here to try it out."

There were four doors, two freight doors on the side and two facing front and back, that could be secured against entrance by large oak cross beams that could be pulled out from the sides.

The oak running from the ceiling to waist high was not just decorative, but at two feet thick, could also absorb gun shots. Up top, one chimney was operative, while the other was a snorkel that could supply air in an emergency. There were shutters on the two side windows, that would close at the pull of a lever. To the rear, there was a small desk, with a telegraph stand. It could be connected to the underneath of the car to wires that ran through the iron plating.

# # #

"So who gets to use…"

"Usually dignitaries, sometimes myself," says Jemm. "This was one of the first projects I worked on with Mr. Pinkerton…"

"I knew you worked for him, but you actually worked with him in the field?"

"Before this war ever started," Jemm says. "He brought me up here from South Carolina after my manumission. He knew Monsieur Perroneau, who owned Orange Grove, and sponsored me as a servant at the War Department. When the war started, I enlisted, and Pinkerton kept me on, to interview servants and new freedmen, who might not otherwise talk with a white man or at least reveal the entire truth. "

But Lt. Ollie Henry knew there was more to it and wanted to hear.

"At the start of hostilities, Pinkerton had an agent, more like a younger brother, named Timothy Webster—who was found out and hanged. One of his field agents, named John Scobell, was a freedman who was brought up to Washington before the war, just like me. Allan really liked him, and—well he disappeared right after Webster got the rope. No one ever figured out what happened to him —at least not yet."

Henry looks at Jemm, who could tell immediately what he was thinking.

"Allan is like a father I never really had," Jemm says, looking downward.

"So Buchanan used this…"

"Not once. Never had to," says Jemm. "The first time this was used was to smuggle Lincoln into Washington through Baltimore."

"So those stupid cartoons…"

"We're right. There's a degree of truth even in some of the most vicious rumors. But it wasn't a matter of Lincoln's cowardice, as much as it was a carefully laid plan by Colonel Pinkerton," Jemm says.

# # #

When Lincoln was first elected, Pinkerton uncovered a plot to assassinate the new president before he ever took the oath of office, Jemm explained. The site of the attempt, Pinkerton learned, would be the City of Baltimore in the heart of Maryland, a state under Union control, but with a large population that had decidedly Confederate leanings.

When Lincoln was met by the crowd at the President Street

Station where he had to stop to change trains, there would be a host of men interspersed throughout the crowd who would be armed with knives. They would descend upon the newly elected president there, stabbing him to death.

# # #

"It sounds like something out of Julius Caesar," Ollie Henry says. "Was Booth involved?"

"It does sound like something dramatic that he might concoct, but we don't have any proof that he was actually involved, although there is ample evidence he knew one of the conspirators, an Italian barber at the Barnum Hotel," Jemm says. "I always suspected that he may have planned it, but I couldn't uncover anything—especially since he comes from Maryland."

"So Lincoln did sneak in through Baltimore in a Pullman?" Henry asks.

"Like I said, he didn't exactly sneak in, but he wasn't in the Pullman car like the newspapers said, either."

# # #

The most dangerous part of Lincoln's passage through Baltimore was at a point where the railcars had to be horse-drawn through the downtown between the Camden Street and President Street stations, said Jemm. This was done due to noise ordinances that prohibited rail lines operating at night in the middle of downtown.

Pinkerton sent out dispatches through Baltimore that Lincoln would be secreted through the town on a Pullman car, which would be horse-drawn through the town at night. He then cut all the telegraph lines at the main, so no further information could get out one way or another. The conspirators, who Pinkerton knew would intercept the electronic missive, would target only the Pullman car, which carried a decoy of Lincoln who wore a top hat—not a very convincing disguise up close, but from a distance, in the dark, convincing enough to provoke an attack. Once attacked, the Pullman would empty its cargo of Union agents, who would be joined by soldiers and police from Baltimore, who would capture the conspirators. The public was kept in the dark, so everyone turned out to see the newly elected chief executive when he made his Baltimore stop. They crowd was obviously disappointed when Lincoln didn't show up and they were told that he had already passed through Baltimore, Jemm said.

But the attack never came, either. The conspirators had gotten spooked, or had been tipped off by the Baltimore police, so they never attempted anything—just like the failed kidnap attempt in March. Meanwhile, Lincoln had been pulled through the city in Pinkerton's Post Office much earlier than the Pullman, which was a trap for the conspirators, said Jemm.

# # #

"If they had noticed the eight draft horses it took to pull an ordinary mail car, they would have known something was up," says Jemm. "People tend to dismiss the ordinary and every day, choosing instead to believe more extraordinary stories, or people, when, in fact, the most obvious conclusion is best. It's called Occam's Razor. The same mistake many detectives make."

"Kind of like the way Pinkerton uses you to get information from servants and freedmen," Henry says.

"And the same way he makes use of women as operatives, one of his best was Kate Warne, who was instrumental at getting Lincoln through Baltimore."

"So Pinkerton cut the telegraph lines…"

"The same way the lines were cut out of Washington last Friday," Jemm says.

"You have to suspect that someone in the War Department could have been involved," Lt. Ollie Henry says.

"Let's just say, it's very easy to make that assumption."

"Now I can't get those cartoons of Lincoln peering out from inside a Pullman car in his nightgown and stocking cap," Henry says. "Do you think…"

"If Pinkerton would have been here last Good Friday than our beloved president would still be alive?" Jemm asks finishing his thought. "Maybe. He certainly thinks so—burst into tears I heard when he heard the news, and is still wracked with guilt."

"Stanton and Baker…"

"Are hiding something? Stanton, but not Baker, but I don't have anything," Jemm says.

"If Stanton and Baker knew so much about the conspirators, why didn't they do more to stop them?" Henry asks. "Why did they leave the Navy Yard Bridge open as well as the Port Tobacco Road, when they knew they would be heading in that direction?"

"Perhaps they wanted them to flee in that specific direction," Jemm says.

"So this trip…is it a fool's errand?" Lt. Henry asks.

"Do you remember what I told you the first day in Stanton's office?"

"To keep my mouth shut so I only look like a fool before I speak up and remove all doubt?" Lt. Henry asks.

Jemm smiles, puts his head down and chuckles. Hearing it thrown back at him like that makes the moment appear a lot more serious than it was.

"That the Secretary doesn't suffer fools," Lt. Henry says, the realization coming to him.

"Or fools' errands," adds Jemm.

# # #

The first attempt at Lincoln's life in Baltimore was the first of several audacious plans by the Confederates to tip the fortunes of the war. The stacked files on the desk in front of Jemm, were filled with just such attempts. There were also personal dossiers with background information on relative suspects.

Another, more ambitious plot was uncovered in 1864 at Camp Douglas in Chicago, Jemm explained. The Sons of Liberty, Confederate sympathizers and Members of the Knights of the Golden Circle, would liberate some 8,000 Confederates held at Camp Douglas, and then march on to other camps at Rock Island, Springfield and Alton liberating prisoners and supplying them with arms as they went. They would capture major towns and capitals in Northern states, where they would comprise a second front creating a Northwestern Confederacy that would attack Union armies from the rear.

Creating an alliance with pro-Southern sympathizers in the North had long intrigued the Confederacy to the point where they had sent agents north to Canada to Toronto and Montreal where they would coordinate operations.

Originally, the Camp Douglas takeover was slated for July of 1864, but somehow Union Intelligence had gotten wind of the plot, through two turncoat Colonels inside the prison, who smuggled information out through one of the newly assigned colored servants. It was, of course, Jemm, who had been dispatched by Stanton to work his magic and move with freedom among the captors--who generally treated him as though he were deaf and mute—although he never led them on that way.

On Jemm's advice, and National Detective Police insistence, the guard at Camp Douglas was doubled, so the entire escapade was postponed.

A second attempt was made during the Democratic National Convention on August 29, the Confederate spies relying on the expanded presence of pro-Southern sympathizers like the Sons of Liberty and the Knights of the Golden Circle who attended the event. The attack was to be coordinated from Lake Michigan by refugees and mercenaries from Canada, but once again the authorities were alerted, and the entire plot called off. Another attempt was tried on Election Day, November 8, but this time the plot called for fires to be set across Chicago.

A week prior, one of the Confederate turncoat Colonels known as the "Texan" was allowed to escape with the help of Jemm and got in contact with the conspirators who then concealed him. The Texan, called Shanks, uncovered a long list of conspirators. Two days before Election Day, arrests started being made at a furious pace. The subsequent investigation turned up over 100 conspirators, including a Captain Hines who had organized the entire plot. Other captors included an English Colonel, who got life imprisonment for his involvement, and on the Dry Tortugas at the end of the Florida Keys.

All in all, the Chicago plots seemed amateurish at best, with Union Intelligence way out in front of any plot.

# # #

"But it was a plot in September of 1864, a plot that also ultimately failed, that really put us on edge, but I had forgotten about it, because I wasn't involved," says Jemm. "This time, however, the conspirators and spies got away—as well as a very precious cargo that no one wanted to talk about. It may provide another powerful link between Booth and Boyd."

In September of 1864, Jemm says, Confederate spies working from Canada had attempted to capture the U.S.S. Michigan on Lake Erie, at 450 tons, the largest gunboat on the Great Lakes, to free more than 2,000 Confederate officers held at Johnson's Island in Sandusky Bay.

"The Michigan would easily give the Copperheads, the Sons of Liberty and Knights of the Golden Circle control of all the Great Lakes, opening up a supply chain through Canada while giving the Secesh a Northwest front complete with 2,000 Confederate officers," adds Jemm.

The plan was to commandeer a sidewheel steamer out of Sandwich Island on the Canadian side as she made her usual run to Sandusky. Then the pirates would take over the Michigan sitting in Sandusky Bay with the help of a Capt. Cole, a Confederate Captain posing as an oil baron who was on board the Michigan.

"I suspect that whatever happened in February, was somehow related to the ill-fated attempt to take the Michigan."

"But the plan failed?" Lt. Henry asks.

"Turns out the redoubtable Captain Cole was also one of our men," Jemm says. "So if they went through with it, we would have captured the whole lot."

"So they got spooked again?"

"No, this time there was some sort of mutiny among the pirates," Jemm explains. "The crew on the Michigan wrongly thought Cole had tipped off the pirates, and he was arrested. But according to eyewitness testimony, they found something of value on the sidewheel steamer and their plans abruptly changed. They also took possession of a 'special cargo' as near as I can tell from the report."

Nobody officially knew what it was, but it sure pissed off Secretary Stanton to no end. From that day forward, Stanton took a very special interest in the workings of Confederates running operations out of Montreal and Toronto, including a man named Jacob Thompson, who was rumored to have a bank account of at least $600,000 to fund operations, as well as access to other funds that could amount to 40 percent or more of the Confederacy's treasury.

"That's probably why Stanton wants us to follow Boyd's trail up to Canada," says Jemm. "To establish some sort of link."

As the train heads north, Jemm walks Lt. Henry through the various dealings of the National Detective Police with a ring of Confederate agents and spies that was being run out of Montreal and Toronto under the tutelage of Jacob Thompson, the former U.S. Secretary of the Interior, who had resigned at the beginning of hostilities to join the Confederacy.

Jemm hands Henry two lithographs that Lafayette had given him, one of Surratt and one of the actor John Wilkes Booth. Pocket sized, both had wood backings.

"These are all I could get, so I had them put wood on the back so they wouldn't get too wrinkled," Jemm says. "If they get confiscated, you're out of luck until we get back in D.C. When we get to Montreal, you'll want to ask questions about St. Helen or Surratt," Jemm adds, pointing to his photo. "I'll ask the servants about Boyd, if a different man exists. See if you can find the names Boyd or St. Helen on the register at St. Lawrence Hall, it's a big hotel up there, but be discreet about it. Don't drop any names unless you're sure it suits your purpose.

"Think only about collecting answers to the smallest empirical questions. Don't think about anything over-reaching or broad—I have my own questions for that. Here's a daguerreotype of Thompson, the best we have, but still not very good," says Jemm.

Thompson is a man with a full flock of abundant black hair, with a meaty face and strong chin, and thick eyebrows that spread across his forehead. As Inspector General of the Confederate Army, Jacob Thompson has unlimited funds at his disposal, including unfettered access to the Confederate Treasury. As Inspector General, he is also the man who performed all the audits and accounted for all funds distributed and spent.

"You'll also want to study these," Jemm says, handing over several personal dossiers held in tan file folders. "Study what you can about Booth, his childhood, who his friends were, who his pets were, everything. Remember, sometimes the smallest detail can have a dramatic impact on the overall investigation.

"We'll also be working with a contact I have in Canada," Jemm says.

"Aren't they having their own Civil War up there?" Lt Henry asks.

"The difference is that they are voting about it, not killing each other," Jemm answers. "They have already voted on a Confederation between Upper and Lower Canada, but it won't actually take place for a few years."

"Our contact is Billy Cao, who works for two agencies aligned with the Montreal Police, but are provincial in their scope," He works for a Gilbert McMicken, a shrewd and very capable constable and magistrate out of Upper Canada."

"Where do we meet?"

"We don't, he'll find us," Jemm answers. "Now let's get back to our studies."

As the train rolled on, the two men studied files. Lt. Ollie Henry, however, found himself getting tired, almost dozing off to sleep several times.

CHAPTER 18
Switchbacks

As the train pulls into Jersey City Station, both Lt. Henry and Jemm are unaware that the whole day has passed while they were cloistered in Pinkerton's Post Office studying. For Jemm, study is an avocation. For Ollie Henry, a necessary evil. It is early evening and the sky to the east is overcast, with the setting sun bathing the clouds behind the city in pink and reflecting bright golden light of the windows of the buildings.

The Agent Beckwith at the front of the postal car comes back into the office.

"Jersey Station, we're switching over," he says.

"That means we probably have at least a half an hour," Jemm says. "You might want to get out and stretch your legs."

"And clear my head a little," Lt. Ollie Henry says.

"They got a great Romani food stand here, run by an old woman. Sells the greatest sausages. Says the come from Vienna," Jemm says.

"And hopefully not the stable," Henry answers. "No thanks, I'll wait until we get into Montreal later."

"That might not be until well after midnight," Jemm says, "and there might not be that much open."

"I'll take my chances."

Jemm bounds out the front door and walks the few steps up to the station platform. Porters are ferrying hand dollies into the station, some filled with luggage, others with cargo. Small booths line the platform across the station wall, selling popcorn, chestnuts, sausages and more, the smells reminding Jemm of the whirligigs for the colored down south when he was a boy.

Lt. Henry isn't so lucky. Beckwith grabs him by the arm just as he was starting to leave car. His grip is firm, strong, but not disrespectful.

"Sir, I'll need you here to test the telegraph lines once we get 'em connected," Beckwith tells him.

"But I don't know the first thing about..."

"It requires an officer, sir," Beckwith says, a broad smile coming across his stern face. "All you have to do is listen to see if it's clicking. I'll come in and receive the dispatches. The message repeats every three minutes until we respond."

Lt. Henry watches Jemm, who waves back at him from the station platform and smiles. It isn't the first time Lt. Ollie Henry had been stuck with extra duty by someone who got the jump on him heading out for liberty—as brief as that would be at the Jersey City station.

As Jemm walks toward his favorite sausage stand, he smells the meat grilling along with onions. A fainter smell of fresh rolls gnaws at his stomach, and he realizes that he hasn't eaten since Marnie had sent him off earlier that morning.

But as he approaches the stand, a strange feeling comes over him. There is a gnawing from his arumbo, not hunger, that bothers him. That somehow close by, there is an answer.

The old Romani Woman is standing at her booth, a pastel gypsy scarf around her head, shooting him a look that says: "don't ask." But it only piques Jemm's natural curiosity.

"I see you come back to me again" the old woman says with a broad smile. "But not just for the sandwich, maybe some questions this time?"

As he had many times before, in other places, Jemm has the feeling that he is projecting his thoughts into her head, and that she can hear them just as clearly as if they are spoken, even shouted.

"Your thoughts, once again, are loud. Why do you want me to answer thine questions, questions that thou knowest the answer, if only ye could search your own mind," the woman says. "Why dost thou test me, Moorish prince?"

"Give me one the same way you always—"

"Ahh with the onions," she says, putting a sausage between a roll and dolloping a small heap of onions on top. "Why have you lied to your friend on the train. Hast thou told him he is under a spell? Why does he travel under a spell, Perhaps I should tell him."

"No please don't," Jemm, pleads. "He is under a spell for…

"A reason that suits you," the woman says. "But perhaps placed by another?"

"Yes—it's something our people do."

"It is something our people do as well. Why dost thou journey?"

"I am on the trail of a man," Jemm says. "A man, who…"

"Again another man, but this time the man with no future," the Gypsy Woman says. "This is of no use to you. Nothing good will come of it."

Jemm smiles and hands her the money. For some reason he wants to talk more but a sharp whistle crackles through the air. Jemm looks over at Pinkerton's Post Office to see Lt. Ollie Henry with two fingers of his left hand in his mouth. He uses the same to fingers to motion for Jemm to come over, which he tries to, gobbling only a few bites of the sandwich before most of it falls beside the rails.

Jemm hustles over to the postal car.

"What's up Ollie," Jemm says slightly out of breath.

"You've been ordered back to DC at once," Lt. Ollie Henry says. "I'm to go on to Montreal alone, and you're to go back with the car."

"By whose orders?" Jemm asks.

"Baker."

"I'll need to send a ciphered message to our contact before we leave," Jemm says.

"How will I know how to find him?"

"Like I said before, he'll find you," Jemm says.

CHAPTER 19
Back to the Hunt

Lt. Henry was well on his way up the Hudson River Valley toward Montreal by the time the Jersey City yard handlers had turned around Pinkerton's Post Office. Indeed, it was at least nine in the evening before they had the postal car turned around and another half hour before it was mated to a cargo train headed south to the Capital.

Jemm waited the entire time, dozing off occasionally on the postal car's bunk, wondering what might await him when he got back. When the postal car was finally dispatched, it was linked up with a cargo train that would make the trip express, pausing only to let other traffic pass in the other direction.

At least there won't be all those stops, Jemm thought, as he drifted off into a fitful sleep of nightmarish images. Sam, crying, "Fathers been shot". The news spreading across the town in concentric circles, reaching his window just as the sisters' bell began to toll. Then, Father's been shot again, the bell tolling this time louder. And Stanton saying, Sic semper something, the bell tolls, no the bell avenges. What does the bell avenge?

There are evil priests just as there are evil men, Stanton told him in his dreams. But Stanton never said anything close to this to him, as near as he could recollect. He saw one of the young kidnap conspirators, John Surratt, dressed as a Swiss Guard at the Vatican. But what role would the Vatican have to play?

"He was here talking about Massa Robert," Aunt Cordelia said in the ethereal. But why would Stanton talk about Robert Lincoln?

He awoke only when the postal car lurched forward. Jemm staggered over to his desk and plopped a stack of files down in front of him. Surely, there had to be something else here in the files. Even the smallest detail could be crucial to the overall investigation. The car gave another annoying buck, as it started on its voyage south, and the top half of the files fell over. As Jemm began to re-stack the files. One caught his eye, and he didn't know why. Coincidence? It had to be. But such happenings shook Jemm's confidence in science and deductive reasoning.

It was a simple report from the National Detective Police Files, from the Jersey City Station dated Feb. 12, 1865. It was wire message, taken by Charlie Dana Assistant Secretary at the War Department. It wasn't classified, nor marked Secret, nor even urgent. Just a plain missive, a confidential incident report.

CONFIDENTIAL REPORT

The incident occurred at approximately 0302, while passengers were purchasing sleeping car spaces on the Capital Limited from a conductor (Manfrey), who stood at the end of car on the station platform. The train, delayed, was the last to Washington that evening, and spaces were at a premium. According to the Conductor Manfrey, sleeper tickets had sold out, but the crowd persisted and became agitated. Lincoln, (Robert Todd) returning from Harvard, was positioned at the front of the group and was crowded into the narrow gap between railcar and the station platform where he fell perilously close to the cars wheels, which were coming toward him. He was pulled from harm by Booth (Edwin). And the two caught a later train the next morning.

ACTION

Manfrey reports no conspiracy or evidence of crime in Lincoln being forced into his dangerous predicament. NO ACTION REQUIRED.

POSSIBLE CIVILIAN COMMENDATION FOR BOOTH (Edwin).

That Incident Report keeps Jemm up most of the night reading files. He is convinced there is something more in there. But where?

# # #

As the night wears on, the car becomes humid, and sticky. Jemm opens one of the top vents, and asks the agent up front of they can open the doors to get some air flowing.

"If it's what you want, it's okay with me," Beckwith says. "Don't 'spect no trouble headin' back."

And Jemm wonders, when does that man ever sleep? As far as he could tell, Beckwith was up the whole way to New York and would now be up the whole way back.

By the time the train pulls into B&O Station, it is only slightly after half past three in the morning. The City is quiet, and you can hear young frogs from river, streams and small ponds around town, squeaking softly—not yet large enough to be a bother. Their voices will grow and mature through summer, to eventually create a cacophony that will annoy the casual visitor to town.

It won't be long before summer, Jemm thinks. This will all soon be behind us.

As he passes toward the front door of the car, Beckwith hands him a message:

"Walk up New Jersey toward the Capitol. I'll meet you along the way."

--Baker.

As Jemm walks up New Jersey Avenue, he notices that the puddles left by the rains of the previous weekend had dried up, and there are large cumbersome ruts along the street. He hears a wagon rattle up behind him. As he turns, he sees Lafayette Baker at the reins.

"I need a good blood hound, and hear you're the best in these parts", Baker says. "Hop on board, I'll brief you."

"I heard the funeral is today," Jemm asks, hoping to get at least a few hours off for some sleep.

"Your country needs you in the field," Lafayette Baker says. "Besides, I heard you already paid your respects at his death bed. I never had that honor."

The comment brings an odd silence. Jemm doesn't know how to respond at Baker's obvious jealousy. Was the comment made to make Jemm feel guilty about having the Colonel cashiered for stealing from Sam?

"So they're going by Boyd and Smith?" Jemm asks.

Baker looks over and nods affirmatively.

"They're not headed north," Jemm says.

"Knew that," Lafayette Baker says. "They'd reach a dead end in Baltimore. Couldn't head no farther north, nor head west for that matter. We think Surratt was heading up north prior under the name of John St. Helen."

"As I had surmised at Gautier's. So, if…"

"Like I said, I need a blood hound and you're it," Baker says.

"There are no less than four different factions on the trail of the two," Baker adds.

He needs Jemm to move between all of the them and get information—listening to troops, acting as a step-n-fetch it. He could work with Elizabeth Van Lew's cadre of spies if he wanted.

Her group, it was said, had already infiltrated as high as the Southern White House through the work of Mary Bowser, a freedwoman. They worked with Grant's intelligence officers through his headquarters at City Point. But Jemm has his own network of reliable contacts as well—contacts that knew the land, and all its great hiding places.

"They won't have the sense to ask the servants and colored about what they saw, and if they do, they likely won't believe them," the Colonel says.

Which brought about another protracted silence.

"Why did you betray me?" Colonel Baker says, and Jemm could detect a hint of anguish in Lafayette's voice. "Why did you choose that old man over me? That old man who treats you like a boy?"

"Then why do you call me a boy in his presence?"

"For the same reason you don't let him call you by your real first name!" Baker almost shouts. "I treat you like that so he's comfortable that our relationship is in line with our current social relationship.

"Do you respect me, Jemm?"

"I fear you."

"Honesty, again that honesty—you may be intellectually dishonest with that old man, but you're totally honest with me. Why? I had hopes for you—hopes that you would be as noble as the bard's tragic Moor."

It is the second time in 24 hours that he's been referenced as Othello, and it raises Jemm's arumbo. Something is wrong, but he doesn't know what.

"But you'll recall what happened to him," Jemm says.

Again, another odd silence.

"Are you with me on this Jemm? I need to know," Baker says.

"Yes, I'm with you," Jemm says.

Jemm's field contacts will be Major O'Bierne, and a Lieutenant Dana, who is Charlie Dana's cousin from the War Department's. Then there is Lt. Luther Baker, Lafayette's cousin who is the leading contact for the National Detective Police and a pretty damn good manhunter in his own right. Jemm is to share any information with only them, and then only on a limited basis and through cipher-coded messages. Any concrete information, will be sent directly to Lafayette Baker, and then only by a specified runners. The wires are not to be used, unless necessary to send misinformation to direct the troops in the field away from the actual suspects.

"Stay off the wire, there are too many ears—It is imperative that my men take Booth and his companion," Baker says. "If you use Van Lew's network, don't let them know who or what you're looking for…and don't let them send any inappropriate information off to City Point."

"You know who he is?"

"Of course," the colonel says. "So do you. We think both Booth and this Smith, who's probably Herold, are hiding out in the woods and swamps around property owned by Samuel Cox. We're pretty sure they haven't crossed into Virginia yet.

"There's a freedman down there named Noah, and his daughter Elizabeth," says Jemm. "He's a handy man, good with a hammer, fixing wagons, and such. I've never met him, but I'll want to talk to him."

Despite having an abundance of men in the field, "and crossing fields and forests arm-to-arm in formations so tight that not even a rabbit could escape," as the newspapers had said, not one of the units has been able to detect where Booth and Smith are hiding.

If they are still there, Jemm thinks, they will need to be sheltered. They will need food. They will need Noah and Elizabeth, who probably don't have any political leanings, but only want to be left alone.

CHAPTER 20
Thompson's Raiders

At the Canadian border, Lt. Oliver Henry passed into Canadian territory without incident, offering papers that show him on leave and headed for Montreal. It is no small feat, given the political tension between Canada and the United States. Washington had long blamed Canadian authorities for not cracking down on operations from the North that included the raid on St. Alban's, the seizure and pirating of ships on Lake Erie—even the burning of hotels in New York City. And Canada was suspicious of Washington for having placed gunboats on the Great Lakes, including the U.S.S. Michigan, which ruled Lakes Erie, Huron and Michigan.

#

At Rue Saint Jacques just several blocks inland from the Port, but not quite as far inland as the Place d' Armes, Henry catches the first glimpse of his destination, where Jacob Thompson has a room that acts as the Confederate office. Some five stories tall, St. Lawrence Hall is Montreal's grandest hotel, painted white with its name spelled out in black lettering over two stories up.

Lt. Henry's mission, per Jemm, is to only ascertain if Jacob Thompson is still in Montreal. And if so, who his contacts and compatriots are. Lt. Ollie Henry thinks he is more than equal to the task and is eager to uncover even more knowledge than Jemm anticipates.

The lobby is guarded by six large pillars, three on each side, with two smaller pillars designating the entryway. A red carpet at the top of the two stairs of the entryway leads guests to another small set of stairs to the lobby, painted cream with wood accents and a high vaulted ceiling. The entryway is guarded by two doormen in full regal faux uniforms that resembled the Swiss Guards at the Vatican on either side.

Boy does this guy know how to live, Lt. Ollie Henry thinks as he walks up to an empty front desk. There he thumbs clumsily back through the register with his one hand, finding plenty of entries a month earlier for both James Williams Boyd and John St. Helen— but there are too many of them to be made by just Booth. As he comes forward toward the present, there is also an entire page missing. Lt. Henry can see its ragged roots near the binding—clearly someone did not want this page seen.

The front desk attendant steps up and abruptly grabs the register out of Lt. Henry's hand.

"A Thompson, Mr. Jacob Thompson," a startled Henry blurts out when the clerk asks what he could do for him.

"I'm afraid Mr. Thompson is out, and might be out for another week or two," the clerk says. He has wire rimmed spectacles, a thin accountant's nose, and speaks with a bastardized British accent that sounds more like shanty Canadian. He raises his voice slightly as he asks, "What business would you have with Mr. Thompson, then?"

"I'm Mr. Boyd," Henry says, but realizes he had made a mistake as soon as he says it. "That is, I am a friend of Mr. Boyd's and the matter is most urgent."

A large man steps out from the cloak room to the right of the desk. The clerk and coat room attendant exchange looks that are neither malevolent, nor suspicious. Still, the two now fill Henry with a very real sense of dread.

"Well, is there a message that you would like to leave? The clerk finally asks. "Where can Mr. Thompson find you."

Scared, Henry spits out, "I really haven't secured accommodations yet…"

"Well we're full up here," the clerk says.

"No…I mean yes…I mean I can see that," Henry stammers. "I'll return and leave my address once I have secured lodgings."

"The Imperial House is quite nice. Would you like me to have the concierge secure a reservation?" the clerk asks.

"No…No, I'm afraid the Imperial might be out of my range as well."

"On a budget them?" the clerk asks.

"Yes…yes…definitely on a budget."

Lt. Henry left the building so unsure of himself that he almost awkwardly tumbles down the front two stairs and into a black cab below.

He'd seen Jemm's ability to handle people, and, since he was obviously his superior in terms of rank, thought he could handle just about any subject just as well.

Geezus, what do I do now? I completely blew it, Lt. Ollie Henry thinks. They know that I'm aware of Boyd. They know that I've traced him to Thompson. If there's any link between the two, they might…Henry steadies himself against the thought. He had braved one of the bloodiest battles of the Great Conflict. If he would die, then he would die. No use thinking about it. Still, he can't help but blame himself for being so foolish. For being so cock-sure that he was up to the task.

So what do you do now Henry? the lieutenant asks himself.

Stay out of all the big name hotels, Henry thinks. They'll look for you there. Find a place where transients and coloreds stay, something cheap. It might even be close by, but not up any street where they might frequent or look.

But that reasoning would turn out to be a mistake—especially since mentioning that he was "on a budget."

For the first time Henry realizes how Jemm can move so freely, without suspicion or even detection. There's a freedom in being no one, Henry thinks. I'll use that to my advantage. If there is any lesson to be learned, at least he realizes that.

Lt. Ollie Henry ambles almost aimlessly down the street named after St. James toward Rue Saint Urban, hoping to catch a glimpse of Basilique Notre-Dame. A block up from Saint Urban, he asks a man reading a newspaper, if he knows where he might secure affordable lodgings for the evening.

The man, who had a carefully crafted grey goatee, with its mustache ends twirled up at the ends, folds his paper at his chest, his blue eyes inspecting him suspiciously.

"Je ne sais pas," the man says. "Je ne parle Anglais," the man says. He folds the paper under his arm, turns abruptly, almost militarily, and walks briskly away.

"Lookin' for a flop, then," comes a cockney voice from a man leaning against a building on the corner. He has black hair slanting across his face, and a workman's uniform on. But he doesn't look like he's worked in a while. He at least looks friendly. Lt. Henry walks toward him.

"You'll want to turn about and walk straight up St. Urban's, there," the man points, his hand is covered in gloves without finger ends. "Head up the street two, maybe three blocks, to a li'l charcuterie, ya know, one of them places what sells all the tasty little sausages and cheese and meats. Turn right there and walk up a block. I think it's called Gauchetiere. There's a little house there that sells you a room, and even takes in Chinamen. The price is negotiable. Judging by the way you're dressed, they'd probably charge full boat."

"Thank you, thanks," Henry says, smiling.

The man puts his left hand behind his back and stretches out his right hand palm up.

"Now then, it would be nice to get a little something for the effort," he says.

CHAPTER 21
Flushing the Quarry

Jemm knew the route Boyd and Smith would take, heading for the farm of Samuel Cox, a known Confederate sympathizer. But Jemm had his own contact in the area, a Wesort by the name of Aussie Smith, who knew the area like the back of his hand, even in the dark.

Wesorts were tri-racial in their ancestry; Native American, Caucasian, and African American, and they were rated as among the very best guides and animal trackers in the area.

The morning had dawned slightly cloudy and there was a fine warm mist in the air. The deciduous trees were greening, and the pines showing renewed vigor as spring crept across the marshes and forests along the lower Potomac.

Jemm had ridden much of the day before, and a good portion of the morning as well, and was half asleep in the saddle, when he stopped, dismounted from his mule, and rapped on the front door of the two room shack of Aussie Smith, where he lived with his wife and eight children.

#

"Sure they came through here," says Smith after looking at two lithographs of Booth and Herold and identifying them as companions Boyd and Smith. "This one here doesn't have that mustache. Paid me $2 Union to take them down to Hogan's Folly, ya know, the place owned by Mr. Burtles. But Mr. Smith changes his mind and tells me to take them to Rich Hill, Captain Cox's place, and even offers me $5 more to do it. Didn't think another thing of it 'cept this one tells me not to say anything or I won't be livin' long. Spect they's still at Rich Hill, but couldn't say for sure. Lots of woods to hide in round there."

# # #

Jemm doesn't get to the Cox farm until noon on Thursday, April 20.

"Go 'round back, boy," says a voice from inside.

"I'm looking for my Uncle Noah, sah," Jemm says, trying to sound subservient.

"Like I says, go 'round back, boy," the voice says again.

Realizing he wasn't getting anywhere, Jemm walks around back of the white wood-framed farmhouse. The field has been plowed, and there are piles of horse dung stretched along the top of each row ready to be spread into the furrows. Other parts of the farm are tidy as well.

Jemm turns the corner at the back of the farmhouse, and steps up to the back door, knocking politely three times. A voice from inside comes once again.

"Now there's a boy," the voice says.

Samuel Cox opens the door, and almost immediately Jemm can smell the whiskey on his breath. His brown hair with streaks of gray is matted down in places from his drunken sleep, and his face wears a stubble that is at least three days old. He holds a musket. While he looks disheveled, his carriage gives him the appearance of a man of some importance.

"Whatchoo want, boy?" he says.

"I'm lookin' for my Uncle Noah," Jemm says.

"Jus' down the road a peck," Cox says, motioning with the barrel of his musket, "lives in a red shack, with wagons and wheels in front."

Cox squints his eyes and looks Jemm up and down. He tilts his head forward suspiciously, almost as if he is trying to sniff the truth out of Jemm, who purposely clears his head so Cox can't detect any untruth.

"You tell yaw Uncle to get up here and fix my wagon," Cox finally says, pointing to a carriage parked by the barn that looked like it has thrown a wheel.

"Thank you sah," Jemm says. "I'll be sure to do that."

# # #

The Taishi House was perfect for Lt. Henry, or at least he thought so at first glance. Just off Rue Sainte Urbain on Rue de la Gauchetiere, it was within walking distance of St. Lawrence Hall, but was anything but high class. It wouldn't arouse suspicion, or so he thought.

Madame Taishi welcomed Coloreds and Chinamen as well as the wharf riff-raff from Montreal's nearby port, which included teamsters, longshoremen and day laborers—as long as they had the money. They could even find warm companionship with Madame Taishi's stable of sportin' women.

At two bits for two nights, the room was certainly affordable. An additional two bits for one night, and you'd get some company. And despite its outward appearance, Madame Taishi kept the place reasonably clean.

Thursday night, Lt. Henry slept fitfully in his room, its walls so thin he could hear one of the escorts dutifully groaning while her head bucked against a headboard. He was thankful when the man let out a gasp and a slight laugh, mumbled some unintelligible words, and left her room.

Finally, some sleep, Henry thought.

But five minutes later, the groaning and bucking started again.

Geezus, how many times...probably all night, Henry said, answering his own rhetorical question.

Unable to sleep, and not in need of companionship, at least physical companionship, Henry decided to do the next best thing. He got dressed, threw on his coat, actually marveling at how adept he had become at dressing himself with just one hand.

# # #

He leaves the room, without locking it and heads down toward the lobby, bouncing off each stare with a distinct thud.

"If they can make noise" he says of the other guests, "then I can make noise, too."

In the lobby, which is more of a small parlor than a place to greet travelers, Madame Taishi is behind the counter, leaning against the mailboxes on the rear wall. The entire room is decked out in gaudy purple and pink, and Henry is sure he can smell opium coming from somewhere.

She notices Lt. Henry as soon as he hit the bottom stair.

"What's amatter, room no good?" she asks him. A Chinese man with a long grey mustache and bald head, comes out from a room behind her holding a pipe, and Henry immediately knows where the acrid smell is coming from.

"No, no room is fine," he says, truncating his language, as if it will somehow allow him to communicate better with her. "Room is fine—too much noise. Maybe too much noise."

"You want girl," the man says, his beady brown eyes lighting up.

"No. No girl…"

"Boy then?" the man asks.

"No Boy. No girl. Drink. Drink."

"He might not understand but I do," Madame Taishi says to Henry in a voice that told him it was a little insulting to try and communicate with her like she couldn't understand. "You need a drink to fall asleep. Nestor's is right around the corner. Tell Nestor I sent you and you'll get your first beer free."

"I'm sorry, it's just that…"

"You don't expect Chinese to speak the King's English," she says. "To tell you the truth, I really don't speak it that well, but I have been in this city most of my life."

"So Nestor's is?"

"Just up the street, take a right and it's two doors down from the corner," Madame Taishi says.

Nestor's is dimly lit, but has a long oak bar with a single brass rail step that runs its entire length. The center of the room is dominated by a potbellied stove, which is just warm enough to throw out heat, without making the room too warm. A permanent tobacco smoke haze hangs near the tin stamped ceiling. The walls are decorated with the names of boats that have sailed the lakes, as well as the names of certain crews. There are five small wall shrines to boats that the Kinskey Line has lost to the gales of the Great Lakes, remembering the honored dead.

Nestor is tall, with a shock of brown hair that falls across his face, and his smile is warm, but his teeth as crooked as an old graveyard with headstones sticking out in every direction. Henry steps up to the bar.

"I'm from…"

"Madam Taishi's," Nestor says interrupting him.

"She said that if I mention her name…"

"You'd get your first drink free," Nestor says. "That's why I always say it first."

Henry chuckles, pulls out a quarter and flips it on the bar.

"Relax, just havin' a little fun with ya," Nestor says. "We have two ales, dark or light, and this month, straight from Germany mind ya, an authentic German Pilsner."

"Pilsner," Henry says.

"It's more expensive," Nestor cautions. "That's why I'm tryin' to talk you out of it especially if I'm payin."

Henry chuckles again, "I'll pay even if it's a little more than…"

"Relax," Nestor says, "I'm still pullin' ya wagon. I'll pay. I'll pay. You need to relax and smile a little.

"How'd ya lose the wing?"

"Down South, a place called Chickamauga," Henry says.

"The Battle Above the Clouds," Nestor says, with a hint of admiration in his voice. "We read about it in the papers here. Had some great pictures, thick musket and cannon fire above the clouds. Fighting in the heavens."

"I'm afraid I never made it up there," Henry says. "We were ambushed at the base the first day."

Nestor's eyes flew open wide. His jaw dropped precipitously. If it hadn't been attached, it would have hit the bar.

"The Long Walk in the Short Woods?" Nestor asks.

"The same," Henry says, taking a sip of the Pilsner placing before him, wiping his mouth to take off the generous foam.

"Georgy," Nestor shouts to a man seated at the end of the bar. "This man was at Chickamauga…"

Georgy, an old salt who dispatches the teamsters at the port, sweeps up his change, and his mug, and hurries down to where Henry is sitting, spilling some beer on his arm on the way.

Nestor looks back at Henry. "You just got yourself three free beers my friend," he says, pulling the half empty beer from Henry's left hand and refilling it at the keg.

"But I had some left in there, and…"

"That's why I grabbed it," Nestor says, "if I'm buying you three, I'm only going to fill it at half way."

# # #

Noah Carpenter was a freedman widower who lived with his daughter Elizabeth only about three quarters of a mile from the Cox Farm. His domicile was set back into a pine thicket, that shielded the house from the weather and provided shade in the summer. There was a fire burning in the house, and Jemm could smell the apple wood smoke, along with meat on the spit, probably pork, Jemm thought, reminding him that he hadn't eaten that day.

While Noah lived in what Cox described as a shack, it was neat and well ordered. True, there were wagons in front, awaiting repair, but they were parked in meticulous fashion. There was a pile of broken furniture, and furniture parts, to the right of the drive, that had been broken into neat pieces for use as kindling.

Once again, Jemm dismounted and headed for the door, for some reason quietly.

Elizabeth Carpenter, exited the house without noticing him. She had on a long print pink and white dress that hide her slightly plump figure. The dress was worn but clean. She carried a bucket of water, which she emptied off the porch, before turning around quickly, startled by Jemm's appearance.

"Who're you?" she says.

"I just stopped by to ask for some directions," Jemm says. "Is yaw daddy home?"

"I can tell you where to go jus 'bout anywhere around here," she says defensively.

"I do need to speak with yaw pappy," Jemm says, politely. "Is he about?"

"Why do you need him? You wiff dose men?" she asks suspiciously.

"Which men?"

"De Army men, dey come by here yestaday," Elizabeth says.

"Lizabeth, you let that man talk to me," Noah says, interrupting her as he comes out the door. He is exceptionally tall, and broad shouldered with streaks of grey along his full head of hair and beard. He is wearing grey leather work apron over a brown work suit, that is frayed along its seams. He eyes Jemm suspiciously as he put his thumbs under the strings of his work vest. Jemm can see his well-muscled arms, built from so much manual labor.

"You don't fool me," he says to Jemm, "I seen you in the capital. I know who you are. You're not welcome here."

"I'm afraid I do need to talk to you," Jemm says, his voice now becoming more precise and official. "If you know who I am, you know I can make things very uncomfortable for you."

"Please don'," Elizabeth begs. "This land is all we got. Don't make us say, they'll take it all away. If it ain't the one side, it's the otha. We only want peace."

Jemm feels for her. Many freedmen lived in these parts, enjoying their freedom only at the acquiescence of white men. Northerners treat them as second-class citizens, always pressuring to have work done for free or at least for cut rates. The Secesh allow them to live as long as they stay in line, but always threaten them with repatriation to the South, which meant being thrown back into servitude.

"Don't give me that freedman, shit," they would say. "Someone ownt you at one time or t'other."

Elizabeth stood with her lower lip trembling like a small mouth bass on a hook. Jemm looks not so much at her as into her.

"Tell me what I want to know, I'll make sure nothing happens," Jemm says to her. He looks Noah straight into his deep brown eyes as well, and somehow Noah knew he could trust him. Noah shakes his head slowly.

"Come in then," Noah says. "I'd invite you to supper, but that ham won't be ready until this evening. Lizabeth, why don't you fry up some fatback and make a mess a biscuits. This man looks hungry."

# # #

From the thicket in the woods, the men could see the two talking on the porch of the shack. Four days they had been hiding under a broken down chicken coop in an area shoveled out to hide slave runaways chasing the Northern Star and freedom. The gray coop had long been swallowed up by the pine and underbrush, and sat in a twisted thicket that was almost impossible to penetrate, except from one entranceway.

"See, I told you, some boy, probably just hungry beggin' for food or work," Smith said.

"Horseshit, I know that boy," the man on crutches said. "I recognize that boy from Mary Surratt's place... that nigger's some sort a federal agent. We need to move and we need to move now."

# # #

Lt. Henry soon becomes a local legend, at least with the denizens of Nestor's, which is another miscue. He visits the bar the very next day, not so much to drink, as to talk, and get the lay of the land.

It isn't long before he asks Nestor about Jacob Thompson. It is Friday night, and the bar is crowded, everybody at the port getting paid, and the sailors of several ships on liberty.

Madam Taishi's girls are peppered throughout the bar, getting the newly rich to spend their hard-earned cash on iced tea, which costs twice as much as a regular drink, but is passed off as whiskey. The trade-off being that they will sit with them, rub their legs, and hopefully get them to repair to Madam Taishi's for a quick tussle between the sheets.

"Have you heard of him?" Henry asks.

"Some sort of a swell from down south," Nestor says, "spent a lot of money in here, and other places...but I wouldn't be askin' too much about him, at least not around here."

"Why, I'm just trying to find an old friend, who might have worked with him," Henry says.

"Just as bad," Nestor says, "people around here asking about Mr. Thompson, usually go missing in a day or two."

"What 'bout these two," Henry asks, passing the lithographs of Surratt and Booth to the bar tender. "Boyd and St. Helen?"

"Don't know 'em," Nestor says. "I wouldn't go showin' those

about—or asking too many questions."

In the shadows of the corner of the room, a lone figure sits nursing a beer, his ears finely tuned on the conversation between Henry and the bartender. His black hair falls across his forehead. He grabs his beer with two hands, wearing gloves without finger ends.

It isn't long before Georgy shows up with some friends and invites Henry over to tell stories of the great Battle Above the Clouds. But more importantly, Henry listens as the sailors tell their stories, of working the Great Lakes of Ontario and Erie.

Lt Henry listens as Georgy talks about valuable cargo coming through the port, from England and Germany. Quinine, laudanum, chloroform and ether, sent by train out of Montreal to New York, for distribution to Union troops under Grant's command in the eastern theater, or shipped across Canada to Windsor, and Malden Island, where it goes to Ohio and Michigan to be shipped to Sherman and other forces in the Western theater.

"And sometimes, those shipments never get through," says one sailor wearing a bandana to keep the sweat off his brow, "lots of hijackings, lots of money to be made."

"And sometimes a lot of lookin' the other way, if you get my drift, sir," Georgy says under his breath.

"And dangerous if you don't," the sailor adds. "There's been many a man disappear, who wouldn't cooperate."

All this time, the lone figure sits in the corner, whisps of tobacco smoke shielding him like a night fog coming off the Port.

"Now then," the cockney voice says under his breath, as he stands and leaves the bar without being noticed. "Looks like we got aweselves another payday."

# # #

On Friday night at the War Department, Lafayette Baker received a ciphered missive from Jemm in the field. Six riders had carried the packet marked "Strictly Confidential Top Secret" through the night, Pony Express style, covering the 40 miles. The message had already been deciphered. Baker was pleased. Even though it was ciphered it was still cryptic—Jemm really knew how to do that. His cousin Lt. Luther Baker had already reviewed its contents.

Near Cox property. Guests close by. Noah daughter fed two for four days. In a chicken coup hidden in a pine thicket. My presence I fear detected. Probably headed for our next stop. May intercept there, or next stop down. O'Beirne closing in so hurry. Happy hunting.

Yours,

The hound

#

Anxious to grab as much reward money as possible, Lafayette Baker assembles his team, meeting with Stanton inside of the Secretary's Office. Stanton sits behind his desk, with Baker barking out his demands behind him, the Secretary almost cowering in his chair.

"I want Lt. Doherty to lead a detail of 24 men from the 16th New York," Lafayette Baker says. "Make sure they are the same ones I had from the 25th New York. Have them meet outside the Willard Hotel."

"I'm afraid Conger will insist on command," Stanton says.

"You can't talk him out of it?" Baker asks.

"He doesn't trust you," Stanton replies.

"But do you sir?"

"Absolutely, but…well it's a question of military politics,"

Stanton says. "It would be better if you designated him to command."

"Fine, but have my cousin Luther assigned to head the detail on our behalf as well," Lafayette Baker says.

"That will give us more officers than warranted," Stanton says.

"I think you'll agree this is a special detail," Baker says.

"When do we move?"

"James will have this figured out in a day or two," Baker says using the name Stanton was most familiar with. "I expect a missive from him—"

"There is one more thing," says Stanton. "Take Sergeant Corbett along as well…"

"You told me that already…'How could you not question his devotion to the cause,'" Baker says, repeating what the Secretary had said earlier.

# # #

But even as the words left his lips, he knew that Boston Corbett was trouble. He would be Stanton's eyes, making sure that nothing went wrong with the capture of the two assassins, who absolutely must be taken alive to reveal the true scope of the conspiracy.

While he had used Corbett during interrogations at the War Department from time to time, and with the interrogation of Jocy Peanuts, he really didn't know the man, only that he had been captured by Mosby's Raiders, and served a five-month stint in the Prison at Andersonville. And of course, there were the usual unsavory stories—especially the one from Boston.

After his release from Andersonville, Corbett hated any Secesh, Confederate or anyone or thing sympathetic to the Southern cause.

After enduring the tortuous existence of Andersonville, who could blame him? Still, Lafayette Baker thought it wise to get to know the man better. Why was he called, the "Glory of God man?" So Baker sought out his service record and dossier from Charlie Dana, and read it from cover to cover.

Sergeant Boston Corbett was a religious zealot who was also fanatically dedicated to the cause of the Union. But before the Great Conflict, he was simply a religious fanatic, the dossier read.

Born Thomas Corbett, he worked as a hatter, or perhaps a mad hatter would be more appropriate, in the City of Troy, New York. But it wasn't until after his subsequent marriage that he truly became deranged. He lost his young wife and child during childbirth, cursed the Almighty, and started drinking heavily, becoming a reprobate, and later simply homeless, somehow ending up a derelict on the streets of Boston.

One day, he was on the way home from a three-day binge, he was confronted by a street preacher, who sobered him up, and persuaded him to join the Methodist Episcopal Church.

Under the influence of church, rather than the bottle, he soon found employment once again as a hatter. But his employer found him disruptive, often interrupting the workday to proselytize, preach the Sacred Word, or even encourage his fellow workers to sing hymns. Corbett even changed his name from Thomas to Boston, after the city where he had found salvation.

That's not so strange, Baker thought. Many men feel they are directed by their Creator. But as he read on, he became appalled. Baker sat back, his mouth dry. He reached for a glass of water, and downed most of it. He can obviously endure pain, Baker thought. But he's obviously unbalanced.

But Baker also knew it was too late to have Corbett reassigned, especially if Stanton insisted upon his presence in the detail. But why would Stanton want someone such as Corbett involved?

#

On Monday, the 24th, after crossing the Potomac at Snead's Ferry, the crossing designated for freedmen, Jemm headed for Claydael, the home of Dr. Richard Stuart, where he had a contact named Jaleel, a freedman who worked in the house. It took him the better part of the morning to get there. The sun was just reaching its zenith when Jemm showed up at the servant's quarters to the rear of the house.

Jaleel was a quiet man of advancing years, who stuttered slightly and shuffled when he walked. But his mind was as clear as a bell. While he was a unionist through and through, his subservience to the Stuart family masked his true intentions.

"They come by here just yesta day, but this one here has no mustache now," Jaleel said, when shown the lithographs of Booth and Herold. "But madame says they can't come in or even stay here. So da Master he hires Johnnie Lucas to take them farther down."

Jemm set out for the shack of John Lucas arriving that night, where he was told that the pair had forced the family out of the shack at gun point—not wanting to share their lodgings with "a bunch of niggers," as the man with the crutch had said.

"Try to give a little hospitality, and this is how they abuse you," John Lucas said. "I know they's headed for Port Conway. Hired my son Charlie to take 'em there in the mawnin.' Spect Billie Rollins be helpin' them cross the river there."

Jemm headed for Port Conway where he prepared a second ciphered missive to the War Department, this time breaking orders and using the wires to make sure Lafayette Baker got it in time.

That day at 2 pm., Lt. Edward Doherty and Lieutenant Colonel Everton Conger and their detachment of 26 men, were dispatched and road out of Washington, boarding the steamer John S. Ide, for the 70 mile trip to Belle Plain, Virginia.

They rode to Port Royal, where they learned that the two fugitives and three other returning Confederate soldiers had been ferried across the Rappahannock by William Rollins, who had given up one of the soldiers named William Jett—who in turn directed them to the path of the two, one of whom was named James W. Boyd.

# # #

Lt. Henry headed out to Nestor's the night of the 24th, much as he had done for the last four nights. He felt at home there and had made many friends. But there were eyes on him the whole time.

After only his second mug, the lieutenant wasn't entirely sure, he became dizzy, then woozy, the room whirling left and right each time he turned. He almost fell off his stool when two men approached him at the bar. The first, he recognized as the man in the street who had directed him to Madam Taishi's. The second was a large man with a scar on his cheek and a brutish brow that held a single hairy eyebrow.

"I'm John St. Helen," the man with the unibrow said. "I heard you have been asking for me."

Henry could tell that he was in some sort of trouble. This man was certainly not Surratt, and definitely not Booth or Boyd. His friends at the bar were now turning their backs on him.

"Let's suppose we step outside so we can have a more confidential conversation," the brutish man suggested under his breath, grabbing Henry by the lower collar of his coat.

Henry's mind was spinning. Even though he was disoriented, he was aware that if he left the bar, he was as good as dead. Then all at once, the bald Chinese man from Taishi's showed up with two constables.

"There he is, that him!" the man shouted as the two gendarmes walked over to Henry at the bar.

"He no pay for boy!"

The bar erupted in laughter.

"So after all this our war hero is nothing but a boy-chasing dandy," said one of the lieutenant's former bar friends. As the two policemen walked Henry to their wagon, Henry passed out.

The next morning at Madame Taishi's, a strong rap came at Henry's door, his mind still clouded from the night before. He took a drink from a pitcher of water on the stand at his bedside, bypassing the formality of pouring it into a drinking glass first.

He walked to the door in his under garments, opening it to find the bald old Chinaman.

# # #

"No. No," Henry says, truncating his voice so he could be better understood. "I don't want a boy. I want to sleep," he continues, trying to shut the door. But the man forces his way into the room, with suddenly surprising strength.

"Dress. Dress now," the old man says. "Hurry. Hurry. No time to explain. There is much danger for you here."

Henry starts to dress as quickly as he can, but finds it slightly awkward using his left hand, while trying to clear the cobwebs from his head. Then he recalls, through the fog, the embarrassing way he had been rescued the night before.

"If I might remember…"

"I'm surprised if you can," the old Chinaman says, this time without any accent at all.

"You besmirched my reputation with everybody in Nestor's…"

"Sorry about that old man," the Chinaman says, now almost

sounding British. "Absolutely necessary. Hopefully, next time you come up, you won't have to visit places like that."

Henry picks up his suitcase, and looks inside checking its contents: pass (check), cash (check), leave orders (check), second suit and shirt (check) but they need laundering, wait a second, where are the lithos of St. Helen and Boyd? He steps outside into the hallway.

"Come! Come!" the old man says, as he stands by an open window at the end of the hall. "Hurry."

Lt. Henry hands the man his suitcase and climbs awkwardly through the window and onto a platform. It is still dark but dawn is quickly coming. Iron steps led to the street below, where a wagon is waiting. The old man hands him his suitcase, and motions with his head toward the wagon. The man closes the window behind him and follows Henry to the wagon, picking up the reins, the horses jolting forward as Henry throws his suitcase in the rear.

"Who are...why am I even here?" Henry asks.

"You don't know why you came to Madame Taishi's? the old man asks. "No briefing?"

"No I was given directions from someone on the street, and it sounded like..."

"Sounded like?" The old man asks as the wagon made its way up the alley and out to Saint Urbain, where it heads inland. "It sounded like a good place and something inside you made it seem familiar?"

"Right, the same feeling I had with you a moment ago," Lt. Ollie Henry says, genuinely bewildered. The wagon passes a newspaper wagon, unloading its papers at a newsstand. News boys cut open bundles that they will later carry on the street. "Back to the original question, Who the hell?"

"Billy," the old man says, "Billy Cao, I work with Gilbert

McMicken and am affiliated with the Montreal Police through a temporary assignment program with the Upper Canadian Provincial Police, but we're still working with the Lower Canadian constabulary…"

"Sounds like you're having your own conflict up here," Lt. Henry jokes.

"The difference being is that we're voting on it, and you're shooting," Cao says.

It is the second time Lt. Henry has been shot down. No use bringing it up a second time.

"We were formed after some of your country's rebels thought it would be a good idea to conduct raids," says Cao.

"So selling flesh is a second career?"

"I do what I can to keep my cover," Cao says.

Kind of like the Chinese Jemm Pender, Henry thinks.

"Being Chinese is great, because no you can always hide under the guise of not understanding what people say," Cao explains as the wagon rumbles along the cobblestone street. "The trade-off is that your life is cheap if your identity is uncovered. Once found out, you're as good as dead."

"Where are we headed?" Henry asks.

"I'll be circling back to the station. You gotta get the hell out of Canada, and right now," Cao says. "You accidently stepped into our investigation of Jacob Thompson, and his Confederate Raiders. They could be running some sort of counterfeit operation…

"Thompson and his friends may also be running some sort of smuggling operation out of Canada, stealing drugs, and reselling them in your country, or even ours, on the black market."

"What kind of drugs?"

"Mostly chloroform, but also laudanum, morphine, opium all of them invaluable on the battlefield—and not in small amounts. And it's not just the drugs they hijacked. With the end of the War down South, we're expecting that most of the money and gold held in the Confederate Treasury will soon be headed our way, on its way to Europe. There could be tens of millions of pounds, er, a dollars involved. These men will stop at nothing. Once you…"

"Spouted off about Boyd at St. Lawrence Hall…"

"They were immediately suspicious. You have been followed the whole time," Cao says. "Once they found out you were an officer, well, I needed to get you out of there before they came back. They would have gotten any information out of you…"

"I wouldn't have talked."

"They would have drugged you with ether to a soporific but conscious state, and then fired the questions at you," Cao says, "Unless maybe Jemm has you mesmerized. Then you would only get fuzzy-headed and forgetful. But you wouldn't know that, would you? But under drugs, especially soporifics, you would have thought you were dreaming while you were giving them everything they want…then they would have slit your throat and left you for dead."

"I guess you have my thanks, then?"

"My pleasure," Cao says. "Here's a nice bit of info for you Yank. Brother Thompson took out $184,000 from his personal account about a week back. We suspect it was traveling money for John St. Helen, but we're not sure. We do know that he bankrolled several kidnapping attempts before, money for arms and wagons, sundries, things like that. We're expecting a big load of Union currency to come through here, maybe even gold…it may have already happened…I have a couple of presents for you as well."

Cao pulls out two pieces of paper from his front pocket.

"The first is a page is from the register at St. Lawrence Hall," Cao says, handing over the missing paper, that Henry had wondered about. "It has a copy of both Boyd and St. Helen's signatures on it. And you can see they are not at all alike.

"This second one is a little more interesting," Cao continues. "It's from the sign-in log and cargo manifest from a passenger ferry and sightseeing sidewheeler called the Philo Parsons out of Windsor —it places your Capt. J.W. Boyd on board in September of last year —which may turn out to be important to Jemm's investigation. If you compare it to the hotel register, you'll see the similarities.

"By the way, I took your lithos last night—they are now mine. They could be helpful for us here. When you get back to Washington, tell Jemm I asked 'hey why do you have to mesmerize all your associates?'—that outta get his goat. And make him take you out from under that spell."

# # #

Less than two days later, inside an old tobacco barn on the nearby Garrett's farm, the man called Boyd, with crutch at his side, sleeps soundly on a blanket provided by the lady of the house. There's a spring rain outside, and the man's broken ankle wakes him up, throbbing. He pulls a bottle from his pocket and takes a sip of the red/brown syrup inside.

"Lovable laudanum," he says out loud.

He lays back down on the blanket spread out on the floor, which has an agreeable smell of seasoned tobacco, even though the leaves have long since been swept up and into the corner. The man listens to a light spring rain clicking against the roof of the barn, its smell sometimes overpowering the tobacco.

Sweet spring rain, the man thinks. It's full-blown spring in Old Dominion.

The laudanum starts to take its effect, numbing the throbbing pain in his ankle and sending his head into a pleasant euphoric state. Just as he's about to doze off, his traveling companion slides open the door, steps through, and closes the door softly behind him. He awakes, slightly startled.

"I didn't mean to wake you Wilkes," the man says. "I got some papers from a farmer up the road."

"What news of Washington, then," the man asks, pulling himself up to a sitting position.

"It's not good," his traveling companion says. He has on a worn hat, bent at the corners, and a triangular face with an unkempt mustache.

"Wilkes," the man with the hat said.

"Please, Boyd, we must maintain that even here, Boyd," the man with the broken ankle says.

"The papers are calling you a monster," the man says.

"But surely…"

"Even the papers from Richmond, the man with the hat says again. "Especially, from Richmond."

He hands the man calling himself Boyd the papers but continues to give him the short version as he reads.

"Johnson has been sworn in like you said, but he has no allegiance to the Confederacy," the man with the hat continued. "There's even talk of Grant or Sherman taking over and martial law in the Capital continuing well into fall."

"No mention of parole for Confederate officers?" the man with the busted ankle asks, as he searches the papers frantically for a clue.

"They say it's a grand conspiracy, designed to take down the whole government," the man with the hat continues. "Johnston in North Carolina has even come out against it, but still hasn't surrendered. Sherman is chasing him all over the Carolinas."

"Do they not know what I was trying to accomplish, at least for my country," the man called Boyd says.

"That's not the worst of it," the man with the bad mustache says. He handed Boyd a copy of yet another paper.

As Boyd reads, a look of abject horror comes over his face.

"Stanton, who has been in charge of Secesh prisoner parole since February, has said he will deny all matters of parole until a full investigation of the conspiracy has been completed."

"You know David, I'm right at the end," Boyd says. "I'd rather surrender now and tell my story. Set everything straight. We all need a confessor, and I think mine should be the American public. We all need an absolution."

"And I think we should move or we'll end up shot, or at the end of a rope," Smith says.

"You must move, and move this minute," Boyd whispers. "David, if you are captured, remember that my name is Boyd, and you only helped me travel for a wage. This is my fate now, not yours."

"But Wilkes, they'll likely hang you on the spot," Smith answers.

"No they won't," Boyd says. "They'll be a big trial, a great stage where I will explain my deeds for all posterity. My journal will be taken into evidence."

"I will not leave you, Wilkes," his companions says..

"If not tonight, then at first light tomorrow," Boyd says. "It is my most fervent wish."

###

The men known to the Garrett's as Smith and Boyd, are suddenly awakened by a great clamoring outside. Lt. Doherty is calling for all in the house to answer and surrender, as the man known as David Smith looks out the slats of the barn.

"Union troops, looks like a whole detachment of cavalry," he says to Boyd.

"I told you to leave earlier," Boyd says. "Stay here, do not make a move. The Garrett's will have to give us up, and we want no further bloodshed."

"But Wilkes, they're making so much noise, we owe it to them to escape," Smith says.

"It's Boyd, start saying it now, and start believing it now," Boyd says. "It means your life. Boyd. We met up north and you have been traveling with me as a paid companion."

Smith helps Boyd up on his crutch.

"Do not arm yourself," Boyd cautions. "I don't want your innocent blood on my hands, enough has been spilt already. Surrender, and we won't be harmed. And I'll testify as to your innocence."

Through the slats, both men could see the Garrett family, children in tow, all brought out to the front porch of the whitewashed farmhouse. A black servant stands with them, pointing toward the barn, as the eldest Garrett boy, named Richard after his father who is absent on business, chimes in, pointing to the barn for the Lieutenant in charge.

"Won't be long now," Boyd says.
"Away there in the barn," Lt. Doherty calls, as his detail

dismounts and starts surrounding the barn in quick order. They light torches and hand them out to each other until they completely encircle the barn. "You are surrounded. We want no bloodshed, especially with innocent children about."

"I will not give up," Smith says to Boyd quietly.

"It is my most fervent wish," Boyd repeats. "Please, do me this honor. Go first.

"There is one in here who is innocent," Boyd calls out to the Union detachment. "He will come out first, and I will follow, unarmed!"

"I'm glad we can settle this like gentlemen," Lt. Luther Baker calls back. "Surrender or we shall have a bonfire and a shootin' match."

Smith heads out first, his arms in the air.

"Lez burn him with perditions flames," Boston Corbett says, tossing his torch toward the base of the barn.

And with that, all the soldiers start tossing their torches toward the base of the barn as well.

"Hold on. Hold on. I am coming out. I surrender!" Boyd says from inside, as the barn quickly catches fire.

Boyd stands, has trouble with his crutch and tosses it down. From the barn slats, the soldiers looking inside could see him drop one of the crutches and, bent over at the waist, makes for the slightly open door of the barn.

Peering through a slat, Corbett sees the man known as Boyd making his way for the door. He raises his weapon and fires, hitting Boyd directly in the back, a mere seven inches down from the skull. Once he sees that it wasn't an immediate "kill" shot, Corbett moves quickly in.

"Dammit. Dammit," the lieutenant screams. "Who shot that? Who shot that?"

"I was the avenger," Sergeant Corbett says.

"Why did you disobey my direct order," the lieutenant says.

"Providence directed my hand," Corbett snaps back. "I did it for the 'Greater Glory of God.'"

As other soldiers look on, the barn starts to burn more ferociously, Corbett and two other soldiers run inside.

"Pull him out. Pull him out," the lieutenant orders, his horse circling, and becoming fractious at the building flames.

Before the men can even grab Boyd, Corbett is on him, searching his pockets, pulling out a billfold with more than $1,000 dollars in it, a red journal, and three newspaper clippings.

The other two soldiers grab Boyd by the armpits, his legs dangling.

Boyd sees red, then white. As they lift him up, he comes to and feels his neck bend awkwardly to one side. Nothing is working.

Boyd sees red then white. As the soldiers pull him up the steps to Garrett's porch, he comes back once again. He tries to spit up the blood and phlegm gurgling in his throat but is unsuccessful. He starts to choke.

Boyd sees red then white. He coughs up blood and wakes. His breath gurgles, as he continues to spit blood and phlegm from his mouth. Doherty stands over him.

"The wound looks fatal," he says to Boyd. "Do you wish to make a last statement."

Boyd looks at him, realizing his situation, and tries to nod his head as best he can.

"Smith, Smith is, paid…paid companion," Boyd says, as blood flowed from the corners of his mouth. His eyes roll back in his head. "Not a part of this."

Boyd sees red, then white.

One of the two soldiers who had carried him, speaks up.

"Corbett, grabbed some personal belongings," he says.

"True," says Corbett. "Looky here, what we got. More than $1,000 in U.S bills, plus some clippings here."

"Garrett, I need some brandy, a sponge," Lt. Baker says. "I want a final confession."

Richard Garrett dutifully steps inside the house, his frightened family and man servant still on the porch as the first pink and grey slivers of dawn can be seen on the horizon.
Boyd sees red, then white.

"Anything else?" Lt. Doherty asks Corbett as Garrett steps inside, but Corbett ignores him.

"I said anything else sergeant!" Lt. Doherty shouts, bringing Boyd back to consciousness.

"Journal. My journal," Boyd says, passing out again. He comes to as Garrett applies the brandy to his lips. "Journal explains," he says, as his eyes roll back in his head. "Bell, Bell."

"Ask Not for Whom the Bell tolls," Lt. Doherty says, quoting John Donne's immortal poem and hoping to give a man he saw as an actor a great last line.

"He musta dropped that journal in the barn," Corbett says.
But Boyd shakes his head and coughs. Blood begins flowing

freely from the corners of both lips.

Boyd sees red, then white. His sister comes down the steps of his home in Maryland and smiles at him. His mother comes out from the kitchen, a concerned look on her face. "Why?" she asks. "Why so short and exciting?"

Boyd sees red, then white. A sharp pain comes from the base of his neck, and he regains consciousness.

"Tell my mother I died for my country," Boyd says. "Raise my hands. Please raise my hands, that I may see them one last time" he pleads.

The soldier that helped carry him to the porch raises his hands up to Boyd's gaze, and Boyd shakes his head slightly.

"Other, other side," he gasps.

The soldier turns Boyd's palms toward him, and the man known to the Garrett family as Captain Boyd whispers his last words on earth and dies.

CHAPTER 22
Assassination of the Assassin

Colonel Lafayette Baker wasn't buying it.

"I don't believe that old man's story, and I certainly don't believe Corbett's," he tells Jemm inside his office at the War Department. "This was a classic assassination of the assassin. Every man in that detail was told to take Boyd alive and did so…except the one requested by Stanton."

"How can you be sure that your orders were even heard?" Jemm asks him, sitting next to his desk in a wooden chair that is usually used for witness interrogations.

Baker's office is as Spartan as the man. His wooden desk, devoid of anything except a few files and a stack of clean paper. No inkwell or pen either, just an old cup holding pencils, which the Colonel used for taking notes. He often visits another office to borrow a pen and inkwell to sign orders and other important documents. Similarly, the walls are bare, accept a calendar, scribbled with pencil marked notes.

"I know because I specifically asked that old man if my cousin Luther could be a part, just to keep an eye on things," the Colonel snaps. "Conger knew, it too. I even asked Mr. Secretary if there would be a court martial for Corbett. You know what he said, 'How can we court martial such a patriot?' think of that, 'How could we court martial such a patriot?

"Now that asshole is being celebrated all over town. Did it for the 'Greater Glory of God.' I don't like the looks of this. Just too neat. Neatness is always the result of planning. You more than anyone should know that."

For a second, Jemm wonders if this is just professional jealousy. But the Colonel is genuinely agitated, and for the first time, Jemm can detect a furrow of worry on Baker's strong brow. No, this time it isn't petty, his concern is real. Jemm's arumbo tells him so.

"Is there any word on Lieutenant Henry?" Jemm asks trying to change the subject to a topic that was equally worrisome to get the Colonel's mind back into the game.

"I sent for him. He's due back in tomorrow morning, detained at the border after what happened, or so I understand. The Canucks don't exactly like us these days, especially with the Michigan still prowling Lake Erie," Baker says. "When he gets in, both of you head down to Garrett's Farm. I want to know exactly what happened down there."

"Has he heard yet?"

"Not unless the Canadian gendarmes told him," Baker says. "I was going to leave that to you."

"How do you think he'll take it? I mean the man did save…"

"He's a soldier, Jemm, he'll take it fine," Baker snaps back, standing to look out his window at the Executive Mansion.

"If it's any consolation, I don't think…"

"Well I do, now more than ever!" Baker says. "We may have hastened a man's demise with those lithos—you were right. It's a tool too powerful to have its use just thrown around like that…"

"Men often look toward invention for an answer to the future without an eye toward the past," Jemm says, trying to calm the colonel down. "Besides, Mr. Henry may carry some of this fault as well."

"Not to mention our beloved Secretary…Do you realize the power he wields? That old man could have planned this whole thing.

Why else would he leave the Navy Yard Bridge open? "

"Maybe just to offer our Captain Boyd an avenue to the south, where he could be more easily tracked by our operatives?" Jemm says. "But he thinks if he heads south, he disappears into the Confederacy…"

"But he didn't disappear," Baker says. "He was caught, and that rat Herold with him. Don't tell me that's not Herold. Smith, a paid traveling companion, that's rich. You think these folks could come up with better lies."

"Did you turn over his personal effects?"

"Had to, the old man wanted them right away?" Baker says. "A lot of money, about what you would expect from Booth, but that probably won't make it to an evidence locker. A candle, compass, some nice girlie pictures—but there was also a journal that's missing. Booth asked about it at the end. Lt. Doherty had it in his report. Corbett had it, or so I'm told. Now, I suspect that Lt. Colonel Conger might have it. If he does, I'll find out and inspect it before he hands it over to Stanton."

Jemm, thought for a while. The two men sat in silence.

"Where is the body now?" Jemm asks.

"It was taken almost at once to Belle Plain, and from there to Alexandria aboard a tug where it was surrendered to the Montauk in the Washington Naval Yard," Baker answers.

"Any chance of a postmortem examination?"

"I already asked," Baker shoots back, his agitation growing. "The old man says he does want any darkie…uh freedman…"

At that point Baker realized his mistake and cuts himself off.

"Sorry 'bout that Jemm," he says after a brief silence.

"I hear way worse every day," Jemm says. "So what exactly did he say? Just give it to me…"

"Says the Booth family wouldn't want a darkie carvin' up their next of kin. There's no chance you can even get a look at the body."

"Not even at night? I could be a janitor…"

"Forget it Jemm, jus' ain't gonna happen," Baker says. "The family is gonna want the body soon, and the old man is gonna hand it over."

"But then, that means my investigation is, for all intents and purposes, at an end," Jemm says. "There's no reason for us to ascertain whether Booth and Boyd are one and the same."

"That's not the way the old man sees it," says Baker. "In fact, he seems more intent now on your investigation than ever before."

"That doesn't make sense," Jemm says. "It means that the old man suspects they shot the wrong man in Garrett's tobacco barn. But if so, then why wouldn't he allow an examination, the hell with the Booth family and how famous they are."

"It could also mean that the Booth family and other witnesses have identified the remains as Booth so as to throw suspicion off John Wilkes, who is already in Canada heading for Europe," adds Baker.

"But why the urgency to see if Booth or Boyd is still alive, if they believe the man in the Garrett's barn actually shot the president?" Jemm asks. "What great secret does Booth or Boyd hold? What bit of evidence does he carry that could be of such great importance to our government, or perhaps more importantly our Secretary?"

"The ole man says he wants a motive. Says that if we can find a motive, we will know for sure who is on the Montauk getting cut up at this very moment."

"But without an examination of the corpse, I will have to rely almost solely on circumstantial evidence…"

"Then let your precious investigation rely on circumstantial evidence!" Baker says, becoming even more impatient. "We're not exactly taking this evidence into court. We can't really convict anybody…We have everything we need to proceed at this point. All the conspirators are captured. Booth or Boyd is dead, and the Secretary is in a big hurry to make sure that a postmortem happens before you could ever get down there. Almost as if he doesn't want you to see the body…"

"Even if I uncover the circumstantial evidence that uncovers a motive…without a reliable and definitive postmortem…it will only give rise to future conspiracy theories involving misidentification," Jemm says. "The assassin will live on, at least in legend. And other opportunists may even claim to be the assassin, as a means to garner fame…"

"But your real objection is that it relegates your investigation strictly to motive," Baker adds, almost happy that Jemm is being thwarted.

"Exactly…I'll have to ascertain if there's any relation between Booth and Boyd…"

"Bennett Burley, one of the Lake Erie pirates, is in custody in Port Clinton. The old man told me about it earlier," Baker says. "He's said to have served with the enigmatic Captain Boyd up in Canada. We could have Lt. Henry or even you interrogate him, take his affidavit."

"Looks like we'll be heading out to Ohio," Jemm says.

"We might also find something in that journal," Jemm says, searching for answers. "We could verify that there was a journal by talking to the Garretts…even if it was destroyed in the fire…"

"Well, if Corbett has the journal, he'll never tell anyone about it, except the man that gave him the order to take it, and like I said, it could be Conger," says Baker. "I'd rely on the folks in Ohio."

"Aside from his prison stay at Andersonville, what makes you think Corbett can take interrogation better than any other man?" Jemm asks.

"This makes for rather interesting reading," Baker said, holding up a dossier on Corbett, which includes his service record.

"He comes from Troy, New York. His family comes from London. His given first name is Thomas. He enlisted in Company I of the 12th Regiment of the New York Militia. He was subsequently discharged for refusing to apologize for insubordination. Seems he chastised a colonel, one Daniel Butterfield, for taking the Lord's name in vain and using profanity. "

"Interesting."

"He was court-martialed and given the opportunity to apologize to the colonel, but refused to do so," says Jemm as he reads. "So he was sentenced to be shot. But it looks like his sentenced was reduced and he was discharged in August of 1863.

"Later that month, he re-enlisted as a private in Company L of 16th New York Cavalry Regiment, and in June of 1864, was captured by Colonel Mosby's men at Culpeper, VA and held prisoner at Andersonville for five months."

"That would certainly account for his attitude," adds Jemm. "He was exchanged last November. He went to the Army Hospital at Annapolis, treated for scurvy and malnutrition, and was promoted to sergeant, a rank he holds to this day."

"Keep reading," Colonel Baker says, as he hands Jemm the service record of one Boston Corbett.

"Notice anything strange?" Baker asks.

"Sounds like he's very motivated and dedicated to the cause," Jemm says.

"The earlier confrontation with Colonel Butterfield raise any questions?"

"Well, he's obviously a man of strong religious convictions. After his court martial, he was allowed to reenlist, so somebody up top is obviously pulling strings for him I mean refusing to apologize, even under threat of a firing squad…

"He's fanatical to say the least, but maybe not balanced."

"He's literally mad as a hatter," says Baker. "At 13, he was apprenticed to be a milliner, working on beaver top hats, and as such was exposed to fumes of mercury nitrate, which can cause madness, hallucinations and the shakes.

"And he's a religious zealot of the very worst kind. His confrontation with Colonel Butterfield started with his proselytizing the troops. He carried a Bible with him constantly preaching and quoting scripture."

"That's hardly a reason for calling him mad," Jemm says. "But it is a very good base for social conditioning."

"He was married for a time, lived in New York, but his wife and child died at birth," says Baker, "and he took to strong drink and found himself destitute and living in the streets."

"Which is understandable under the circumstances. Like many men he no doubt blamed himself for his wife's demise. You're really not telling me anything."

"He later moved to Boston, and after a night of heavy drinking, was confronted by a member of the Methodist Episcopal Church. He stopped drinking. Got baptized, and officially changed his name to Boston. He took up lodgings at a local boardinghouse. And later earned a reputation around town as a street preacher and religious fanatic, who would offer up sermons in the streets of Boston."

"You're not really telling me anything that would raise any further suspicion," Jemm says, getting ready to toss aside the dossier.

"The real problem started after he was confronted by two prostitutes while walking home from a nightly prayer meeting…"

His prurient interest piqued, Jemm continues to read as Colonel Lafayette Baker stares out the window.

CHAPTER 23

If it Offend Thee…

Along a dark and musty back alley in Boston's North End, Boston Corbett walked back to his room at Emma's Boarding House. It was well past midnight, and many of the bars that cater to the sailors have closed their doors. The night was unusually foggy, and you could hear the halyards clacking against the masts of the schooners, as they moved with the harbor waves, that were crashing but a few blocks away.

As he headed down Fulton Street, two ladies of the night stepped out of the shadows.

"Fancy a frolic, love?" one said to him as she stepped directly into his path.

"Tis been a slow night," the other said coming up alongside.

"You might even get double the company, for the same price," the other said, as she intentionally pressed her breasts against him.

Corbett lost his breath, and started to shake, as the other prostitute puts her arm around him.

"Let's just see what we have here," she said as she reached into Corbett's britches. "Not too excited are we," she said, "but oh now lookey here," she added as his member rapidly engorges. "You are willin' aren't you."

Corbett felt his testicles ache and turn as his manhood stiffened. And then that warm feeling in his lower abdomen, just before he shot a load of his jism into pants. He felt his face flush with embarrassment.

"Little quick aren't we love," she said pulling out her gooey hands and wiping them on his coat. "Looks like you won't be needin' a tumble after all."

They both started to laugh, as Corbett hit his back against the wall in humiliation. As they walked away, he's horrified. Looking down at his soiled britches, smelling that sickly fresh smell of fornication, he ran to the boarding house, being careful to cover his mess with his waistcoat as he climbed the stairs to his room.

The next day, Corbett was back in the North Square early, preaching and proselytizing, reading Matthew Chapters 18 and 19 to all that would take notice and hear:

"And if thy right eye offend thee, pluck it out and cast it from thee," Corbett shouted. "And there be eunuchs which have made themselves eunuchs for the kingdom of heaven's sake."

But his mind raced back to the night before, and he began to feel shame and a tightening in his newly washed britches. A lady standing nearby notices his growing bulge, covers her mouth and started to giggle. Before he can become fully aroused, Corbett ran back to his room at the boarding house, bounding up the stairs before other boarders could stop him.

Once inside his room, he pulled out the chamber pot from underneath the bed, and the wash basin from the cupboard. He found his milliner shears in the bureau, took off his trousers and sat on the overly plump bed. His full erection was staring back at him, throbbing with each beat of his heart.

"And if thy right eye offend thee, pluck it out and cast it from thee," he whispered, as he placed the wash basin under his groin. "And if thy right eye offend thee, pluck it out and cast it from thee," he whispered again. Taking his razor sharp shears, he started at the top of the scrotal sack, and barely pierced the skin, before he ejaculated.

Corbett cried and slid to his side, whimpering. But he soon found the strength to continue.

"And if thy right eye offend thee, pluck it out and cast it from thee," he whispered again.

Taking a deep breath and focusing on the wall straight ahead, he started at the top of the scrotal sack, cutting his way slowly downward, each snip causing excruciating pain. He stopped and placed the shears down, as blood flowed copiously into the wash basin.

Corbett took another breath, this time using his fingers to widen the incision, and let the two soft grey-white eggs flop out and lie against the side of the porcelain bowl. He was surprised at how white they are, and how the cords and vessels were surprisingly long. Corbett sat for a moment and closed his eyes, then, looking down, severed the cords to his manhood, grabbing the pillow from his bed to stem the bleeding as he fell back.

# # #

"It's a wonder he didn't die," Jemm says finishing his reading. When did they find him?"

"They didn't" Baker says. "As near as we can tell, he got up 30 minutes later, and went to a prayer meeting. It wasn't until the good reverend saw the blood coming through his trousers that he sought medical attention…but not until the prayer meeting was over."

"Stanton and Thompson could have planned this whole thing. If not for power, then at least for profit," the Colonel says.

"I doubt we ever find a journal, but if we do, they'll be pages missing."

The Colonel whirls from the window and looks directly at Jemm.

"Now why the hell would you think that?" he asks.

"I only thought that if there were pages missing, it would confirm your theory about a cover up. And that Stanton, at least at some level, is involved. If we can prove that Booth was under a spell, then almost certainly, or at least circumstantially, we can link Stanton, Booth and Thompson. If he's only socially conditioned, those links will be much harder to prove."

"We need to find that journal," the Colonel says. "Intact."

Jemm gets up immediately, antsy and turns around. He walks briskly to the door.

"Where are you going?" Baker asks, "we still have work to do."

"I'm going to the wife. I just got to see if everything's working."

"Listen Jemm," The colonel says. "I forgot to thank you for your work helping us corner them at Garrett's…"

"I suspect they would have closed in on him sooner or later."

"But I might not have been able to close in on him sooner than the rest—I won't forget that," Baker says. "You know, after all this is over…"

"We'll probably hate each other even more," Jemm quips.

The colonel let out a loud guffaw, relieving the tension in the air.

Leaving the Baker's office that evening, Jemm feels strangely relieved by the meeting. Baker knows more than he let on, especially when it comes to Booth's journal, but at least he isn't a part of any deep conspiracy involving the Secretary of War or Jacob Thompson and Jemm can sense his frustration. He doesn't have to worry about assassination by Baker, indeed, he may soon be a trusted ally and valuable resource in the investigation.

# # #

As Jemm climbs the stairs to his fourth-floor home, he feels strangely exhausted. The revelations about Boston Corbett have put him strangely ill at-ease. He finds Marnie sitting at the table humming what seemed to be a happy melodic tune with no real direction or focus. A small candle in front of her throws flickering shadows against the wall. When Jemm comes close she looks up and smiles.

"You look like you could use some good news," she says.

"Come over here and put your hand right here," she says, placing his hand on her abdomen.

Jemm can feel the slight but subtle movements of life inside of her.

"That's you growin' inside of me," Marnie says, smiling. "Cordelia say it's a boy by the way he's ridin' and kickin'."

Jemm is overcome with joy, that turns to fear and finally guilt.

"Why you so troubled?" Marnie asks.

"I can't leave you alone anymore."

"Oh nonsense, they's plenty of time. Sides, Cordelia say she may be losin' her position at the Mansion, now that Mary Todd no longer there."

Cordelia would be a welcome addition to their home. Still, Jemm feels he has to stop the dangerous work.

"This will be my last case…"

"What we gonna do for money?" Marnie asks.

"You leave that to me," Jemm says. "Money is nothing more than an exchange for goods and services. I know how to make money…Life, life is the most precious gift of all."

CHAPTER 24
The Blizzard Monster's Little Red Book

The next morning dawns purple, red and gray against the magnificent spire of the B&O train station, a sign which meant storms later in the day.

Jemm waits for Lt. Ollie Henry outside the rail station, sitting in a canvas covered Army wagon drawn by two mules. Inside, there are provisions enough for a week, including hard tack, tinned beef, jerky and water. Jemm looks like many other of the freedmen livery drivers waiting for fares at the station, especially with the lack of military designation on the side of the wagon's canvas.

While other drivers shout out and call to each other, Jemm is focused on the task before him, waiting patiently, as the train out of Baltimore pulls in 20 minutes late, unusual for its run. He doesn't spot Lt. Henry coming out the main gate, but sees Agent Beckwith back by the freight entrance, motioning with his chin. It is then he realized that Henry had been riding back in Pinkerton's Post Office supplied by Colonel Baker.

Lt. Henry comes around the corner with his haversack slung over his right shoulder, holding it with his left arm crossed in front. He looks bright and well rested and smiles broadly as he approaches the wagon.

"Still can't get them to give you anything more than a mule," he teases.

"Hop aboard Ollie, there's some bad news," Jemm says, as Lt. Ollie Henry climbs awkwardly up. "Billy Cao is dead. They found him with his throat slit from ear to ear and his tongue pulled out from under his jaw."

"Geezus." Henry didn't know what else to say. He sat in stunned silence as Jemm slaps the reins down and pulls the wagon away from the station.

"Don't worry, it' s not all your fault," Jemm says.

"I blew it up there," Henry says. "I felt like an amateur."

"You are an amateur," Jemm answers. "But don't let it bother you. We all have to start somewhere."

"Still, a man is dead, and I likely hastened his demise," Lt. Henry says dejectedly.

"The key word being 'hastened,'" Jemm shoots back, "they were likely on to him already."

It is a long drive down to the Garrett's farm in Virginia. It might take light cavalry 24 hours riding day and night, but is at least two days by wagon, and maybe another day when that wagon is drawn by mules.

But there was no real hurry. Booth, or Captain Boyd, is now aboard the Montauk. And there will be no postmortem, at least by Jemm. And Burley's court date in Ohio is at least three weeks away.

So the two can take their time, sleep in the wagon. Or if Lt. Henry liked, he could get a room at a tavern or inn. Jemm, of course, is relegated to a wagon, not afforded common courtesy or dignities, even close to the Capitol.

Regardless, Jemm and Ollie Henry share a singular mission to retrace the steps of a dead man, to ascertain what the most valuable witness might be able to tell the world from beyond the grave.

"We're looking for a book," Jemm says at last, "a journal, that might shed some light on Booth's last days, maybe even a motive."

"Or maybe even more," Lt. Henry says, hopping on board with the idea.

Jemm gives him an inquisitive look, "What you got Ollie?" he finally asks as a soft rain began to fall.

"Boyd is supposed to be joining Jacob Thompson up in Canada," Henry says. "A man named John St. Helen is already with him. Cao said Thompson already withdrew $184,000 from his personal account.

"Trust me, it's just one account of several."

"They're supposed to be leaving Canada for Europe in a few days…don't know why they didn't leave as soon as they got the news…I suspect they're waiting on Boyd."

"Or waiting for something else…" Jemm adds. "This John St. Helen person, is it Booth or Surratt?" Jemm asks. "Did you show the lithos, at least get a description?"

"Cao stole the lithos, while I was drugged," Lt. Henry says. "I left them in my room, and he…."

"YOU DIDN'T KEEP THEM ON YOUR PERSON?" Jemm shouts.

Once again, Henry feels like an amateur, and this time Jemm doesn't offer any encouragement or solace.

"A lot of times, the person's name or alias is associated with the mission," Jemm explains. "So when Captain Boyd comes down from Canada, his close associates know what his mission is. Similarly, if he is going by St. Helen his ultimate mission may be quite different, even though he is the same person, and the name may actually have a destination or a direction of travel associated with it…

"Did you find out anything about the bell the 'avenging bell'?"

"Nothing. But Cao did give me a page from the register at St. Lawrence Hall. He also gave me a register from a passenger ferry out of Windsor called the Phil Parsons, and.."

"The WHAT?"

"The Philo Parsons out of Windsor, it seems our Capt. Boyd was on it last September…"

"I think you found our priest," Jemm says. "Good work Ollie!?

Jemm thinks that he may have gone a little overboard with the compliment. Henry is at least partially responsible for blowing Cao's cover—and the fact that Cao had been disposed of meant the lithos are now in the possession of the spies out of Canada, making it easier to adopt a change in appearance or even a disguise while traveling.

"Cao said I should ask you why you always have your partners mesmerized," Lt. Henry says, "Am I mesmerized?"

"Just a precaution, I can assure you," Jemm says. "We'll have it remedied once we get back to Marnie. In the meantime, you may get a little fuzzy-headed from time to time—don't worry about it. It's natural. The spell is already broken."

Lt. Henry doesn't know whether to be angry or relieved. The revelation does spark some resentment.

"Mesmerization is only a tool," Jemm explains. "Europeans are starting to call it hypnosis—but my people have been using it for centuries to calm and control not only people, but animals."

Still, Jemm, realizes that the breaking of a spell in this forced way, may create false realities or narratives within the mind of the subject.

"To control people?"

"To control situations," Jemm answers. "And sometimes animals —even the great cats of the plains. Let me explain what it is. By putting you under a spell, you become compliant. It was initially thought that you may have been hypnotized by Stanton or his associates. But even under a spell, a subject will not do anything that they object to morally. So it wasn't like we were forcing you to dance around naked after Easter supper. You simply became more compliant to offering up information---more willing to open up— which was essential to our investigation, especially in light of the fact that you were put in charge…"

"So that's it. This is revenge for my promotion? If you think that…"

"That's not it at all, and what's more you know it."

"I still feel like I've been used! Why couldn't you just come out and tell me?"

# # #

As they headed farther south, the forest and underbrush along the road thickened green quickly covering the gray that blanked the countryside all winter. In two weeks, it would be virtually impenetrable. The rain began falling harder later in the afternoon, slowing their progress along the muddy spring road. The tension between them palpable.

Jemm's mind swirled as they rode. Every time something new was learned two more questions pop up. Did Booth head north? If so, who was the man that was shot in Garrett's barn? Was it Booth, or Boyd? How could he prove that the two were one and the same? Surely the register of the St. Lawrence Hall and the Philo Parsons showed similarities in the cursive style.

Was Booth just an actor sympathetic to the Confederate cause? Surely, the person who shot Lincoln knew it would be suicide. Then the same question came back: Why would someone like Booth throw away such a promising career, riches and future happiness for a political cause?

It didn't add up. There had to be more to it. Maybe Booth was mesmerized. It was beginning to make more sense. But how could he prove it? And how could he tie it to Stanton? Most certainly, he was socially conditioned to the task. Proving that would be still harder.

Jemm's arumbo came back, telling him about the tension his silence was causing Lt. Henry.

"Don't worry Ollie," Jemm says. "You brought back a ton of information. I just have to sort through it all. Your information about Thompson is spot on—it's just as we expected. And the comparison of the handwriting samples might be the only concrete evidence that we have connecting Booth and Boyd.

"Here, I want you to re-read the history of John Wilkes Booth. Remember, even the tiniest bits of information can be crucial—especially if we're going on strictly circumstantial evidence.

"I suspect we'll find a lot of answers in that journal," Lt. Henry says, hopefully.

"We'll be lucky to find it, if it exists at all," Jemm says.

They continued to ride in silence, which was now a lot more comfortable. Lt. Henry finally finds the courage to ask Jemm for information that had seemed incomplete, that had been gnawing at him for some time.

"How the hell did you ever get into this business…I mean I know you're well suited for it…"

"But why would Allan Pinkerton choose a darkie?"

"That's not what I meant, but, well, I guess it is…"

"I did tell you that Colonel Pinkerton is a chartist…"

"And as such would really not regard color as a barrier…"

"But there's a lot more to it than that," says Jemm. "Women and colored make the best spies. The same reason Webster used John Scobell—who was always singing songs and acting like a friendly darkie. Remember what you learned in Canada? Cao and Madame Taishi's girls were all operatives."

"But are they just better suited to it?

"Not at all. Thery'e just not noticed or even considered as a threat," says Jemm. "Women, have been used in this conflict repeatedly—especially by the South. We even used a network of women who assisted us in cornering Booth."

Jemm told Lt. Henry about how, Rose O'Neal Greenhow, a southern socialite, was friendly with William Seward, and may have passed information on Union Troop movements. Belle Boyd was known to have smuggled intelligence to Stonewall Jackson during his valley campaign, while Bettie Duval dressed as a farm girl, and passed union sentinels on the Chain Bridge leaving Washington then moved on to Fairfax delivering her ciphered message to P.T Beauregard, dooming Union efforts at the First Bull run.

But the Union also had their female operatives as well. Richmond's Elizabeth Van Lew was said to have infiltrated the highest level of the Confederacy, one of her slaves Mary Elizabeth Bowser, who was educated by Quakers, held a position in Richmond as a servant to Jefferson Davis. Because they thought she was illiterate, she was able to read action dispatches during state dinners, often times reading them upside down. Mary also perfected a technique of hollowing out eggs inserting ciphered messages in the empty shells, and placing the empty eggs in a basket that would pass by sentinels undetected.

"But the use of coloreds and women was also very well documented during our revolution," adds Jemm. "During the British occupation of New York City, Robert Townsend established a network of women operatives, who eventually uncovered Benedict Arnold through something called the Culper Spy Ring.

"I suspect that's where Pinkerton got the idea to use women and coloreds," says Jemm. "Most people don't think they're too bright, so most people don't think them a threat…"

"But also, there has been a terrible failure of white male field agents…"

"Like mine in Canada?"

"Let's just say you were working at a disadvantage," says Jemm. "Lafayette Baker failed miserably and was almost put to death in Richmond. And one of Colonel Pinkerton's favorites, Webster, was hanged—after that, Colonel Pinkerton wanted to give all of his agents the best possibility of survival—something Lafayette Baker knows all too well. But there is a long history of agents being discovered and put to death…"

"Like Billy Cao," says Henry.

"Who had a pretty good cover," adds Jemm.

"Not with any help by me."

"Like I said, they were likely on to him," Jemm adds.

By early evening, the rain became a steady downpour, the mud caking against the wagon wheels' wooden spokes. Finally, they pulled to the side of the road, partially under a copse of large pines, listening to the rain plink and click off the canvas of the wagon as they drifted off to sleep.

The next day dawned sunny, but everything in the wagon seemed to be wet or at least damp. Lt. Henry pulled down the canvas from its supporting wooden hoops and with Jemm's help folded it and placed it in the back, hoping the sun would dry the contents of the wagon.

After about an hour, they came across Noah's place. He was in front changing a wagon wheel, when Jemm steered his wagon onto the drive.

# # #

"Carnsound it boy, you know better than to move a wagon with mud drying on its spokes like that," Noah says to Jemm, only acknowledging Lt. Henry with a quick nod. Actually Jemm didn't know that dried mud would dislodge a spoke and throw a wheel.

"Lizabeth, fetch us some buckets with water," Noah calls over to the house. Soon his daughter is busy filling buckets at the red pump well out in front of the house.

"Watchoo up to this time boy?" Noah asks Jemm, "they done caught your man and his buddy—same ones hidin' out in the chicken coup, from what I understand."

"Did you know who they were?" Jemm asks

"We all believed his name was Boyd," the freedman wagon master and sharecropper says. "I don't think anyone is gonna talk to anyone right now, and who can blame them? Everyone thinks they was hidin' this man. But I knows different.

"We don't get too many papers round these parts, so how could they know? They was just bein' hospitable."

"What sort of man was Boyd?" Jemm asks him.

"A good looking fellow, lean, good head of hair, too. His partner who went by Smiff, looked like he could use a bath…smelled like it too."

"Did your daughter give them anything besides food?"

"Not that I know of, just the cornbread and chicken that first night. Said they was real hungry," Noah says. "They lit outta here just after your visit. Spect they seen ya?

"And that's the last you saw of them," Jemm asks Noah.

Elizabeth shows up carrying two buckets of water, placing them at the front of Jemm's wagon.

"You'll need two more Lizabeth, one more for each wheel," Noah tells her.

"Wait, I'll help," Lt. Henry says climbing down and following her back to the pump.

"Actually, I'd like to talk to your daughter," Jemm says.

"You a married man?" Noah asks.

"It's not like that," Jemm says. "I'd like to ask her a few questions about the two that hid out in the chicken coup."

"No reason for that, they been caught, and one is shot dead," Noah says. "It only means trouble for her."

"Still, I'd like to ask her…"

Elizabeth and Henry return each carrying full buckets, placing them next to the others by the front of the wagon.

"Lizabeth honey, this man here wants to ask you a few questions about those men in the coup. You okay with that girl?"

"You took them food a couple of times didn't you? Jemm asks.

"It was only on accounta they's hungry, scared, too…I didn't mean…"

Jemm can sense the fear in her voice, and the reason Noah wants him to interview her while he is present.

"Oh no, no, it's nothin' like that," Jemm says, his tone and accent falling back to the vernacular of the freedman. "I just' want to know if you saw them writin' anything, the one with the crutches, writin' anything…"

"He had proper writin' things," Elizabeth says. "And was always puttin' things down in dis pretty little red book."

"Did he take the book with him when he left?"

"Wasn't nothin' but some chicken bones left in that coup when they lit outta here," Elizabeth says.

"Is this the two men you fed in the chicken coup," Jemm asks, showing her the two lithographs he still has in his possession.

Elizabeth looks over at her daddy, then sheepishly back at Jemm, then back at Noah, who nods slightly.

"That's them all right," she says.

"Which one had the writin' things," Jemm asks.

Elizabeth points to Booth.

"Okay, honey, that's all he needs know," Noah says, cutting the interview a little shorter than Jemm would have liked.

Noah looks over at Jemm.

"Better get your rear skin on those buckets and wash down them spokes," Noah says to Jemm. "I don't want to get news later that you're stuck somewhere on the road with a broken wheel. I'll charge ya twice as much just for bein' stoopid."

Noah watches in amazement as Lt. Henry shares the chore. After they both wash down the wagon wheel spokes, Jemm and Lt. Henry are soon back on the road.

"Sumpin' ain't right about those two," Noah says to his daughter as they pull away. "Which one's the boss?"

#

About a mile down the road, the two meet their first rendezvous at the Potomac with a military paddle steamer ferry. The captain of the vessel comes down to the bow loading plank to greet them.

"Lt. Henry?" he asks, holding out his hand.

Lt. Henry reaches for it with his left hand, always feeling a little awkward at having to shake hands that way.

"No man, your orders!" The captain snaps at him. He has an orange beard that stretches along his chin, but no mustache. His uniform looks like he's slept in it.

Jemm reaches in his front trouser pocket and hands the crumpled orders to Henry, who in turn hands them to the captain, who is growing impatient.

"You're late!" the captain snaps again, "and you're holding me up! And you're letting a nigger carry your orders! What kind of an officer are you?"

"I'm new to the rank," Lt. Henry tells the captain.

"You *are* an amateur, sir," the captain tells him. "There's a man inside the main salon wanting to talk with you."

Lt. Henry looks over at Jemm, and shrugs his shoulders, but soon becomes a little fuzzy in the head.

The mules balk slightly at crossing over the loading plank, but with some gentle encouragement make it across fine, the wagon and its team leaving behind a thick trail of mud from the road—which doesn't go unnoticed by the captain. Jemm gets down and grabs blankets from the back. He heads over to the mules placing the blankets on the mules' eyes to calm them as they ride across the Potomac, an almost two-mile voyage at this section of the river.

Jemm waits with the mules and wagon in the cargo hold, until Lt. Henry comes back down.

"So who was your friend?" Jemm asks innocently.

"Some man, I can't really place him," Lt. Henry says, his mind only now beginning to clear.

"That's okay, don't worry about it Ollie," Jemm answers, a half smile coming across his face. "I'm sure it wasn't anything, at least anything important."

It was a wise precaution to mesmerize Henry.

Lt. Henry and Jemm disembark on the other side at Point Mathias, finding the road ahead a little drier and sandy, which makes for easier going. They stop at John Lucas' place to interview Charlie and enlist his help as a guide to Garrett's farm. But Charlie really can't help much, except re-identifying the two men from the lithographs that Jemm has.

The next morning the three set out, Jemm and Henry in the wagon and Charlie on his own mule. It takes most of the next morning before they come across Garrett's Farm, where Charlie bids them farewell, and heads back on his own mule.

Garretts's farm has a proper Virginia frame house, painted white, with a long broad porch with and roof held up by four large white pillars in front. Children of all ages are in the yard and running about—the youngest a little girl of no more than three years, the eldest a young lady in her late teens or early 20s. There are still some sentries on site. Jemm recognizes a couple from the New York 16th. But there are no officers. About 200 feet from the house, Jemm sees the charred remains of the tobacco barn, it's sooty smell still in the air.

An old sergeant, with grey hair sprouting out from under his blue cover at the temples holds up his hand to stop the wagon as it approaches the house coming up the drive. He doesn't look like he'd take nonsense from anyone.

"No tourists, curious visitors, souvenir seekers or civilians at all beyond this point," the sergeant says. "You'll have to turn around."

"Orders," Lt. Henry says, holding his left hand across his body, until Jemm supplies the necessary papers, which were a little damp, but still readable.

"That's Colonel Baker's mark all right," the sergeant says, as he examines the papers. He steps back and snaps Lt. Henry the proper salute, then realizes that Henry can't return the favor, but smiles as Henry salutes from his left, as is the custom.

"Lost it during the Chickamauga campaign, Lookout Mountain," he says to the sergeant.

"Have your boy pull the wagon up over here," the sergeant says, motioning to one side of the white frame house's porch. "National Detective Police is it?

"I'll get young Richard for you. His father Richard, is still away, but due back in a couple of days, if you need to talk to him," the sergeant adds. "You can come with me inside, but your boy has to stay out here in the wagon."

"But he's supposed to accompany me…"

"I didn't see anything about anybody accompanying anybody else in them orders, lieutenant. And I'm not about to subject this poor family to any more…"

"Relax dar, Sir, I just stay out her and talk with the chidrens," Jemm says, once again letting his dialect slip into the comfortable vernacular that puts the sergeant at ease, but it seems almost comical to Henry. "You go on an talk with Massa Garrett inside."

And then under his breath so only Henry could hear, "I'd rather talk to the chidrens anyway. And the younger, the better."

As the sergeant leads Henry inside, the children in the yard, especially the younger ones, became naturally curious. They are family, no mistaking it. The two boys are about five years apart, the youngest about seven or eight, but they shared faces cut from the same cloth; dark brown hair, blue eyes and a protruding lower jaw. They are dressed like twins, in almost identical black outfits, but of obvious different sizes.

The smallest girl, who has to be only two or three Jemm surmises, is dressed in white and red pantaloons. She is towheaded, but her two sisters about six and nine, have hair that is turning dirty blonde. The oldest sister, sitting on a porch swing watching the other children, has grown into a beautiful young woman, with light brown hair and a slender figure. The soldiers on duty stare at her but avert their gaze whenever she looks their way.

The little girl in pantaloons approaches the wagon boldly, her right hand almost completely in her mouth the only sign of any trepidation. Her older sister grabs her before she gets too close to the wagon.

"Leave that man alone, Cora Lee," the older girl says.

"Hey mister, are you a soldier man too?" the seven-year old boy asks.

"That we are," Jemm says, his tone taking on a little more authoritative tone.

"Yous been in and out of here, asking questions all along," says the older boy, as he steps up to the wagon.

"Hey mister, they botherin' you?" Anna Garrett calls from the front porch. "You kids leave that man alone while he waits!"

"Oh I don't mind mam, kind of like the chidrens," Jemm calls back.

"Well if they bother you, you all just let me know," Anna calls back. "Can I get you a drink, some water maybe."

"I'm fine mam, I have water here in the wagon," Jemm yells back.

"Can I jump up?" the seven-year old boy asks.

"Bobby, that ain't polite," his brother says, "he don't want you…

"So it's Bobby is it?" Jemm says, offering the boy his hand to help him up.

"Can I get up too," his six-year old sister blurts out as she climbs up without any help at all. She looks like a tomboy.

"And what's your name?"

"Henrietta," the little girl says, "but everyone just calls me Henry."

"That's my lieutenant's name," Jemm laughs.

"Are you here about Captain Boyd?" the 11-year old asks.

Jemm nods.

"Died right there on the front porch," the boy says pointing toward his older sister on the swing, "Wanna see the blood stain? They's still some left."

"He was a nice man, why did they shoot him?" Henrietta asks innocently.

"And why do you think he was nice?" Jemm asks her.

"We was playactin' with him," the little girl says.

# # #

"Here comes a blizzard," Johnny Garrett said. He's dressed in a blue suit, with short pants. His ill-fitting white socks falling down into his brown shoes.

The little girl is no more than three is dressed in white with a yellow sweater. She picks up a handful of white apple blossoms, which are carpeting the ground. She plastered Captain Boyd directly in the face and runs away giggling in delight. As Boyd raises his hands, contorts his face in mock pain, and falls back on the ground feigning injury.

The little boy in turn picked up a handful of blossoms that are mixed heavily with mud and dirt, he tried to hit Captain Boyd in the face, but is well off his mark. Boyd grabbed him about the waist and picked him up as the boy squealed and laughed.

"If you're going to go about fighting monsters, you must perfect your aim," Boyd said, setting the boy back down. "Now go get some more ammunition."

The little girl came back, pausing directly in front of Boyd.

"He can't aim so well because he needs spec taters," the little girl said.

"You mean spectacles, my blue-eyed beauty," Boyd says correcting her. "Your brother suffers from a very common condition known as myopia. Many great men suffer from such a condition these days."

The sun, which was starting to set, casting an orange glow over the white apple blossoms on the tree. Mr. Smith walked up from the road.

"It's not good Wilkes," Smith said. "They're definitely closing in. We need to move out of here tomorrow, latest."

The little girl, becoming bored, picked up some more apple blossoms, hitting Captain Boyd directly in the face.

"Another blizzard," she squealed, as some of the fallen blossoms find their way into the Captain's mouth. He made a comic face as he spit them out, and then picked them out one by one.

"You know David, I'm right at the end," Boyd whispered. "I'd rather surrender now and tell my story. Set everything straight. We all need a confessor, and I think mine should be the American public. We need an absolution for history's sake."

"And I think we should move or we'll end up shot, or at the end of a rope," Smith said.

A woman came out of the Garrett House and shouted to her children.

"You two leave Captain Boyd alone," Mrs. Garrett said. "You've both had enough playacting for today…

"Captain Boyd, do you and Mr. Smith want some supper?"

"Some biscuits would be nice," Boyd answered.

"I'll get you both blankets for tonight, it's supposed to be colder, and that barn doesn't hold too much heat," she said to her guests.

"Thank you so much," Captain Boyd said struggling to stand up on crutch, "You've been much more than just kind."

He turned to Smith and said under his breath, "We'll leave at first light."

Boyd and Smith head toward the old tobacco barn at the southern corner of the Garrett farm.

# # #

"Aside from just eatin' vittles and playactin' did Captain Boyd do anything else? Jemm asks.

"Aside from hobblin' around you mean?" Johnny Garrett asks.

"Did he talk about anything? Mention anyone?"

"Wonderin' if we heard anything. Kep askin,'" Johnny says. "And he was always writin' in his little red book for prosperity."

"You mean posterity."

"Yeah, that's it," Johnny Garrett says.

"What happened to that little red book?" Jemm asks.

"The squeaky sergeant took it. Said he's given it to the colonel."

CHAPTER 25
The Trial

In early May, with entire nation wrapped up in the trial of the conspirators, Jemm and Lt. Henry headed for Ohio. Stanton had favored a quick military style trial and execution, which was opposed by Secretary of Navy Gideon Welles. Stanton wanted the conspirators to be tried and executed before Lincoln was buried in Springfield, which aroused Jemm's arumbo.

While Lincoln was interred on May 4, the trial of the conspirators didn't start until five days later, when General Hartranft visited each prisoner's cell to read the charges and specifications against them by lantern light.

Prior to the reading of the charges, the prisoners had been treated cruelly. Mary Surratt and Doctor Mudd were jailed at the Old Capitol Prison while the six other prisoners were split between the brigs on board the Montauk and Saugus. They were later moved to the Old Capitol Prison, as the trial approached. Four of the male prisoners, Herold, Powell, Spangler and Atzerodt were in ball and chains with hands held in front by an iron bar. From the time of their arrest, through their trial, all prisoners except Dr. Mudd and Mary Surratt were forced to wear canvas hoods that covered their entire face, making breathing that much more difficult during an early, hot and humid spring.

Testimony began on May 12, with the conspirators offered, if they wanted, defense counsel a scant three days earlier. Stanton saw the trial as an opportunity to prosecute not only the eight charged conspirators, but the already dead Booth, who had been identified almost immediately by the Booth family as well as Surgeon General Barnes, although Dr. Fredrick May who also performed a postmortem actually said the body did not look like Booth. This even further aroused Jemm's suspicion. The case against the conspirators also included Jefferson Davis and the Confederate Secret Service, a good portion of which was still in Canada.

Thanks to the efforts of Jemm and Lt. Henry, the National Detective Police were able to further investigate and produce witnesses that testified that as the war waned, the Confederacy had grown increasingly desperate. There were: the plots in Chicago in the summer and fall of 1864; plans to destroy public buildings, burn steamboats, poison the public water supply and offers of commissions to raiders of northern cities.

Naturally, many of these plots have since been tied to Jacob Thompson and Clement Clay, two men appointed by Jefferson Davis to fund terrorism operations from the North, including a rather nasty attack that came in the form of contaminating clothing with yellow fever, smallpox and other infectious diseases.

One witness testified that the Northern Confederates out of Montreal had appropriated $200,000 for the operation. A man named Hyams, refused to deliver an infected trunk to Lincoln, instead sending on other infected trunks to New Bern, North Carolina, where there was an outbreak of small box that killed almost 2,000 citizens and federal soldiers.

During the trial, it was revealed that the plot against Lincoln had been going on for a long time, at least after the Battle of Gettysburg in 1863, but certainly no later than the summer of 1864, when all the plots along the Great Lakes were unfolding. The goal of Thompson and Clay was to "leave the Union without a head," by killing not only Lincoln, but also Vice President Johnson, Secretary of War Stanton, Secretary of State Seward, and General Grant. But it was obviously apparent that the plan had evolved over time.

Other witnesses testified that Booth had tried to recruit sympathizers to participate in a plot to abduct Lincoln and take him to Richmond, where he would be exchanged for rebel officers. This plan was abandoned in mid-January, but then came back in March, when the conspirators saw an opportunity on March 17th with the knowledge among them that Lincoln would be returning from a play at The Old Soldier's home. It was the same plot that the conspirators had revisited after its inception after abandoning it in Mid-January. But the real question was never asked. Why did the conspirators abandon the plot in mid-January of 1865, then revisit it in March? What had set them off? And why did they abandon the plan entirely on March 20? Did they simply chicken out? Or had they been tipped off?

There were, of course, some questions as to the intentions of witnesses, some receiving clemency for their testimony. Joey Peanuts testified that he had held Booth's horse at the direction of Spangler, who had given him a quarter for the deed.

While the chief prosecutor Judge Advocate General of the Army Joseph Holt tried to press his case against Jefferson Davis and the highest levels of the Confederacy through Montreal, his case was reliant on the testimony of Sandford Conover, who it turned out had perjured himself and was unreliable. That line of argument in danger of bringing down the entire case, Holt was forced to abandon it to obtain the prosecution of the more obvious conspirators. The case became dependent on another key witness, Louis Weichmann, who was both a border at Mary Surratt's and a good friend of Booth, Powell, (or Paine), and other folks who frequented Gautier's. It was rumored that he, too, was involved with the Confederate spies out of Montreal. He denied any involvement in the kidnap plot. However, he did take credit for exposing it to authorities. On the stand, he was said to have done a better job of acting than anyone in the Booth family, explaining his innocence, while deftly pointing an accusatory digit at everyone else.

Weichmann also testified that John Surratt had already headed north on or about April 6 with a ciphered letter detailing the president's assassination plot. That was the obvious reason Thompson withdrew over $184,000 from his private Montreal account which had over $600,000 in it. But there was no trail of where the money went after its withdrawal. And it was well known through the National Detective Police that Thompson had access to a much larger sum from the Confederates placed in separate accounts across Canada.

Mary Surratt had been taken into custody to try to lure her son John back into the country. While she had been involved at the very highest levels of the conspiracy, a woman had never been tried for murder, at least since the United States had declared its independence. By Stanton's reasoning, John Surratt would return to save his mother from the gallows. However, Surratt would not come back if he was a part of a much larger conspiracy. In fact, John Surratt did not return until several years later, but only after being apprehended in Europe.

As for the ongoing investigation, there were still some very real questions that needed to be answered, and many of them involved Secretary Stanton.

Why had he rushed the postmortem on Booth's body? Why did he want only the Booth family and Surgeon General Barnes involved? Would the Booth family mis-identify the body to take the heat off a still escaping John Wilkes Booth?

Why had Stanton rushed the prosecution of the conspirators? Were there any direct ties between Stanton, Thompson and Booth? These were all ancillary questions, that would eventually help Jemm answer his two empirical questions—once those were answered, all the other questions would fall into place, and help develop a fact pattern.

Aside from funding Confederate terrorist activities, the Northwest Conspiracy and other missions, the boys in Canada also seemed to be running a business out of Montreal that turned an attractive profit—what other businesses were they in? The answer to that could be found with Bennett Burley, the man in Port Clinton Jail that Jemm was heading out to see.

Prior to its stop in Sandusky, Jemm had arranged to have Pinkerton's Post Office dropped at the Collinwood Yards near Cleveland, so Lt. Ollie Henry might have two days of leave to help determine what was going on at his family's property in Ohio. When Lt. Henry returned the next morning on the final leg onto Sandusky, Jemm could tell he was, as Aunt Cordelia liked to say, "Troublin."

# # #

"It's worse than I had thought," Lt. Henry says to Jemm. "I almost wish I had never ventured out there."

"That bad?"

"I must be losing my mind," Henry answers. "I don't even have a grandmother named Marnie, it's Mamie and she's been dead these many months. There haven't been any ghosts either—it's almost as if I made the whole thing up. But it seemed so true, as if it were a part of my past.

"Kids or hooligans are playing tricks on my cousins and the help out there, and the entire property is falling into a sad state of disrepair," Henry says. "I fear someone is trying to run them off so they can buy the property at a reduced price—there's no other explanation. But I can't explain how I got everything so wrong."

A false reality concocted by the trance, Jemm thinks.

"After this, we'll try to get you a couple of weeks leave so you can sort things out proper."

"It won't be necessary, at least for a while," Henry says. "Why did I think my grandmother was trying to talk with me from beyond the grave?"

"After intense human conflict, and death in a family, it's only natural that people try to seek answers, to reach out for explanations or try to reconnect with the dead," says Jemm.

"I don't believe in such nonsense," Lt. Henry says.

"Nor do I," Jemm says. "But they do…Here, let's do a little

studying, that'll take your mind off things."

He hands the Booth dossier to Henry.

"Re-read this," he says to the lieutenant. "Remember, even the smallest detail or relationship could be important."

As the train trundles through the flat farm country that marks the start of the Great Plains west of Cleveland, Jemm can see the rays of the rising sun casting a pink hue over the white farm houses, each surrounded by what seem to be the same copse of deciduous trees, just starting to come into full leaf.

Invariably, the trees are dotted with the white blossoms of shorter dogwoods. And here and there, Jemm can pick out the purple blooms of rhododendron.

The air is warm, and pleasant, even in early morning. And there is a hint of freshwater in the air.

"Beautiful isn't it," says Lt. Ollie Henry, coming up from behind.

"The topography is a little flat for my taste," Jemm says, looking up from his reading.

"It's farm country, just smell that air," Lt. Henry says, taking in a deep breath.

"There's a hint of fish to it," Jemm says.

"That's because we're just south of one of the greatest sources of freshwater fish in the world," Lt. Henry says proudly. "Sandusky is home to the largest freshwater fish market in North America, bet you didn't know that."

"I prefer seafood to lake food," Jemm says, still unimpressed. "This is just one of the seven seas of the seven tribes."

"You mean the Iroquois?" Lt. Henry asks.

"And Lake Erie is named after one of those nations," Jemm says.

"Weren't they annihilated by the Iroquois?" Lt. Henry asks.

"And think of all the knowledge that was forever lost—knowledge that could be used to further the human condition—all for not paying their taxes," Jemm says. "It seems the Iroquois shared food with the Erie Indians when they suffered a drought, but the next year they wouldn't return the favor. So the Iroquois invaded and killed off most of them and took the rest into slavery. A steep price to pay for tax avoidance."

"I guess they took it a little personal," Lt. Henry says.

"All history is personal," says Jemm.

"We're set up with the coach wagon out of Sandusky, and it's a bit of a trip over to Port Clinton," Lt. Henry says. "Figure on the better part of the day before we get into town. That should get us there right in time for supper."

"A little early to think about anything but breakfast," Jemm says.

"But wait till you try Percy's Fish House," Lt. Henry says. "It's the best in the world, walleye and perch, fried in peanut oil. They make this sauce out of egg yolks and chopped pickles—it's like nothing you've ever had."

Outside the window, a blue heron takes to majestic flight across the Huron River, soaring high and then out of sight.

"Peanut oil?" Jemm asks. "How are they...."

"It's against the embargo, at least during the Rebellion it was, but no one ever questioned them on it."

"Okay enough about fish houses, pickles and dead Indians, we have work to do," Jemm says. "Tell me what you learned about Booth, aside from his family theatrical connections?"

"Went to Miles Boarding School. Brilliant but often distracted student. An accomplished horseman, even at a very young age. Went on to the University of Virginia, but dropped out and joined Botts Greys…"

"At the beginning of hostilities?"

"No, before. His unit was involved in the arrest of John Brown at Harper's Ferry. If he was with them, and I think we can establish that, he saw John Brown swing."

"I need to know more about the man, than just a litany of where he's been, if we are going to connect Boyd with Booth."

"Well, he's very athletic, fancies himself a swordsman, and is prone to strong drink."

"That's it? You're not telling me anything about the man."

"Apparently, Booth is extremely superstitious. He often has to carry out a series of complicated tasks so he feels safe for some reason."

"Tasks?"

"Positioning objects in a certain way, or order. Grooming. He's very concerned with his appearance but washes his hands just about every chance he gets, as if trying to rub something off in the process."

"Read it again. This time try to link his actions with superstitions."

Meanwhile Jemm picks up another file on the arrest of one John Yates Beall.

CHAPTER 26
A Fishy Dinner

Jemm and Lt. Henry arrive in Port Clinton a little after five that evening. The Port Clinton jailhouse has grey sandstone walls and flat iron grating bars painted black, with rust bubbling out from underneath. Its smell is dank, but overwhelmed by the fish house restaurant next door, which reminds Jemm once again, that he has forgotten to eat.

In a room just off the number three cell block, Bennett Burley sits at a table, his feet and hands manacled. He has thick brown hair, and a full, thick beard that needs trimming.

Jemm can tell at once he is a powerful man, with a strong jawline and flat but strong nose. He has deep brown eyes and does not show any respect for his guards, or Jemm.

"So I tell them I wouldn't talk to an officer, and they send me a nigger?" he asks as Jemm sits down.

"Let's get one thing clear, I wasn't sent to you," Jemm says, as he opens up the dossier he'd carried in. "I'm conducting an investigation into..."

"I tole them I wunna answer a thing," Burley shoots back looking away from his interrogator. At that point Jemm can see his quarry's arms, thicker than most men's lower legs, and almost as thick as a thigh. Clearly, Burley has lived a life of physical strife. His thick brogue making him either a farmer or a miner, Jemm thinks.

"You said you would cooperate...."

"But only aboot certain topics," Burley says, "As long as we donna talk about me robbin' anybody or Mr. Ashley..."

"Why do you have such a problem with that?" Jemm asks.

"Well now, I am accused of certain crimes which may or may not have occurred on those vessels, and wouldn't wanna incriminate myself now would I? As long as we donna talk about the Parsons, Island Queen, the Michigan or any of the events surrounding September of last year, I'm good with it."

"Okay, so I'll keep it to the man you knew as Captain Boyd. When and where did you first meet him?"

"It was about a year before, at St. Lawrence Hall in Montreal."

"Were you two alone?" Jemm asks.

"No, there were actually several men in the room."

Including?

"Jacob Thompson, Clement Clay and a Commander in the Confederate Navy who was going by the name W.W. Baker. But that wasn't his real name."

#

A man with a thick broad face and full black hair, Jacob Thompson sat in a broad-back chair at a large desk in a hotel room that has clearly been converted into an office. To the side of the desk, sat Clement Clay, with a thin scraggily beard that accentuated his pointy chin. The two traded documents, as Burley stepped up between them.

"Mr. Burley, meet Commander W.W. Baker of the Confederate Navy, he will be in charge of this operation," Thompson said, as he handed a file over to Clay, who seemed more intent on the papers than the men at hand.

"We know each other well," Burley said. "You shoulda known that. So it's W.W. Baker now, is it?"""

Behind Clement and Thompson was a map of the Union, with various ports of entry from Canada and ferry schedules of vessels crisscrossing the Great Lakes.

W.W. Baker wore a long brown overcoat with sleeves that are cut about an inch too long for his reach. A man with darting blue eyes and dirty blond hair, the information hanging out in the open was not lost on the Commander.

"Forgive me Mister Thompson, but do you always hang out your personal business like so much dirty laundry?" W.W. Baker asked.

"Simply window dressing I can assure you," Thompson answered, a little taken back by what he considers an insubordinate nature on the part of his guest. "Union spies know we are here, but we know when they are watching. When there are no operations, we run people in and out of here, just to watch them scramble and use up manpower, or use it when it could be better used elsewhere. It may even keep them awake a night or two. It may sound petty, even immature. But please forgive us our dalliances, we are so far from home and welcome such amusements."

Thompson stood and walked past Commander W.W. Baker toward the windows, bracketed by long full green drapes. He looked out onto a sunny day three stories down on the streets below. A fishmonger was passing by with a cart laden heavy with fresh fish.

"We also happen to believe that the cleaning ladies are in their employ," Thompson said still facing the window. "So, we constantly feed them misinformation so they misappropriate resources to aid in our operations. It really is quite convenient."

Thompson stepped up from behind and gently grabbed a file

held under Commander W.W. Baker's arm.

"What really surprises me is that someone of your reputation would be walking about with such a detailed file," Thompson said, opening it and reviewing its contents.

"I can assure you Mr. Thompson, I am not so easily taken."

Thompson walked back to the broad back chair, sat and reached for a derringer hidden under the desk.

"Then how do you know that I am indeed Mr. Thompson?"

Before he can even touch the derringer, Commander W.W. Baker straightened out his right arm, revealing a sawed-off shotgun held under his sleeve. It was pointed directly at Jacob Thompson's head.

Thompson held up his hands immediately removing any threat. Clement Clay dropped a stack of files spilling their contents onto the hardwood floor.

"Geezus Jacob, would you stop playing your petty games, you'll get us both killed!" Clay said.

"My, you're as good as your reputation," Thompson said rather sheepishly.

# # #

"Right at his head? Was all business in Canada conducted like this? Jemm says, interrupting Burley's story.

"Thought he was going to shoot him right then and there," Burley answers. "The Commander was always heavily armed and always had a trick or two up his sleeve or in a sock. You really never know what a man like that is capable of. I was ready to bail on the whole operation."

"When did Captain Boyd show up?"

# # #

"According to your own records, you are exactly the kind of man that we are looking for," Thompson said.

"Served with Botts Grays, Company G—wounded in action and found incapable of military service—I find that rather hard to believe..."

"I can assure you sir that I am fully capable of..."

"Don't worry Commander, you have as much demonstrated that —later commissioned an active master in the Confederate Navy, acting as a privateer on the Potomac and Chesapeake Bay with The Raven and The Swan—with Mr. Burley here as your second...

"That is correct, sir."

"Mr. Burley, it says here that you did a little stint at Fort McHenry after capture."

"Not a cherished memory, I can assure you sar," Burley said.

# # #

"We actually have information on the Commander W.W. Baker," Jemm says, interrupting once again. "But there is some doubt as to whether or not he is actually a Confederate officer."

"You mean, was a Confederate Naval officer," Burley corrects. "Mr. Thompson was supposed to supply his papers for him if ever captured. But he was hanged earlier this year in New York for being a common brigand."

"I wasn't aware of that," Jemm says. "So let's cut to the chase, I'm more interested on whether Boyd was involved and to what degree. Was he under orders from Thompson?"

"Worked directly under him. Even identified the Commander,

not that Thompson needed any convincing after having a shotgun stuck in his face. He came into the room about five minutes later... Turns out the Commander and Boyd were old classmates. I think they served together somewhere too...At least it sure sounded like they did...

# # #

"Hello John, what news of Old Dominion?" said Boyd as he crosses the room toward the man who is traveling under the name Commander Baker.

"Captain Boyd, I presume," W.W. Baker said. "I might have known it was you. It's been a while."

"Two years," Boyd said. "You haven't changed. Your limp is better."

"Nor you. Sic Semper Tyrannus."

"Sic Semper Tyrannus," Boyd answered.

"A reunion like this calls for some brandy," Thompson said. He stood and walked over to the table to a brandy decanter and snifters waiting to be filled. Burley stepped over and immediately put a snifter under the direction of Thompson's pour.

"That's as eager as I have seen you all day, Mr. Burley," he quipped.

Clement Clay, who has been busy reading Baker's file looked up.

"I do have a few questions," Clay said. "actually for both of you. You started out with Botts Greys?"

"Both of us," Boyd answered. "We were both at the execution of Brown under the command of Lee.

"Back then it was the Richmond Greys," said W.W. Baker correcting him.

"That was my first real experience in the military," said Boyd.

"But not your first with an insurrection," W.W. Baker said. "At least an insurrection of sorts."

"I've never heard this story," Clay said, putting the dossier back down.

"In school he led a revolt against the faculty at St. Timothy's Hall over the killing of some chickens," W.W. Baker said.

"They were pets," Captain Boyd said. "And I wasn't alone. My brother Joe helped."

"Is that where you matriculated in the theatrical arts?" Clay asked.

"No but it's where he learned to ride and shoot," W.W. Baker said, answering for Boyd.

"It's also where I learned to handle a sword."

# # #

Burley raises his nose into the air. "It cood help matters if I had a plate of that fish, I haven't had me dinner yet."

"Only if you don't mind if I join you," Jemm says. It was a good way to feed his belly, and may loosen Burley's iron jaw, hidden by his beard.

"My last dinner mate in the cell, was a rodent, so donna think you might be somptin' special," Burley says.

Jemm instructs the guard to have Lt. Henry procure a plate of fried perch and walleye with Percy's special sauce, which brightens

Burley's mood almost immediately.

"I dinna thin' you would actually do it, but thank ye all the same," he says. "Ya know how long I've been smellin' that smell? Enough to make a man batty it is."

#

In a room down the hall that is both clean and well ordered, Lt. Henry is questioning Walter Ashley, the Master of the Philo Parsons. Henry reads a copy of Ashley's affidavit before he began questioning him.

"I, Walter O. Ashley, of Detroit, Michigan, do solemnly affirm that the information contained in this deposition is truthful and correct, and that I will testify to the same in upon court."

"For the record, please state your profession."

"I am the clerk and part owner of the steamer Philo Parsons, which runs between Detroit, Michigan and Sandusky, Ohio, usually offering sightseeing and day trip access through connections there to the Lake Erie Islands. We also carry cargo from Detroit through to Sandusky."

"Tell me about the run that day, as well as you can recall," Henry says.

"We usually stop at Amhertsburg and occasionally at Sandwich Island on the Canadian side on our way to Sandusky, but we stop off at a number of islands, including Kelley's Island to pick up cargo.

"On Sunday, the 18th of September, at 6:05 in the evening, I was in the Pilot House, when a man came in and asked to see Mr. Ashley, to which I responded that I was Mr. Ashley. He informed me that he, and three friends intended to go down to Sandusky in the morning. He also requested that we stop at Sandwich, where those friends would get on. I agreed, but only if he agreed to board at Detroit and let me know for sure that his friends would board at Sandwich. He went away without offering to pay any fare in advance for such services.

"We left promptly at 8 o'clock the next morning, and five minutes later, the man came up to the pilot house to remind me to stop at Sandwich to pick up his friends. At that point he paid the fare for his friends from Sandwich all the way through to Sandusky.

"Having not identified himself to me as yet, and curious to his identity, I left the pilot house, with my second taking control of the vessel, to at least identify who the passenger paying the fare was. It was then that I found out that his name was Mr. Bennet G. Burley, of Toronto, but judging from his accent I assumed he came to Canada from either Scotland or Ireland."

"When you stopped at Sandwich, were Mr. Burley's friends there?" Henry asks.

"They were. Well-tailored in their appearance, I could tell right away they were men of means. I asked if they had any luggage, to which they responded no. At that point, I should have asked their names for the register, but as this was a personal favor to Mr. Burley, I decided not to, because Mr. Burley had already paid their fares."

"If you put their names in the register, you would have to report their fares, isn't that correct?"

"Well yessir, but it's only that I forgot…"

"Never mind, Ashley, please continue."

"They said that they may take a short excursion at Kelley's Island or another island if we had to pick up cargo there. Being that they didn't have luggage, I never suspected."

"What happened from there?"

"The day was quite uneventful. We pulled into Malden, the port for Amherstburg about 15 miles down river, where we took on 25 passengers—a rough looking lot—except two that were clean and looked like proper gentlemen.

"Could you describe those two men?" Henry asks.

"Yes, one had sandy brown hair and a small beard at the end of his chin. The other had dark brown, almost black hair and a mustache. Other than that, both were very well kept, almost as if they had come direct from a barber."

"And what made you suspect these men were the leaders of the group?" Henry asks.

"Aside from their appearance?"

"Yes."

"They pointed out men and gave hand signals and the 25 men followed their orders implicitly."

"Such as?"

"They had an old trunk tied up with rope, and my first mate asked them what was inside and they said it was for a picnic on Kelley's island, which caused them all to chuckle. That's when the man with Sandy hair and a beard pointed at two men and then the trunk, and the two obediently grabbed the trunk and brought it up the aft gangway. But it looked a lot heavier than just food for a picnic, or even ice and beer."

"And your first did nothing?"

"Being that they weren't going to cross the border where they might have to declare, he did not press them further. Two of them put the trunk inside the cargo hold. But they took their time about it and I became suspicious. I told my first, Wilson, to hurry them out, and they came out immediately. I thought at the time they might just be curious as to what was in the hold, so I dismissed it at the time. I know now that they may have been sizing up the cargo to see if there were any valuables.

"At 9:30 we headed down toward the lake…"

"By that you mean Lake Erie?"

"Correct. Everything went off fine. At 2:30 that afternoon we dropped off Captain Atwood on Middle Bass Island, as he has a home there and it was usual for him to take his days off there."

"Who was in charge of the Parsons at that time?"

"I was. But I'm no sailor. My first was at the helm. We then headed for our next stop, which was Kelley's Island…"

"And where is that?"

"About six and a half miles north of Sandusky. We were scheduled to take on cargo there as well as two passengers who had booked their passage two weeks before. Except that 25 men that had come on board, did not get off at Kelley's Island. I informed the man with the dark hair and mustache, who appeared to be one of the men in charge, that I would need the balance of their fares as we stepped off in Sandusky, to which he agreed."

"And who was this man?"

"They called him Boyd, but I heard one of them slip and call him Captain."

"And that didn't arouse any suspicion?"

"No sir, I thought they may be men home on leave just looking to relax. It's very common on the islands, very good fishing there. And a casino on South Bass Island, too."

"What happened next?"

"Two miles out from Kelley's, the three men that got on at

Sandwich came up to me brandishing revolvers. They said if I gave them any trouble, I was dead."

"Where were you at this time."

"Up in front by the office."

"Was Mr. Burley among those men?"

"No but he soon joined them, along with more than a dozen others who had gotten on at Amhertsburg. He pointed a revolver at my head and told me to get back in the office."

"And you?"

"Complied of course. I stayed there for at least 50 minutes."

"Did you try to come out?"

"No, Mr. Burley had two of his confederates stationed at the door. But from where I was I could see Mr. Burley take an axe from the trunk, which a few of his men had opened. He smashed the cargo door, and then began smashing the cargo. Just after three of his men threw a racing sulky overboard, he became enraged, as if he were searching for something that wasn't there. Right around that time, the man with sandy hair came in and asked if I was in charge of the Parsons' papers. I told him I was. I gave him the papers."

"Did he identify himself to you at that time?"

"No, but when I begged him not to sink the Parsons, he asked that if I was a Union soldier and had seized a Confederate vessel, that I would probably destroy that vessel. But he never identified himself as a Confederate soldier."

"Where was the Philo Parson at this time?"

"We were just off Kelley's Island but heading for Sandusky. We then came about and headed back toward Middle Bass Island, where the man with sandy hair told me we would get more wood and let all the passengers off."

"Were you relived that your passengers might be spared?

"Of course, but I was even more fearful that they meant to scuttle the Parsons."

"What happened on Middle Bass?"

"We took on wood, and then the Island Queen came along side and asked to tie up alongside. I was in the cabin with Mr. Burley, he nodded in the affirmative, so I gave them permission. They weren't alongside for 10 minutes, when Burley's men seized her and made prisoners of everyone on board who had not already disembarked. About 30 minutes after that, the man with sandy hair came back into the office and said all passengers were allowed to disembark. I tried to disembark myself but went back to the office to get the ship's papers and cargo manifest. As soon as I came out of the office, the man with sandy hair and Mr. Burley came along side. I asked permission to keep the boat's papers. The man said that everything that belonged to the boat was now theirs."

"Burley motioned with his revolver to open the ship's cash drawer. I looked over at the other man, and he nodded in the affirmative. I opened it and gave them the money in the drawer, but it wasn't much, maybe ten or 12 dollars. Then Mr. Burley said, I know you have more than that, let's have it. And he poked the revolver right at my liver."

"And did you comply?

"Yes sir, in addition to having a revolver, Mr. Burley had a very intimidating presence."

"Did you surrender any more money at that point?"

"Yes sir, I had become accustomed to keeping the fares on my person, so much of the money was in my vest pocket."

"How much was handed over?"

"More than 100 dollars, perhaps one hundred and six."

"And who took the money?"

"The man who had identified himself to me the previous Sunday as Mr. Burley."

"What happened after that?"

"The Island Queen was scuttled just after leaving Middle Bass but didn't sink completely. The Philo Parsons continued on toward Sandusky, but I didn't know her fate until later."

"Did you ever see Mr. Burley again?"

"Not until I saw him in the cell at Port Clinton."

"Did you ever see anyone else from the piracy again. I recently saw the man with sandy hair. I was brought down to New York City to identify him. It was then I learned his real identity was John Yates Beall, although he had identified himself as W.W. Baker.

# # #

Jemm comes over and sits with the prisoner face to face, careful to face his chair a quarter turn to the side, a less confrontational posture designed to put his subject at ease. There is no going through this character, but easy ways around.

"So, Mr. Burley, it's says on one document that you came by way of Montreal, but in Ontario, you registered in the Montrose in Windsor, as being from Toronto—which is it?"

Neither, Jemm thinks. He sounds Scotch, but not the lowlands, and just a tad stronger than a highlander, maybe from Islay.

"I know ya figured out that one by now." Burley says, his fingers tapping on the table in anticipation of his coming repast, his eyes darting around the room, looking for avenues of escape.

"How did you come to be aboard the Philo Parsons?" Jemm asks.

"I booked passage the Sunday afore, but I truss ye know that," Burley answers.

"Was Commander W.W. Baker a member of your party?" Jemm asks.

"Wasn't among the passengers I paid for," Burley says.

"Are you an officer in the Confederacy?" Jemm asks.

"No sar," I am not."

"Then what is your relationship with W.W. Baker?

"First of all, Baker is an assumed name, ya know for the mission," says Burley.

"We know that," Jemm says. "We have a complete dossier on him. His real name is John Yates Beall. We've known about Beall and his relationship with Captain Boyd for some time. We know that he was taken under the name W.W. Baker to New York but he was properly identified later.

"Then why are you callin' him Beall, like a peel?" Burley asks. "Because it's pronounced Bell, you know, like a church bell," Burley says. "You've been mispronouncing it. That poor man was a Confederate Naval officer—and he was unjustly hanged—"

"Do you remember when that was?" Jemm asks.

"Right around the end of February, in fact February 24," Burley says.

There is an odd silence, as Jemm remembers the date. Right around the end of February—the timing is perfect—then "avenging bell." Everything was becoming clearer now. As clear as a bell.

Burley notices the consternation on his inquisitor's face, and quickly seeks to change the subject before Jemm can make any connection.

"How did you know Captain Boyd?"

"Let's just say we were associates," Burley says.

"How so?"

"Working by the same means, but sometimes toward different ends," Burley says.

There is a brief knock at the door, as the sheriff's deputy brings in the fish, perch and walleye, steaming hot, with two cups of the special fish sauce which made Percy's so famous. Burley requests to have his manacles removed for the feast, but Jemm sees it is easy enough for him to feed himself with them on, the request being nothing more than a ploy to give Burley an advantage—which he is always looking for.

But Jemm is hungry too, and a brief respite will give Burley time to make some small talk that may reveal a clue, something that Jemm seeks. It will also give him a chance to digest that last piece of information about Commander Beall.

As Jemm begins to pick up small piece of perch from the plate, Burley eats like a wild animal, more primate than human. Picking up the fish and jamming it into the creamy, sweet sauce. But he is occasionally leaving small pieces of fish and breading in the sauce, which at times he rescues with his thick, dirty fingers, and stuffs into his now greasy mouth and beard. Jemm decides he will just forego the sauce, even though it smells delicious.

Jemm has seen men eat like this before in his early years at the

Pender Plantation. Starved all day and forced to work under the Carolina hot summer sun, they care little for formalities---it is all about expediency—getting as much into the gullet as quickly as one can, gulping down food and washing it down with pitchers of water, a half pitcher at a time.

Definitely a farmer or a miner, Jemm thinks.

"So what do you know about Beall, aside how to pronounce his name," Jemm asks.

Burley looks up from his meal and takes a breath.

"Well, I worked with him on the Chesapeake. He was a Confederate Naval officer, if that's what you're asking," Burley says. "And he was acting on orders. So your boys at Governor's Island murdered an innocent man, a prisoner of this conflict."

Jemm thinks back to Burley's earlier answer. If they were working at cross purposes, to what ends? What were Commander Beall's orders? But he didn't think Burley would answer that. Besides, he already knew that the taking of the Parsons was just one step in rescuing Confederate officers from the prison on Johnson's Island, and seizure of the Michigan and eventually the western end of Lake Erie.

"Why did Commander Beall, give in and decide to scuttle his plans to rescue prisoners at Johnson's Island?"

"Got spooked, I suspect," Burley answers.

"Doesn't seem to me to be the kind of man to get spooked," Jemm says.

"Well that's my story and I'm stickin' to it," Burley says.

Burley looks up, then back at the fish in his hand, shrugging off the question before dropping a piece of Wallleye into his mouth. Burley knows, of course, and Jemm can sense that Burley is starting to become deceptive in his answering. Time to take a different tack.

"Beall and Boyd knew each other, of course," Jemm says, as matter-of-factly as possible. "They were both officers."

"Correct sar."

"But they were close friends, too?"

"That they war. Maybe even closer than friends, if you get my drift sar," Burley says, picking up the last piece of perch off the plate.

"How so?"

"Well sar, if you ask me, they were both a couple of dandies, if you ask me. Always primpin' in a lookin glass, eatin' together, never very far apart."

"That doesn't necessarily mean they were dandies, looks can be deceiving."

"Like yar skin color and yar intelligence," Burley posits. "Yar one of them thinkin' darkies aren't ya?"

Jemm doesn't know whether to be offended by Burley's remark or complimented by what it meant and he re-traced his own New World lineage, as the two dined in silence.

#

Before being sold into servitude in Africa, Jemm's ancestors migrated north into the Kazanze in Africa, where they were converted to Catholicism by Portuguese missionaries. Many Ovambo embraced the new teachings, which were said to be almost identical to their own beliefs of Kalunga the Creator. Once converted to the teachings of Rome, the Ovambo lived in peace, but only for a short time.

Jemm's ancestors were eventually taken by the Imbangala, who were cannibals and fearsome warriors. They raided and burned their village, as was the habit of the Imbangala, conscripting strong young men to their ranks, raping all the good-looking women, and then enslaving, torturing or eating the rest as they saw fit.

So, when Jemm's ancestors were told upon capture by the Imbangala that they were being sold to the Portuguese, they reasoned they were being sold back into freedom. The Portuguese were Catholic. How could one Christian possibly enslave another?

Yet despite their pleas, even in the Portuguese tongue, Jemm's ancestors were betrayed once again because of their pigment. The Portuguese didn't want the sin of enslavement on their souls, but they did want slaves to own and sell in the New World.

The Imbangala had been working for them all along.

As their range started to become hunted out, and Ovambo village militias began to grow against them, the Imbangala took to enslavement of captured soldiers who might have been fierce, but wouldn't convert to cannibalism.

It's rumored that's where the Great Cato came from. He was a Catholic general who led a militia against the Imbangala. Eventually captured, he later led raids for them, But he didn't have the taste for human flesh. They eventually tricked Cato, and sold him to the Portuguese, who brought him to the English colonies, a man in chains, but still a man whose soul would forever breath free.

When Cato died after the Great Slave Rebellion in South Carolina in 1739, most plantations owners were anxious to eliminate the rebellious Kongoese and Ovambo blood lines. Their future chattel would be more subservient. So Jemm's family's forced migration to North Carolina was ordained, if not by actual law, then by sociological imperative.

Jemm's family eventually took their New World name from Master Robert Pender, who owned a small 1,000-acre tobacco farm in Edgecombe County, North Carolina. Having fallen on hard luck with weather, Robert Pender was looking for Ovambo lineage for his slave stock, for it was rumored they were intelligent and possessed the gift of precognition—if only with the females. So, after the Great Rebellion and the subsequent Great Purge of 1740, Jemm's family was sold north to Robert Pender, the family completely intact—almost unheard of in the day.

It was a risky move for Master Pender, who was advised to buy maybe one or two, but disband the rest, or resell them into Virginia. While Jemm's family hadn't taken part in the Great Rebellion in South Carolina, they were rumored to have the blood of its leader, Cato flowing through their veins. Further proof was their Catholic heritage, and the fact they all spoke fluent Portuguese, in addition to their native Oshiwambo and slave English tongues.

While he paid top dollar for Jemm's family, Master Pender was confident that he would get more than enough money in return using their gift of precognition. And that the future issuance from the lineage would yield high profits.

But Master Pender fell on hard times, and had to sell some of his property, including his slaves. After less than 43 years with Master Pender, the family was once again sold to a plantation along the Ashby River in South Carolina—the Accabee Plantation in Charleston County. The property had been acquired by Elias Hory, after Ann Elliot married Lewis Morris and moved off with him to the Hope Plantation.

Master Hory was converting crops from mostly rice to tobacco, and Jemm's family's expertise was in high demand. It was rumored that Robert Pender got a price that was too high. But that also came as a blessing. Jemm's family was once again allowed to pass down their matriculation in both language and healing skills, and treated better than their contemporaries—even the house help.

In 1832, Edward Perroneau took possession of Accabee and all her persons and property. He renamed the property Orange Grove, which it's still called to this day. When Jemm's father Thomas died in a carriage accident in 1834, his mother moved into Orange Grove House and became the head cook. Jemm was born two years later in 1836.

So Jemm's father wasn't his real father, only the man that his mother had loved. Which was accepted, the lineage in the Ovambo being matrilineal.

Like many freedmen of the day, there was miscegenation in Jemm's heritage. It came from Monsieur Perroneau, who had taken Jemm's mother as a companion, after his wife died in the same carriage accident that killed Jemm's father.

Coincidental? Who's to say. We only know that Master Perroneau raised Jemm as his own, and Winnifried Pender, Jemm's mother, seemed content with it.

# # #

"So they were good friends?" Jemm says at last.

"That they war. From boyhood from what I understand. Joined up together before hostilities ever started."

"At Harper's Ferry?"

"Sure. Went to school together, from what I understand, University of Virginia or a high school that sent its lads on to the school, ya knoo Sic Semper Tyranus and all that shite."

The last remark sent shivers up Jemm's spine. The information Burley is offering up would not have been shared by Beall nor Boyd, especially if Burley isn't an officer.

"Who were your friends, that you had Ashley pick up at Sandwich Island?"

Burley just smiles.

"Why did the Parsons, turnabout and head back to Middle Bass?"

Again silence.

"What were you looking for when you smashed up that sulky?"

"Heard 'bout that did ya," Burley says, smiling again.

"Was the Parsons carrying any money, gold or script?"

"There are things in this life more valuable than gold or money, like life itself," Burley says. "You canna spend much money when you're in the ground."

Burley's words seem far less than casual. And his demeanor changes abruptly.

"Are you threatening me, Mr. Burley."

"No just warning you," Burley answers back. He sits back in his chair and regains his composure.

"If you aren't a Confederate officer, why did you use Commander Beall's identity when you were first arrested?"

"That's not somethin' I will answer," Burley says.

"Why did you rob Ashley?"

"Never said I did," Burley says.

"So they were dandies?"

"A closer pair I never saw," Burley says. "Brothers to the end. Overly fond of their mothers…Dandies for sure."

"What else do you know about Jacob Thompson?"

Silence.

"Clement Clay?"

Burley simply licks his greasy disgusting fingers.

"How about John Surratt?"

"Sure, you're a thinking man, aren't ye?" Burley says. "Thinkin you can tie this whole thing up, but ya canna. You're a slick one, I'll give ya that.

"Where er your people from?" Burley asks.

"What difference does that make?"

"I'm guessing West Africa," Burley says. "Voce fala Portugues?"

"Sim," Jem answers.

"Thought so," Burley says. "Ovambo. They call you James, but your name is Jem, after Jem Cato. Your masters know that?"

"I think we're done here," Jemm says, standing up and placing his notes back into the file. It was almost as if his gift had shifted and he was planting ideas in Burley's head.

"I dinna mean to offend thee," Burley says.

"Thanks for your time," Jemm says, as he packs up his notes.

"Thank ye kindly for dinner," Burley says.

"We might do it again sometime," Jemm answers.

"Better make it quick," Burley says, smiling broadly. "No goal kin hold me."

CHAPTER 27
Back to DC

Following Burley's informative although appropriately evasive interview about the operations of the Confederate pirates on Lake Erie, Jemm and Lt. Henry return to Pinkerton's Post Office, although the carriage ride back takes almost until sunrise.

In his interview with Lt. Henry at the Port Clinton Jail, Ashley has basically confirmed much of the information on the affidavit, although he did mention that something was taken from aboard the Parsons.

"He said it was a special package," Lt. Henry tells Jemm, "But didn't know its contents. Only that these special packages came through at regular intervals, usually by way of the Port of St. John in Nova Scotia and later through Montreal."

"What is more precious than gold, or gold script or money?" Jemm asks.

"I suppose life itself. "Lt. Henry responds almost immediately. "I mean, how many robbed men, when asked for their money or their life, so easily give up the money."

"Precisely. So what saves lives?"

"Water, if you are in a desert," Lt. Henry muses.

"Or doctors, if you are on a battlefield," Jemm adds. "You look like you could use a good rest. Now, then Ollie, I want you to see something. Agent Beckwith brought us this beautiful rose. Sit down here and take a look at it. Relax, and put everything out of your mind. How many petals are on that rose? Let's count them together, but let's count backward from 100…

Two hours later, Henry wakes from a deep sleep, remembering and realizing everything that has been said between Marnie, Jemm and the man with the bowler hat. His head aches, and he feels somehow betrayed by the man who he considers his mentor and friend.

Jemm senses his consternation and tries to change the topic.

"You know, there's a branch of medicine now called prosthetics," he tells Lt. Ollie Henry. "They could fit you with an arm, when manipulated properly, might even be able to grasp and hold lighter objects."

Lt. Henry looks up, actually intrigued.

"When we get back to the Capital, I'll look into it for you."

CHAPTER 28
Governor's Island

Armed with the information they both obtained in the Port Clinton interviews, Jemm and Lt. Henry wired Col. Lafayette Baker and obtained orders to take Pinkerton's Post Office into the Jersey City station. From there, they would travel by ferry to Manhattan, down Manhattan by coach, and take another ferry across to Governor's Island.

# # #

"I'm sure Lafayette won't care, but the old man might not like this," Jemm says. "Just tell him I'm going to get a sausage at the Jersey Station."

"Oh that should make him real happy and reasonable," Lt. Henry says. "I'm not sure about how I still feel about what happened and all with the mesmerizing. It was like I was tricked."

"It was necessary," Jemm says. "It might have kept you alive. Besides, someone who is under a spell, mesmerized, won't do anything that runs contrary to their basic morality, like I said.

"Still, the explanation for the hypnotic spell and subsequent suggestions seems trivial and unnecessary.

"This trip wasn't so much about obtaining vital information, Jemm continues, "just sewing up a few facts that might or might not be pertinent to the case."

# # #

Governor's Island was a military outpost off the southern tip of Manhattan, strategically located near the mouth of New York harbor. While its defensive fortifications had become largely obsolete by the 1830s, the federal government kept the land in military service, using it as an administrative center and as a mustering point for soldiers during the Mexican War. It was used during the Great Rebellion for the same purposes, a portion used as an armory, the other converted to a military prison, with cell blocks surrounding a prison yard where there were three gallows.

The file on John Yates Beall's career and subsequent arrest record proved to be interesting reading for Jemm.

Following the ill-fated operation on Lake Erie and what amounted to the mutiny of his operatives who chose to steal a valuable cargo off the Island Queen rather than go through with the seizing of the warship U.S.S. Michigan, Commander John Yates Beall continued with his mission to free Confederate officers from Union prisons.

On December 16, just three months after the seizure of the Parsons, Beall and George S. Anderson tried to derail a passenger train carrying Confederate officers in Niagara, New York, but following a mix up at the Suspension Bridge, Beall was arrested and taken into custody as W.W. Baker.

He was sent to New York City, where he was held in a City Jail. It seems the City also had an interest in the Commander, as a participant in an arson plot for fires that were set at major hotels in the city on Friday, November 25—the very same night that brothers Junius Brutus Booth, Edwin Booth and John Wilkes Booth staged a benefit performance of Shakespeare's Julius Caesar to build a statue of the great bard in Central Park. Indeed, one of the first fires was set in proximity to the Winter Garden Theatre where the event was held.

After their arrest in Niagara, both Anderson and Beall were eventually imprisoned at Fort Lafayette in Brooklyn. During the incarceration, Beall was betrayed once again, this time by Anderson, who agreed to testify against him in return for clemency.

General John Adams Dix ordered a military commission, which began on January 17, 1865—ironically, the very same day Lincoln, in Washington, had agreed with General Grant to allow a renewal of parole for Confederate officers. The commission found Beall guilty on February 8, and he was transferred to Fort Columbus on Governor's Island to await execution.

No mention of Beall's trial was made in the papers. But news did spread among Confederate sympathizers. Not too surprisingly, and just after his conviction, the Commander received a visitor, traveling incognito, among the many dignitaries that came to see him.

Tracing Commander's Beall's trail after his apprehension, Jemm and Lt. Henry decided to visit Fort Columbus, with Jemm interviewing the staff and orderlies, while Lt. Henry interviewed officers and military personnel, including Dr. Weston, the Fort Chaplain and Major Milton Cogswell, the turnkey in charge of Fort Columbus who had eventually become friends with Beall.

After a few quick questions among the staff, Jemm found an orderly named Jimbo that cleaned the cell block where John Yates Beall was held prior to his execution.

Major Cosgrove's office is plush for a warden's. While the walls were of stone, there is a nice patterned red and blue rug on the floor, perhaps even Persian, Lt. Henry thinks. There is a large and very well done portrait of Lincoln behind Cosgrove's over-sized maple desk.

Both Major Cosgrove and Dr. Weston sit on a couch in front of the desk with a short oak table in front, while Lt. Henry is supplied a chair across from them. The men are generally cordial and Lt. Henry detects no hint that they would be untruthful in any way.

"So he was arrested at the Suspension Bridge as W.W. Baker? Lt. Henry asks.

"Yes, he later explained that it was an alias he used while traveling," says Major Cosgrove.

"When did you discover his true identity?"

"He revealed it to me just before he sent a letter to Montreal asking for papers that would prove he was a Confederate officer," says Dr. Weston. "A finer Christian man I have never known. Read the bible constantly, while he was with us."

"As I suppose a condemned man would be inclined to do," says Lt. Henry. "So when did you receive those letters?"

"They never came," says Major Cosgrove. "That didn't help his case much, especially with the upper echelons of our command."

"And who was that?"

"General Dix, he signed the execution order," says Major Cosgrove.

"And that was for 24 February, correct?"

"No, it was originally ordered for the 18th, but something held up the orders. We later heard through the grapevine that Secretary Seward played a hand in expediting the orders."

# # #

Jimbo's housekeeping headquarters remind Jemm of Geoffrey's office at the War Department, although it was much larger. There is a small desk, more of a podium than a desk, where Jimbo writes down his notes and orders supplies and the like. A small gas jet throws what is really inadequate light.

"Sure I saw him…came through 'bout a week 'fore the hangin'," the orderly Jimbo says. "Always a gentlemen, that one. Plenty of visitors—a whole bunch of swells. But always gives thanks for his meals, and such. Even calls me sir once. Can you believe that? Calls me sir!"

"And you heard?"

"I hear everthin' in this prison," Jimbo says. "Makes it my point to. When yaw man came in, I makes it my point to mop jus outside the door."

"So you make it your point to eavesdrop?" Jemm asks smiling.

"Of coss I do," Jimbo says. "Jus' moppin' and cleanin' gets pretty borin' but it's all I have 'cept listenin' in on things once in a while."

"So where did Boyd come in?" Jemm asks.

"You and me knows that wasn't no one called Boyd," Jimbo says, "He signed in the log as John St. Helen. He was jus playactin' like always. I know it right off, of course. He put on that Shakespeare at the Winter Garden, him and his brothers. Saw the picture in the papers. That's why it makes it so interestin' for me to be moppin' right outside the door…"

# # #

In the background, sawing and pounding echoed through the dimly lit prison corridor. As Booth walked toward the Guard Station, a rat scurried long against the floorboard. Through the bars of cells, Booth saw prisoners, some scraggily dressed and unkempt, others seemingly fresher, obviously incarcerated for a shorter period of time. Some prisoners hung their heads, another stared out into the corridor, wild eyed, his hands white knuckled clutching the bars of the cell.

Booth stepped up to a large-red haired Yankee sergeant sitting at a bare black desk with only a small clipboard on top. He handed the sergeant a slip of paper.

"This looks good Mr. St. Helen," the sergeant said. "I'll take you down now there. You have three minutes once I open the cell."

"But I've come a long way, surely…"

"I'm sorry Mr. St. Helen, he's a federal prisoner. That's all we allow."

The two walked down the corridor only a few yards before turning off into a second, even smaller and even more dimly lit corridor. Here the doors were not bars, but wooden, with only crisscrossed iron banding across a window near the top, just enough to peek out. The sergeant's keys were jingling over top of the banging and sawing. A muffled moan comes out of a cell. At the end of the corridor, Jimbo was slowly mopping the wooden floor.

Two doors up from the end of the corridor, the sergeant stopped.

"He's in here Mr. St. Helen," he said. "Like I said, you have three minutes. I'll be back."

The door creaked open, as the orderly moved his bucket closer to the cell. The sergeant shot him a disapproving look, but said nothing, as the orderly began mopping the floor outside of the cell.

Inside, Commander John Yeats Beall was huddled under a gray army issue wool blanket. He looks up. He's unshaven, but his blue eyes still burn with ambition. He was quivering slightly from the cold. As he sat up, he pulled the blanket around his shoulder for a little more warmth.

"How are you John?" Booth asked.

"I've been better" Beall said. "I think they really mean to do it this time."

"Nonsense John," Booth said. "I've interceded on your behalf. Your mother and I went there…"

"How is she?"

"Concerned of course, but she's much better now. She is on her way here. You should be getting a visit any day."

"And Will?"

"Will's fine, actually looking forward to seeing you…and he will see you."

"Everything. Everything I did was for Virginia," said Beall. "It was all done for my country. You know I never saw any of that cargo, nor any of the money. I was all about securing the release of our officers…"

"I know that. They know that," Booth said. "I guess Burley and his brigands made a pretty good haul. He hid it but got arrested in Canada."

"How much?"

"Six cases of morphine with 144 ampules each, 64 liters of ether, some laudanum—enough to make everyone rich—and help our boys in the field."

"And there's been no further investigation?"

"Has there ever been?"

"There's always a first time," Beall said. "I can't help but think that someone in the federal government is getting sick of their shipments getting hijacked, whether on the water or up in Canada."

"Trust me, John, they haven't a clue."

"Then building that coffin is a pretty good bluff," Beall said.

"It's for some other prisoner, John," Booth said. "I've already interceded, and right at the very top."

# # #

The comment sends shivers up his spine. Had that been what Aunt Cordelia had been trying to tell him that fateful Saturday before Easter? Jemm needs to know.

Jimbo proceeds to fill Jemm in on the circumstances surrounding Booth's interview. It is clearly the circumstantial evidence, not only linking the two Confederate spies, but also the reason both men were eventually murdered, even if orchestrated by the government.

"So what happened after that?" Jemm asks the orderly.

"Sergeant Terry come back and took Mr. St. Helen out. Seven days later, they hanged that poor man," Jimbo says. "He didn't make no fuss, neither. Just keep lookin' out on the yard, like someone was goin' a swoop down and save him. They was still hope in those eyes, even as they was bringing down the black hood."

Boyd, Booth and St. Helen are one and the same. Jemm needs to get confirmation from Aunt Cordelia once back in Washington. It also is time to make his final report and confront Secretary Stanton.

CHAPTER 29
The Superstitious

A t the Jersey City station, Jemm stops at his favorite sausage stand. The Romani woman has his sandwich ready before he steps up to order. He tries to hand over money, as he grabs the sandwich wrapped in brown paper.

"There is no need for that this time," the woman says.

"But it's only fair…"

"I fear that this will be the last time I see thee," the woman says, a look of melancholy coming over her face. "You have always wanted to ask me questions…"

"I must tell you, that I don't believe in these kinds of superstitions, I don't believe in soothsayers and the like, never have," says Jemm as he gulps down some more of the sandwich.

"But you don't have to believe, you only have to know. The man you seek, only he has to believe, not you," the woman answers. "It is not your way, but ours."

"I don't want you to read my hands…"

"I didn't ask that," the woman says. "But you have questions. Your thoughts are loud. I hear them before you ever get into the station."

"Okay, let's see if you can help," says Jemm as he throws the used napkin back on the cart. He reaches into his pocket and pulls out the lithograph of Booth and Herold.

"Ever see any of these me come through here?"

"Not that one, but this one," the old woman says, pointing to Booth. "Many times he comes through here, one time asking about my daughter. But he is a man with no future. I see it in his hands…

At the train stop people clamored around John Wilkes Booth, asking for his autograph. The women, in particular, were interested in Booth, who is appreciative of their attention. An attractive young woman with raven hair caught Booth's attention in a nearby Gypsy camp. Making a quick excuse, Booth left the platform and headed over to her. The old woman pushed her into a nearby wagon, decorated with green leaves and yellow flowers.

"I told you my daughter is not for you," the woman said to Booth.

"But if you knew who I am, I might be able to dissuade you," Booth said.

"There is no use, she is not for you."

"Shouldn't we allow her that decision?" Booth asked earnestly.

"All right, come over by the fire and sit that we may talk," the Gypsy woman said. "Give me thine hands that I may gaze upon thy soul."

"And from the hands you can see what's in a man's heart?" Booth asked.

"You, too believe it," the Romani women said.

The Gypsy Woman grabbed Booth's hands, gazing intently upon them. She then tried to wipe something away, and make them cleaner, as if something might be wrong with them. She looked up at Booth, her stare went ashen gray. She can't look Booth in the eye.

"You have nothing to do with my daughter," she said to Booth. "You go now and leave us in peace."

"I've never heard such impertinence," Booth said. "I know my future, and I can assure you that you are clearly misreading…"

The Gypsy Woman grabbed Booth's hands once again, and again she tried to wipe them clean, as if there is something that can be taken off his hands.

"I've never seen such bad hands," she said to Booth. "Useless."

# # #

"I tell him my daughter is not for him, but he is unconvinced," the old woman says. "Then he wants to know his future, but there is no future for him, none that he wants to hear."

"You said he came through here many times, did he ever talk to your daughter?"

"No I would not let him," the Gypsy woman says "But every time he comes through, he wants his future told. And pays well for it…"

"It doesn't make sense, why would he want to pay for a future he already knows?"

"Men with bad futures often try to change their destiny," the woman says. "They can't accept their fate and think that somehow, they might be able to change it through some act they perform, or a favor they do another. But destiny is destiny, there is no changing…

"The last time I told him, there would be no change, I could not charge him, but he asks again, tells me he has taken matters into his own hands. When I look again, I tell him, 'It's just useless' I say. But he curses me a thief and almost hits me.

"Like I said, I don't believe any of this," Jemm says.

"But it doesn't matter that you do," the old woman says, "only that he believes."

Jemm thanks the woman, and tries to turn around, but she grabs his wrist and turns his hand upward.

"You will be confronted by a great truth but be wise and keep these secrets within you. Let me gaze upon thee one last time," she says, as she grabbed both of Jemm's hands. "I wish to remember your face, for I shall never see it again."

CHAPTER 30
The Trip Back to Mars

On the train ride back, Jemm sleeps fitfully. If he is in any real danger, his arumbo will tell him. Still, the old Romani woman is convinced that she would not see him again, and that was disconcerting. Should he take a different way back to Marnie and the safety of home? Should he do something out of the ordinary to throw off the fates? But the Gypsy woman's words came back to him: "Destiny is destiny, there is no changing."

Jemm looks over at Ollie, who is dead asleep on the couch at the rear of the car, his left arm thrown up over his head. If that goes to sleep, it ought to be comical watching him wake up in the morning, Jemm thinks, but he quickly dismisses it as being cruel. He'll help him with the new science of prosthetics when they get back.

Somewhere along the line, Jemm fell into a fitful sleep at the desk. He is awakened by Beckwith, who sticks his big jaw and smiling face back inside the Pinkerton's Post Office.

"Pullin' in gents," Beckwith says loudly, always getting that military kick out of waking people up.

Jemm watches as Henry struggles to get up. His arm has fallen asleep, and he is looking strangely at it, waving it back and forth to get the circulation to return.

"Hey Ollie, when you hit the War Department later on, make sure and give the Booth dossier one more read, if you can find the time," Jemm says.

Henry nods and moves his fingers, watching them as they return to usefulness.

"And Ollie, make sure Baker has Booth's arrest reports from his cousin and Dougherty on hand," Jemm adds. "Also, have him get the information on who signed the actual death warrant of one John Yeats Beall. I'd like to have a preliminary before we go in and confront the Secretary with what we know."

"But what do we know?"

"More than you might imagine, my friend. I think I have this one noodled out. But first, I am going to see my Aunt."

CHAPTER 31
The Last Report

By the time Lt. Henry and Jemm make it to the office of Colonel Lafayette Baker, it is mid-morning. Allan Pinkerton is already there, seated across from the colonel's barren desk. While there has been no time set for the meeting, Jemm can tell the colonel thought they were late and had been waiting for them anxiously, walking back and forth behind his desk as they enter. He stops and stares out the window.

"So?"

"We're you able to get the information on who signed the death warrant?" Jemm asks.

Lafayette Baker walks back to his desk, and briefly reviews some papers.

"Says here that General Dix signed the death warrant at the direction of Secretary Seward," Baker says. "Signed for an execution on the 18th of February, but the execution did not take place to February 24th—the reasons aren't clear.

"I fail to see the correlation of a death warrant for a prisoner on Governor's Island and the assassination of our President," says Pinkerton.

"When I make my report tomorrow, I will tell Secretary Stanton that I believe J.W. Boyd and John Wilkes Booth were one and the same. And that he also used John St. Helen as an alias, especially when heading back north.

"We can surmise that Booth was under the employ of Jacob Thompson, who ran the Confederate spies out of Montreal. And that Booth frequented Montreal, often staying at St. Lawrence Hall. This has been confirmed through a handwriting analysis on two documents supplied by the late Inspector Cao.

"But let's get down to motive—which supports what is mostly a circumstantial case."

"Was Booth under a spell?" Pinkerton asks. "It's probably one of the first things that Stanton will ask. If he was, then surely he was working directly for Thompson."

"Fanatical, yes. But directly under a spell, I believe not," Jemm says.

"You really don't need a spell to turn someone into the prefect fool, for taking the blame, or for actually committing a crime for that matter," says Lafayette Baker.

"But it would certainly help," says Ollie, looking accusatorially at Jemm.

"In addition to working for the Confederates, Booth was publicly a southern sympathizer, so there really wasn't a reason for a spell," says Pinkerton.

"But why would a man throw away such a successful stage career? It's a question that I have been forced to ask myself, especially in light of Stanton's insistence on an investigation," says Jemm. "It's one of the two key questions that could expose motives."

"Like I said, a spell is not always necessary," Baker interjects again. "It can be done by manipulating beliefs, especially if they are strong. Look at Corbett, nutty as hell…"

"More like mad as a hatter," Jemm corrects.

"As such, it didn't take much to have him assassinate the assassin—even though countermanding orders was at the risk his own career," says Baker.

"Then he wasn't mesmerized," says Ollie.

"I don't believe so," says Jemm. "But that doesn't mean he wasn't."

"But you said that someone under a spell would never do anything that runs contrary to their values or morals," says Lt. Ollie Henry.

"Not exactly true," says Pinkerton. "Under a spell and with the proper suggestion, a subject can become convinced they are acting perfectly in line with their own morality. They can be told, for instance, that the world they are in under a spell, is totally different from reality. They can be told that a pistol is actually a flower…

"Or a rose!" adds Ollie looking over at Jemm, "So I could have been dancing around your place naked last Easter!"

"Relax Ollie," says Jemm, "You weren't that impressive."

They all laugh, which does nothing for Lt. Ollie Henry's morale.

"Behavioral modification is what I am thinking," says Colonel Baker.

"And I am inclined to agree," adds Jemm. "But through orchestrated circumstance, rather than conditioning."

Ollie looks confused.

"Let me give you a quick example," says Baker. "A man sees a goose swimming in a pond, but a friend comes along and says, 'You mean that duck over there?' to which the man tries to correct his friend, 'that's a goose.' Well day after day, the man identifies the goose as a duck, until his friend finally acquiesces and calls the goose a duck, just so he can communicate with his friend. He still knows the goose is not a duck, it's just easier to identify it as a duck to expedite communication…"

"The same could be said of sociological expediency…"

"The way you feign a slave accent and speech…" Ollie Henry realizes.

"It does help move things along," adds Pinkerton.

"Okay, so let's start with Booth, or Captain Boyd's behavior, mesmerized or not," says Jemm. "It may be circumstantial, but it's the only evidence we have…"

"I doubt that the now horizontal Booth, or the redoubtable Captain Boyd, would be able to stand before a judge for anything," says Pinkerton sardonically.

"And I'm certain the judge would object—especially at the stench," says Lafayette.

The gallows humor is not lost on the group.

"Okay, okay," says Jemm trying to refocus the group. "Let's start with the actual assassin's behavior.

"The date of execution roughly corresponds with the increase in drinking by Captain Boyd at Gautier's. But let's go back to that Good Friday," Jemm says. "The assassin actual told us his motive as he jumped to the stage from the Presidential Box."

#

Booth leaped onto the stage, tearing down some decorative Presidential bunting on the way. When he hit the stage, he limped to the center, and screamed, "Sic Semper Tyrranus! Beall is avenged!"

#

"I am now convinced that is what was actually yelled," Jemm says.

"But what about the other eyewitness reports?" Lafayette asks.

"Please let me continue," Jemm says. "That observation is but a piece of my conclusion. Let's now turn to the security on that night:

"Why was Major Eckert, a man with a commanding physical presence and proven experience as a bodyguard, assigned to Seward, but denied to the president?"

"Because Stanton is involved with the conspiracy at the uppermost levels?" asks Baker.

"Maybe not," Jemm says. 'it's just too easy. And the motive doesn't match the man. We know that Stanton is an imperious and sometimes capricious man, but I don't think he's as motivated by greed as you think he is. No, there was another reason. Stanton simply expected an attack to come in Seward's direction and was doing his best to protect a member of the cabinet."

"Then why would he leave the Navy Yard Bridge open, allowing Boyd and Smith to escape?"

"Because he knew the real reason that Seward would be attacked," Jemm answers. "And if it were made public, Stanton, who still has political ambitions, might be disgraced for his actions."

"And what about the telegraph lines?" Ollie Henry asks, chiming in.

"The telegraph lines were never cut," Jemm says. "When I came to the Secretary's office the next day, those lines were clicking at a breakneck pace—and the office was fully staffed with cipher operators, who all looked like they had been at it all night."

"But that just confirms my theory…Stanton's says the lines are cut, and it gives Boyd and Smith the time they need to make it across the Navy Yard Bridge…" says Lafayette.

"But once again, it is not in the nature of the man. His motive, I conjecture, is purely political. But there is a secret that he is hiding, there's no doubt about it. I always wondered why he wanted me to investigate, especially if he realizes that I will find out that secret or confirm that Boyd and Booth are one and the same—which he already knows. Then it came to me, he wants me to figure out that secret—not so much as to discover a crime, but as an absolution, to uncover his ultimate innocence…that Booth acted of his own volition, without being mesmerized…and that would somehow dispel the notion or theory of a larger, grand conspiracy that involved the theft of the Confederate Treasury. This would give our Secretary of State an appearance of innocence."

"I think you're confusing innocence and a lack of guilt," Baker says.

"Good point, Lafayette, and an important distinction."

"What about the matter of denying your postmortem examination, didn't you say that it limited your investigation to circumstantial evidence, that it might even cast doubt on who was actually killed at Garrett's farm?"

"There were solid political reasons for that as well," Jemm answers. "Not wanting a freedman to touch a famous white dead actor, or to offend his famous family—the First Family of the American Theatre mind you—would have been very important to Stanton, who has a keen awareness of societal hierarchy. So no, while I agree the postmortem would have put all questions to rest, I still believe Stanton had faith that I would uncover the truth without it."

"So, what is this great…"

"Uncovered truth?" Jemm asks rhetorically. "I wasn't able to ascertain it directly, but I did uncover it during my trip to Ohio and later New York. And it does help dispel the notion that Booth was mesmerized into the assassination attempt—even though he had agreed to an earlier kidnap attempt. You were right in assuming it might have to do with the Confederate spy operations out of Canada, Lafayette," says Jemm. "On that one you were spot on. Booth under the alias Boyd, or I should say Captain James William Boyd worked for Jacob Thompson out of Montreal with a Captain W.W. Baker, who later became known to us as Captain John Yeats Beall an officer in the Confederate Navy."

"Did Burley tell you this?"

"Yes, he also confirmed the actual identity of W.W. Baker, and that he was a Confederate officer."

"And you believe him?"

"I have no reason not to disbelieve him. In fact, I think the identity was made to define the execution as illegal," says Jemm.

"Burley did confirm that Boyd and Beall knew each other and knew each other well. Burley isn't a Confederate officer, but I believe he was working for Jacob Thompson out of Montreal."

"The same man you think planned the assassination of Billy Cao?" Baker asks.

"The same. Burley is what you would describe as a political opportunist, an adventurer. Not allied to any one side, but to the enrichment of his person. He was working for Thompson."

"But weren't Beall and Booth working for him as well?"

"Yes, but I believe that Burley and his three friends that got on at Sandwich and Boyd, were actually working against Beall, who thought they were going to free prisoners on Johnson's Island as was the original plan. When Burley entered the hold of the Parsons, and smashed up that sulky, he was looking for something."

"But there was no gold on the manifest." Baker says.

"And there wouldn't be," Jemm answers. "But I don't think he was looking for gold, he as much as admitted it."

"Like Cao said, drugs; laudanum, quinine…" Ollie Henry interjects.

"That can save lives, even more valuable than money on the battlefield," Jemm says. "They weren't on the Parsons, but Burley thought they would be. He found them on the Island Queen, and that's why they commandeered her as well."

"So then as the Parsons sets sail…"

"There's something of a mutiny on board between the two parties, Beall wanting to complete their mission and seize the Michigan, while Burley and his friends decide to make off with the treasure that's already in their hands. But he thought there might be even more aboard the Parsons."

"But you have a couple of dozen men, led by two officers, and only four including Burley?" Ollie asks.

"I suspect that at least half of those men were in league with Mr. Burley," Jemm says. "I suspect Burley also knew that the plan to take the Michigan had been discovered, and that they were all walking into a trap…And once that was revealed…"

"It was easy to persuade the entire party to turn back," Ollie Henry says.

"Scuttling the Island Queen, and later the Parsons before they made their way back into Canada," Jemm adds.

"So the ultimate order came from Thompson?" Baker asks.

"Precisely, and so did the betrayal of Beall, which was most keenly felt by Boyd. The fact that the piracy was key in getting his friend hanged also weighed heavily on his soul, getting Booth, to act on plans to get him freed from imprisonment."

"But how do you know that Booth used these three names?" Baker asks.

"The names were not to hide the identity, but code for the actual mission. Confederates have used this system in the past. Booth, or any other Confederate courier like Surratt, used the alias John St. Helen when returning to Canada or heading north with money, regardless of the ultimate destination or contact. Booth, or anyone else, used the alias Boyd when smuggling drugs usually from Ohio down to Memphis for the Western Theater and in the east from Montreal down the Hudson, through New York, and later along the train line. Boyd was code for carrying cargo or drugs to Dr. Mudd, who then dispersed by rider the drugs along the Eastern Theater of War. So basically one name was used for getting into the Confederacy, while the other was used to get out."

"The same Dr. Mudd we have in custody, I take it." Baker says.

"The same. Remember, he claims that he didn't know it was Booth, but someone named Boyd, which could be at least partially true. He may not have discovered Boyd's true identity until after the assassination."

"And it was the same alias he used with Noah's daughter when he was on the run." Henry points out. "But other than that, how can you tie those three names together?"

"Once again, using a document acquired by Inspector Cao from Canada, we know that our enigmatic Captain Boyd took a ride on the Philo Parsons back in September of 1864. I ascertained from Burley and your interview with Ashley, Ollie, that Captain Boyd and Beall knew each other, possibly from childhood. They both went to school with each other and both enlisted in Botts Greys, where they helped put down John Brown's rebellion at Harper's Ferry.

"When I went through the enrollment files at St. Timothy's Hall, which is a preparatory school for the University of Virginia, I saw that there was no one with a last name of Boyd, and indeed, no one with a first name of Boyd at the school…

"There was, however, one John Wilkes Booth, he left school to enlist in…

"Botts Greys," says Lafayette.

"Correct."

"And the University of Virginia's motto…"

"Is the same as the state's and St. Timothy Hall: 'Thus be it ever to tyrants.'"

"Then how did you ascertain that St. Helen and Booth were one and the same?" Lafayette asks.

"At first I was unsure, given that Burley never heard the alias used. But the Guards at Governor's Island heard the name and saw that it was also used at the sign in register of visitors, which…"

"On the same date corresponding with our Mr. St. Helen's visit to Governor's Island in February," Ollie Henry says.

"I didn't get a chance to tear out the register, but the style of writing is very similar with both Booth and Boyd," says Jemm.

"Beall must have known the alias." Baker adds. "So when the guards told him he had a visitor named St. Helen, he knew that it was Booth, and he knew that it was some matter relating to some sort of payoff from inside the Confederacy.

"The subject of their conversation was a giveaway as well," Jemm adds. "According to my interview with the orderly on Governor's Island, St. Helens said that he had interceded on his behalf at the highest levels of government—something suggested by my Aunt Cordelia at the beginning of my investigation—in the kitchen of the Executive Mansion. Lincoln promised Booth that he would spare his friend Beall and commute his sentence after hostilities."

# # #

Inside the cell on Governor's Island, John St. Helen or more properly John Wilkes Booth, was speaking with the federal prisoner, John Yeats Beall:

"Your mother and I. we saw the President. He agreed to see me. We told him the circumstances surrounding your incarceration," said Booth. "And he agreed that you should be treated as a Confederate Naval officer, not a common brigand."

"You'll forgive me if I don't celebrate until I'm out of here," Beall said.

"You might not get out of her until the cessation of hostilities," Booth said. "You'll be paroled then."

Beall shot Booth a look of genuine concern. And Booth knew why.

"Once he gave his word, I had to give my word as well," Booth said.

"You mean you betrayed Old Dominion!?" Beall asked.

"Lives are more important than money or political causes," John," Booth said. "You must survive this conflict: for your family, for Virginia. Who knows what hell she must suffer once this conflict is over. Old Dominion will need leaders like you then, John.

"Besides John, I think they brought you here, blaming you for the fires we set. I had to do something. Especially after siding with Burley on that last haul—that was Thompson, not me John—he gave the order. We had to go that route. That guy Cole, on the Michigan, was said to be a turncoat—a federal agent. No one can find him right now."

"I hope you're right about that coffin," Beall said as the pounding and sawing continued.

The two men embraced, and through the cross-hatched iron, Jimbo the orderly was looking in. Over Booth's shoulder, the orderly could see the worry on Beall's face, his bright blue eyes staring off in the distance.

"Just keep the faith, and I'll write you as soon as I get back to Baltimore," Booth said.

# # #

"I have a hard time with your reasoning here, Jemm," Lafayette says. "Why would Lincoln agree to a midnight meeting with Booth. I heard that Booth once spurned the President's invitation to visit the Executive Mansion after a performance...the Marble Heart at Ford's...there were other invitations as well. Why would Lincoln accept such an invitation, especially after it became known that Booth was such a rabid southerner?"

"I thought so as well. But then riding back from New Jersey earlier this spring I found this missive in our files," Jemm says, handing over the innocuous incident report. "It describes how one Edwin Booth saved Robert Lincoln...

"At the New Jersey train station! I remember that!" Lafayette says. "Pretty easy to grant an audience..."

"When Booth's brother has saved the life of your son..."

"And especially after losing Willie only a few years ago."

"Well that certainly explains why Lincoln would accept Booth's audience," says Lafayette.

"And why he would probably further offer a commutation of his friend on Governor's Island," says Jemm. "That commutation was something that was later communicated to Stanton at the War Department, according to our sources there; Charlie Dana and

Geoffrey."

"But the stay of exaction had been later countermanded by Seward, of all people, who communicated this to General Dix, who signed the death warrant," Henry adds. "So they basically went behind Lincoln's back?

"Or perhaps simply didn't follow through, at least in a timely fashion, on the commutation of sentence."

"Then why wasn't there an attempt on Dix?" Lafayette asks.

"There may have been, but it failed, or they simply didn't have the resources, or there was too much security—he is a General and is always heavily guarded…we'll never really know," says Jemm.

"The death warrant had to be read to Beall ten days prior to his execution," says Baker.

"So he would have been able to communicate who countermanded the order of a stay of a federal prisoner, and who issued the actual order…"

"So Booth knew that it was Seward, and not Stanton—and there was no attempt made on Johnson nor Stanton," Jemm says.

"And that's why Stanton put more security on Seward than Lincoln, figuring the attempt would come there and possibly end there."

"Stanton orders the execution of Beall, but forces Seward to sign the paper. But Stanton is scared into thinking that he has unbalanced Booth, which he has. Then our President and the unsuspecting Mr. Seward become primary targets," Jemm says.

"So Stanton was actually doing his job, trying to protect a government official that he thought might be in danger. But where does Thompson fit in?" Lafayette Baker asks.

"We have hard evidence and interview testimony that he

conspired with the now missing John Surratt to loot the Confederate Treasury."

"The whole idea was to create action that would not only decapitate the Union, but if failed, would also serve as a diversion to actually abscond with funds, or at least move funds to a more secure location in Europe," says Jemm "We're not sure whether that was to the Royal Family in England, other contacts, or possibly to the Vatican…"

"Which would then be used to set up another Confederate Government either out west or in Mexico?" Baker asks.

"Probably the latter…We're still not sure," says Jemm. "I often asked myself, 'Why would Booth give up his career, if it was simply political' and 'Why would Stanton want me on this investigation, if he thought I would uncover some dark secret?' That's when the idea came to me that he wanted at least a portion of this information uncovered."

"But I still think that greedy ole cuss was somehow involved with Thompson and the looting of the Confederate Treasury," Baker says. "You said Booth wasn't mesmerized, but they could have very easily used behavioral conditioning…"

"I have to agree," says Jemm. "But we have no strong evidence to link Stanton and Thompson—at least not during the Insurrection."

"What about leaving the Navy Bridge open?" asks Lafayette.

"Protecting Northern egress would prevent Surratt, if he were traveling with Booth, from gaining access to Northern ports and international travel, possibly through Canada," Jemm says. "Keep him in the South where he can get his hands on and question him."

"But the wily Surratt, leaves early and heads North before any assassination attempt is made." Ollie Henry says.

"Knowing that the game is up, and perhaps enriching himself the best way he can," Jemm says. "If what you proffer is true, then we could all be in serious danger if we confront the Secretary on the morrow. There is another very troubling aspect of this fact pattern that I haven't brought up. There also seemed to be a coordinated effort to execute John Yates Beall, both by Secretaries Stanton, Seward and General Dix. Perhaps more troubling is that it also fits well with the motives of our friends out of Montreal."

"It's an amazing tale, but we need hard evidence if we are going to confront the Secretary," says Baker.

"The only hard evidence would be in Booth, or Boyd's diary, which we know exists…" Jemm says.

"But has since disappeared," Ollie Henry adds.

"Corbett has it," Jemm says.

"Which means it's in Stanton's possession." Baker says. "In fact, I know it is in Stanton's possession. Colonel Conger told me so."

"Well I'm making my report to Stanton tomorrow, and I'd like to have you all there as witnesses," says Jemm.

"And we won't be the only ones," Baker says. "I know for a fact that Major Eckert and Sergeant Corbett will be there, as well as some other hand-picked witnesses as well."

"Who will no doubt take us all into custody if we overstep the report," Ollie Henry says.

"In which case, I'll have to amend my report," Jemm says. "Perhaps we only offer what we know about St. Helen, Boyd and Booth."

Ollie, Lafayette Baker and Pinkerton all look at each other, genuinely concerned.

"I'm kidding," Jemm says, letting them off the hook. "I'm almost certain that there are two outcomes to our confrontation with the Secretary tomorrow. If he's involved in a much larger conspiracy involving Surratt, Thompson and the looting of the Confederate treasury, he will hear us out, accept my report and disagree with us."

"And if he does that? Baker asks.

"We leave the office calmly and run. For we each have less than 24 hours to live."

"So we get our affairs in order tonight?" Ollie Henry asks.

"Just be prepared to move," Jemm says. "If he is involved like I think he is in volved, he will as much as admit it. Not by words, but by his actions. Colonel Pinkerton, you always told me that he was a lousy liar. He can lie in words to your face, but his actions always reveal his true intentions. At the President's death bed, when he removed his hat, and then replaced it, like he was crowing himself king, I knew that he was involved in some sort of falsehood. I just had to find out to what extent. I am convinced he inadvertently caused Lincoln's assassination by countermanding an order he had no reason to countermand, other than just pure cussedness. For this he feels guilty, which led to the clumsy theatrics at the Petersen's Boarding House. It's probably why he went through such great lengths with the diary, which no doubt has an explanation in its pages. If he's involved in this way, I suspect that there is some other sort of play he might have in store for us on the morrow.

"Henry, do you have that dossier on Booth?" Jemm asks. "You have given me a lot of background, but you haven't really told me anything about the man. Was he superstitious? Does he believe in spiritualism or fortune telling?"

"What does that got to do with anything?"

"Please," Jemm says impatiently.

"Now wait a minute, it does, I mean he was," Lt. Ollie Henry answers. "Says right here that after he failed in trying to rescue some chickens at St. Timothy's he went to a Romani fortune teller—and after that he visited them almost regularly. According to one of his classmates in grade school, he visited a fortune teller and palm reader at a fair who told him he'd have a short but grand life. After that, he frequented palm readers, gypsies and soothsayers whenever he could."

"And why do you think he did that?" Jemm asks.

"To hopefully get his previous spiritual diagnosis overturned?" Ollie Henry jokes.

"Or to see how close he might be to his ultimate end," Jemm answers. "Very fatalistic. Good Ollie."

"But I thought you didn't believe in that nonsense?"

"It doesn't matter what I believe, only in what Booth believed," Jemm says.

"I have just one more question that will cement my case—at least in my mind. From the reports at Garrett's farm, what were Boyd's last words?"

"He died in my cousins arms, well, almost literally…"

"That's not what I asked Lafayette…"

"He said, 'tell my mother I died for my country.'" Baker says, reading from the report.

"Which were the same words used by John Yates Beall at his execution. "And those were his absolute last?"

"No, he asked that his hands be raised up so he could gaze upon them."

"Did he say anything then? Anything about bad hands? Or hands being useless."

"He simply whispered, 'Useless…Useless.'"

"We have our man. Booth is Boyd, or at least the Captain Boyd who was in Garrett's barn."

"How the hell do you know that, from a man's last words."

"I just know."

"I have no doubt that our assassinated assassin is John Wilkes Booth, or let me put it this way: He was the same individual that had his fortune read by a soothsayer as a teenager, who told him he had bad hands and was born under an unlucky star," says Jemm. "He was the same man whose future was described to him as colorful but brief. He was the same man who regularly visited fortune tellers at virtually every city he visited while on the stage to overcome that prediction. He was the same man who traveled through New York regularly, having his palm read numerous times by a Romani woman at the Jersey Station, who called his hands 'useless.' And he was the same man who visited the Executive Mansion to win a pardon for his good friend John Yates Beall. That was in mid-January, when Lincoln granted Beall's parole at the end of hostilities. He was also the man that had his palm read by my Aunt Cordelia during that visit, who came to the same conclusion of bad hands.

"He was also the same man, who with a group of conspirators, was duped into the assassination our beloved President after he learned of his friend's execution in New York at the end of February. Even when he found out he was manipulated into assassination, he probably went to his death thinking it a noble cause to decapitate the Union.

"But he didn't realize who was really pulling the strings, nor the amount of money involved.

"I am sure I have this one solved. Booth assassinated Lincoln as personal revenge for the execution of John Yates Beall. Stanton needed to know that John Yates Beall was the ultimate motivation for Booth's actions. Stanton wanted me to find that out, for his on conscious, his own absolution.

"Yes, I have this one solved…Can I prove it? No. Do I want to prove it? No. Do I want the investigation to continue? Again no. It could prove too dangerous for the people I work with here. That means you Lafayette—and you too Ollie. Colonel Pinkerton, I know you share my sentiments. It's much too dangerous to raise the prospect of further investigation, if it's based on hearsay, conjecture and speculation that would never be accepted in court."

With that Jemm turns and leaves Lafayette Baker's office. Lt. Henry stands there with a dumbfounded look on his face.

"That's one scary bastard," Lafayette Baker says to Lt. Henry.

"You don't know the half of it," Henry answers.

CHAPTER 32

Confronting the God of War

As Jemm rides his mule halfway home up U Street, his arumbo once again perks up.

"Big day tomorrow, then," comes the friendly voice of Allan Pinkerton, who rides up alongside. "Be careful. Like you said, look to Stanton's actions as a key. He'll let you know if he's lying and how he agrees with you."

"And if he doesn't?"

"Marnie knows what to do and how to get out of town," Pinkerton says. "You have a nice little wagon with a wood cover."

"And what about my fellow detectives?"

"Henry will be fine, but I'm a little worried about Lafayette," says Pinkerton. "He's a little headstrong. "

"And you know he'll never let it go," says Jemm, "that will lead to his eventual undoing I fear."

"Ha, you actually like the bastard now!" Pinkerton laughs. "Work and confide with someone long enough and the strangest of fellowships follow."

"We're talking about a man's life, sir," Jemm says formally.

"I suspect that you now believe that Thompson and Clay used Booth as a patsy, setting him up to effect the assassination on

Lincoln, knowing that he would be distraught at Beall's capture, perhaps even suggesting that he use his influence with the president to commute Beall's sentence. They knew that Beall at the end of a rope would unbalance their would-be operative—which it did, causing him to change the conspiracy from kidnapping to assassination. They also used the feeling of Stanton against himself, knowing that he would never pardon someone who he thought to be a pirate, brigand and drug smuggler—especially one who had operated in his home state."

"The whole objective was not the decapitation of the government by a small band of conspirators, but to do so to create a diversion that would involve our government at its highest levels," Jemm answers, "so the money from the Confederate treasury could be smuggled out of the country. In the end, It was all about the money. But if I tell the Secretary that…"

"And he is in any way involved, then you might a hard time leaving Washington outside a pine box."

"I can't believe that about Stanton," Jemm says.

"Perhaps he got involved, but only partially, and is now seeking forgiveness for his limited part in all of this," Pinkerton says. "You might base your report on that, just to be safe."

There was a protracted silence as the two rode up the avenue. Pinkerton starts to pull off at the intersection of 10th.

"Good luck tomorrow," Pinkerton says. "I'm not going to be there."

# # #

When Jemm, Lt. Henry and Lafayette Baker enter Secretary Stanton's office the next morning, it is much the same as it had been just after the President's assassination. The old patchwork quilt on the lounge replaced by a grey army woolen blanket being the only upgrade.

Stanton sits behind his desk, staring at the three men who will be making the report, while the physically intimidating Major Eckert stands directly behind him, huge arms crossed above two holstered pistols. To his side are Sergeant Corbett and Agent Beckwith, both of whom are not only armed, but have their hands on their weapons as if expecting trouble.

Jemm begins his report, Stanton looks down. As Jemm recites his observations about the personal betrayal and countermand of the Beall execution order by General Dix, tears began to fall from the Secretary's cheeks. Before Jemm can get to the part of Booth's midnight visit to the Executive Mansion, Stanton takes off his glasses and begins to meticulously wipe them off. He stops Jemm in mid-report.

"The fact that Booth believed so religiously in Romani prognostications…That he identified his 'bad hands' at the moment of his death, is as good as a death bed confession…We have also ascertained that he worked with John Yates Beall in Canada, John Yates Beall who was more than a friend, but a mentor. John Yates Beall, whose friendship preceded our Great Rebellion. And that after his execution, Booth became personally enraged…Those are two very real fact that point to the enigmatic J.W. Boyd and John Wilkes Booth being the same individual."

"Were there any other reasons that might have motivated Booth? Was he involved in any greater conspiracy?" the Secretary asked.

"I wasn't able to ascertain anything beyond that he was his friend," Jemm says, obviously leaving out his theory that Stanton's countermand order for Beall's execution was the driving force behind Booth's decision to kill Lincoln.

"I've heard enough," the Secretary says.

"Sir, being as the Great Rebellion is now over, I'd like to be mustered out. My wife is with child, and I want to leave politics behind…"

"It is so ordered," Stanton says. "Good job. Good job as always Jemm."

And Jemm realizes that it is the first time the Secretary has called him by his proper first name, which arouses his arumbo even more so than on that Good Friday night months before.

Stanton pulls out a red book, tearing out a chunk of earmarked pages. Both Lt. Ollie and Colonel Lafayette Baker lurch forward, but are stopped by Beckwith and Corbett, who start to draw their arms. Stanton places the pages in the large obsidian ashtray on his desk, strikes a match against the side of his desk and lights them afire as the witnesses look on.

As the pages burn, Stanton stands, puts his glasses back on and utters the immortal phrase, "Now he belongs to the ages."

But it all seems a little too far-fetched for Jemm. Mars, the great god of War, still has political ambitions. If he sees anyone of us as a threat, it could be dangerous, Jemm thinks.

Afterward, outside the office, Jemm tells both Lt. Henry and Colonel Lafayette Baker that they should resign their commissions and make plans to leave Washington as soon as possible. They walk down the hall to Colonel Lafayette Baker's office in silence.

"So there's no way I can get you to stay on?" Baker asks breaking the silence. "You and I both know that part of Booth's diary was burning back there. Very convenient that you left out the Secretary's countermand for Beall's stay of execution. But I still think that Thompson and Stanton are somehow involved, if not a part of a conspiracy, then at least financially…"

"But now, we'll never know," Jemm says.

"I'll stay on," Henry offers.

"Go home Ollie," Jemm says. "You have your own home and property to look after back in Ohio. "Our job here is done…"

"But it's not, we're letting the main culprits get away..." says Baker.

"The mission of my investigation was to ascertain the identities of three Confederate spies, who are indeed, one and the same, which I have done."

They enter Baker's office.

"One thing I could never wrap my head around," says Baker. "Why did the old man let Booth escape that first night?"

"Needed him to," Jemm answers. "He takes Booth alive, then the accused has a chance to tell his story—and the fact that he countermanded the order of John Yates Beall gets out."

"And there goes our beloved Mr. Stanton's political aspirations," says Lafayette.

"Let him get through where he knows he'll run into our little nest of spies...."

"And he knows he'll be caught. Obviously just buying time, but why?" Baker asks.

"So he can arrange the assassination of the assassin. The true story dies with Booth," says Jemm.

"And then our investigation..."

"Serves as an absolution. No more investigation necessary. General Dix and Secretary Seward are saved any embarrassment," Jemm says. "And the story of the redoubtable Captain Boyd and Booth is relegated for all time to a top secret classified document."

"Brilliant, but that doesn't absolve him of any involvement in the theft of the Confederate Treasury," says Baker.

"Doesn't truly implicate him either...unless...you of course choose to pursue such an investigation…but I would advise against it. It could prove deadly. Besides, I have another life to think about, and you don't have any more kingdoms to sell," Jemm says to Lafayette.

Baker reaches behind his desk for a large trunk case. He hands it to Jemm who offers up an inquisitive look.

"Any ways, here's your surgeon's kit, what are you thinking of becoming some sort of half-assed medicine man? They'll probably string you up and run you through with a blunt deer antler." Lafayette Baker says.

"They might be a lot smarter than you think," Jemm says.

The words cut deep.

"You know, Jemm, this has been very hard for me. I was raised a certain way, and have had a hard time dealing with this war, what it was all about, not just the Union and the freedom of your people, but the actual equality of all men…"

"It was what Pinkerton…"

"Always taught, I know," Lafayette says. "But there's something else, too. Like getting used to the fact that…"

"I'm a better field investigator?" Jemm asks, trying to beat him to the punch.

"Or just plain smarter," Baker answers. "That's just something I'm gonna have to deal with as well…anyways, here's your surgeon's kit. So are you going to join the U.S. Sanitary Commsission or something?

"The kit is a nice thing to have, especially with a child on the way," says Jemm.

"With my compliments and thanks," the colonel answers.

It would be the last time the two saw one another.

CHAPTER 33
Leaving DC

A few days after his meeting with Stanton, Sergeant Jemm Pender was officially mustered out of the military and resigned from the National Detective Police. He sold most of his possessions and gave the rest to Sam the cook.

The next day, well before rosy fingered dawn, Jemm and Marnie loaded up their wagon with the help of Aunt Cordelia, and Sam the cook. There was plenty of food, canned provisions and preserves in jars, sacks of flour and coffee and a full cask of water that both he and Sam had to wrestle into the wagon. Sam kept asking if he could come along. But Jemm declined, realizing that Sam, while great for protection, was so large and foreboding, that he might invite violence, or at least a confrontation.

Still, Jemm couldn't help but wonder what lay ahead, not only for himself, but all of his people. There wouldn't be colonization. There wouldn't be repatriation. There wouldn't be reparations. There might be an initial hint of freedom across the land, but Jemm was equally sure that would be swept away. He was also fearful that the knowledge of his people would be mostly lost, compromised, or stolen. That thought made him sad, but also more determined to write his chronicles of lost knowledge, of lost history, of lost language.

It can only be truly saved through freedom—true freedom, which comes at such a dear cost. More than a half a million lives— and it still had not been won. The tree of true freedom bears fruit slowly. It must grow in the hearts of men, and it must grow within your own first before it ever begins to take seed in the hearts of an oppressor.

The sun was just starting to break the horizon, throwing shadows across U street.

And what might he find at the end of the realm? Jemm wondered. What knowledge might he be able to save? Only the Creator knew. With Aunt Cordelia in tow, he and Marnie headed west into the Great American frontier, and into the obscurity of history, never to be heard from again.

They live on today, if only in legend, among Native American peoples who were visited by a dark doctor, who traded treatments, drugs and medicinal knowledge—for knowledge of native cures and herbal remedies. He was beloved most by the medicine men of the tribes, who saw him as an equal and an associate rather than a threat.

EPILOGUE

Lieutenant Oliver Henry mustered out a few months later and headed back to Ohio and Henry House. He lived in Henry House for more than 20 years, before selling it off to his cousins, the Troy family.

Of the eight conspirators put on trial by Secretary Stanton, four were hanged on July 7, a scant five days after Jemm's report, a sunny hot day by all accounts. They included Lewis Powell, David Herold, George Atzerodt and Mary Surratt.

Her son John never came to her rescue or aid.

Samuel Arnold, Michael O'Laughlen, Edmund "Ned" Spangler and Samuel Mudd—the doctor who set Booth's leg, were all sentenced to life imprisonment at Fort Jefferson in the Dry Tortugas, a dry desert-like island 70 miles off Key West. Captain Samuel Cox, who had helped hide Booth and Herold on their fugitive flight, did not face any charges. Similarly, Noah and his daughter Elizabeth who fed Herold and Booth never faced any recrimination for their deeds.

After two years at Fort Jefferson, Samuel Mudd distinguished himself, using his skills as a physician in helping stem the tide of a dangerous outbreak of Yellow Fever. He was pardoned and moved back to Virginia, where he continued his medical practice and lived out his life in relative peace.

As for the actual pursuit of the assassin, hundreds of the manhunters sought to claim a piece of the reward money, including Conger, Dougherty, Lafayette Baker and his cousin Luther, the latter two who each received $3,750. Richard Garrett, the man whose tobacco barn was burned, made a claim against the government for his barn, but never saw a dime.

Boston Corbett was never punished for either disobeying the order or in the actual shooting of Booth. While he enjoyed a brief period of fame, he eventually went insane and disappeared.

Colonel Lafayette Baker was removed from his office by President Andrew Johnson in 1866 because the president believed he was spying on his office. The colonel admitted that he had spied on the President but was doing so under orders from Stanton—perhaps as a means of buying time while he continued his investigation.

Lafayette Baker never gave up his pursuit of both Stanton and Thompson. He died under suspicious circumstances in 1868. A postmortem of his remains performed later revealed that he had died of progressive arsenic poisoning.

After the Great Rebellion, Jacob Thompson was said to have lived lavishly in Toronto, although he was accused several times of mishandling Confederate funds. While he was indicted by the Federal government for his possible connection in the murder of Lincoln, the Union government was unable to prosecute him. Shortly after the indictment, he fled Canada for England and later Paris, where he lived lavishly for three years at the Grand Hotel.

As rumors swirled about his embezzlement of Confederate funds, he tried to make amends, returning the paltry sum of 12,000 English Pounds to Judah Benjamin, the former Confederate Secretary of State, who was living in London—no one knows what happened to the rest of the money.

Thompson returned to his home in Oxford, Mississippi only to find it destroyed by Union troops during the war. He eventually moved to Memphis, where he died peacefully. He was rumored to be an incredibly wealthy man.

Bennett Burley stood trial for the theft of only $40 from Walter

Ashley, the rest being assumed was a part of the spoils of war, or the amount he had paid for his pirates. After intense deliberations, the jury deadlocked on whether his theft constituted an actual theft of property, or an appropriation of funds for the Confederate War effort. While awaiting his re-trial, he jimmied the lock on his cell door, leaving a note that simply read:

"I have gone for a walk. Perhaps I will be back."

Burley

He is said to have stolen a small boat, and rowed across Lake Erie to Canada, some 20 miles, reappearing in Guelph where he later changed his name to Burleigh.

We do know that he was hired by the London Telegraph to cover a war in Sudan in 1881. He also served as a war correspondent for the Central News Agency during the bombardment of Alexandria in 1882 and was the first to report the failure of the Gordon relief expedition. He also covered the Boer War, the Russo-Japanese War and authored several books. He died in 1914, after a very successful journalistic career.

As for John Surratt, it was later learned that he fled Canada on a steamship to Liverpool and was later found serving under the alias of John Watson in the Ninth company of the Pontifical Zouaves in the papal states before he was recognized by an old friend who alerted authorities. He was arrested and sent to Velletri prison but escaped and posed as a Canadian citizen before being arrested once again in Egypt in 1866 and sent back to the United States. He was tried in 1867, but not convicted because of lack of evidence. He would later go on a short-lived lecture tour, cut short due to public outrage. He later took a job as a teacher, and married a relative of Francis Scott Key, the author of the Star Spangled Banner. The couple lived in Baltimore and had seven children before his death at 72 from pneumonia.

Stanton continued as Secretary of War. He was instrumental in re-organizing the army into two sections; one to handle training and ceremonial duties, the other to fight Native Americans in the west. It was said he was always asking his officers about the whereabouts of "the dark doctor." He also presented his military occupation proposal for the South, which was approved by President Johnson.

Eventually, their relationship soured, with President Johnson wanting to cashier old Mars. Grant opposed the idea, arguing for Stanton's retention and the fact that he might be protected under the Tenure of Office Act.

While Johnson tried to suspend his position as Secretary of War in 1867, the Senate voted overwhelmingly to reinstate the Secretary in 1868. However, the Secretary fell into ill-health. He was named to the U.S. Supreme Court but died just a few days later at the end of 1869 at the age of 55.

To this day, there is still controversy on Stanton's famous deathbed quote. Lincoln's secretary John Hay, who was next to Lincoln's death bed, clearly heard "Now he belongs to the angels." It was also the quote that Corporal Tanner heard as he took notes in the parlor next to Lincoln's death room.

But the most accepted version of the quote today is "Now he belongs to the ages," which was quoted in Dr. Charles Sabin Taft's book, one of Lincoln's attending physicians at his death bed. It was also the quote that Stanton preferred. There is still controversy as to which was said, with many scholars agreeing that both were somehow used.

Being unavailable and lost at the time, John Wilkes Booth's diary was never used in the trial of the conspirators, because it couldn't be found. It surfaced after the trial and is still missing 18 pages to this day. The contents of those pages were known only to Boston Corbett and Secretary Stanton. They are now forever lost.

Jemm was right about the need for a definitive and reliable postmortem. It did give rise to many conspiracy theories, and even opportunists claiming to be the assassin. In fact, the secret of John Wilkes Booth's actual grave site remains closely guarded by his relatives to this day—we only know that he is interred in an unmarked grave at the family's plot in Green Mount Cemetery in Baltimore. The body can never be exhumed or tested for DNA even today.

As for John St. Helen, the man claiming to be John Wilkes Booth, he recovered from his illness and moved to Leadville, Colorado. Skeptical of St. Helen's supposed death bed confession, Finis Bates moved to Tennessee, where years later, he was summoned to the Grand Avenue Hotel in Enid, Oklahoma.

A house painter named David E. George, had poisoned himself and requested Bates' presence. When Finis Bates showed up ten days later, he identified the body as that of his friend John St. Helen. But Bates did not initially claim the body. While Finis Bates claimed he did not believe John St. Helen's tale, Bates did write the War Department seeking to claim a portion of the $100,000 reward.

George's unclaimed body was sent to an undertaker named Penniman, who hesitated to bury it until the body was claimed. While George did have a will, most of the property contained in it proved to be nonexistent. The body remained unclaimed and unburied at the Penniman's, who eventually put it on display, opening its eyes and placing a newspaper in its lap.

The body eventually ended up in Finis Bates' care, who stored the mummy in his garage in Memphis, eventually renting it out to a wide variety of circus and carnival sideshows before World War I.

It ended up being displayed on a potato farm in Idaho, in an abandoned Pullman car of all things. Enraged by the carnival-like atmosphere, the Veterans of the Grand Army of the Republic threatened to lynch the mummy.

It eventually ended up in Philadelphia where it was purchased from a landlord who had obtained it in lieu of back rent.

The sad story of John St. Helen, David George and a mummy nicknamed John remains something of a mystery to this day. It is the tragic, comic coda to our nation's greatest tragedy.

One man and three identities? Who can be sure?

The story of John Wilkes Booth, his friend John Yates Beall and revenge as a motive for the killing of Abraham Lincoln was taught as historical gospel in Texas Public Schools, until its inexplicable removal from all curricula in the late 1870s.

THE END

ABOUT THE AUTHOR

A student of the American Civil War since visiting Gettysburg more than 50 years ago, T.F. Troy has an award-winning journalism career spanning more than 40 years. He currently serves as Executive Editor of Cleveland Magazine's Community Leader as well as the Editor of Ohio Business Magazine. He also writes features for Northern Kentucky Magazine and Dayton Magazine, among other regional publications. His work with those publications has won him numerous awards, taking first, second and third place in Ohio for Magazine Feature Writing. Troy's work has appeared in major metropolitan daily newspapers including the Cleveland Plain Dealer and Pittsburgh Post-Gazette.

In addition to the previously mentioned publications, Troy also held positions as a Senior Editor for both ABC/Capital Cities and ICD Publications in New York. His work has appeared in numerous national consumer and trade periodicals throughout his career. In his first book Cleveland Classics: Great Tales from the North Coast, Troy interviewed local and national Cleveland celebrities such as: Jim Brown, Bob Feller, Patricia Heaton and Arsenio Hall among others. *The Absolution of Mars*, set just after the Civil War, is his first novel.

Follow the author at www.historiumpress.com/t-f-troy

www.historiumpress.com

www.ingramcontent.com/pod-product-compliance
Lightning Source LLC
LaVergne TN
LVHW092014060225
802923LV00012B/409